EAT YOU ALIVE

EDEN O'NEILL

EAT YOU ALIVE

COURT LEGACY: BOOK FOUR

EDEN O'NEILL

Trigger Warnings:

Trigger warnings include dubious consent, degradation, SA, bullying, and scenes of manipulation. There's also a scene of voyeurism that includes MM content but doesn't directly involve the hero and heroine. This is a MF romance with a cliffhanger.

PROLOGUE

Fawn - age 16

I need to get closer.

This was my last thought before leaving the bleachers, my gear on my back. There was no way I was going to get the shot I needed from the nosebleed section.

Knowing that, I pushed my way through fans and class-mates. This assignment may have been shoved on me, but I was still going to get it right.

I hit AstroTurf, the track surrounding the field in the game against Windsor Preparatory Academy. The rich kids were killing us on our own turf, but our team still showed up and were taking it like champs. Honest to fuck, I had no idea what was actually going on on that field, and if it wasn't for the scoreboard, I'd be completely lost. Again, this assignment had been given to me, forced onto me from the editor of the school's paper. I'd rather be taking photos for pieces that actually mattered, but I'd already gotten the actual news assignments done for the week. Football games and other sports-related nonsense usually went to the photographers who just wanted to get into the games for free.

"Steven has mono. You're going in for him."

That was the last thing Doug, my editor, had said before handing me a press pass and telling me I had to make it to a game that started in fifteen minutes. The paper needed shots of tonight's game, and needless to say, I showed the fuck up late.

Hence the nosebleed seats.

I'd dealt with worse conditions, stress. I'd been taught by the best, so pushing through all the traffic, I finally made it onto the field. The players were in a full sprint, our guys blending in with players donned in Windsor Prep's orange and navy uniforms. Their guys were about twice the size of ours, and it wouldn't surprise me if a lot of these dudes went on to go pro. Their flashy uniforms also made our guys look like shit, and I'd care more if I cared about the game at all. I had a job to do, get the shot and make the deadline for my school's newspaper.

I set up my camera on the sidelines, getting it ready. I could do this without the tripod but that made for a better shot.

"Hey. You!"

A man in little pants and a striped shirt sprinted over to me, whistle in his hand. He blew that little whistle, *at me,* and my head shot back when he crossed the sidelines over to me. He pointed. "What do you think you're doing on my field?"

I wasn't on the field, at least not technically. I propped my camera on my hip. It hadn't made it to the tripod yet. "I just need a couple shots of the game."

"Well, you can take them from the bleachers."

"I'm press." I flashed him the badge. "I also got here late, so if you could let me get my shot, I'll be out of your hair. I have a deadline to make anyway."

Not to mention, I was completely over spending my

Friday night here instead of editing photos. I'd taken quite a few over the last weekend of things that actually mattered. Needless to say, a football game against boys who looked like combat warriors wasn't it.

The ref or whatever blew his whistle again, and again, my head snapped back. That shit was fucking loud.

"I don't care if you're the President of the United States. You're on my field, and I want you off—now."

Um, rude and even more so when he got in my personal space. I must have not been moving quick enough for his liking because the next thing I knew, he was taking my tripod and getting it away from the sidelines.

"What the heck do you think you're doing," I growled, but he didn't stop there. He started to reach for my camera next, and I dodged. This dude was *not* getting his fucking hands on my dad's camera. "Back the fuck off!"

"You *will* get off my field," he started, but stopped when someone yelled from the field. The ref whipped around, me too when a player in orange and navy sprinted to the sidelines toward us. It took a second for me to realize the game hadn't stopped, and whoever this player was from Windsor Prep still continued to make his way over.

He was a big guy, real big, tall. In fact, he was probably the tallest boy I'd ever seen, and he obviously couldn't have been more than eighteen. I mean, we were in high school, but the closer he got, he towered over both me and the ref. All of Windsor Prep's players looked like soldiers, but this guy looked like Captain Freaking America.

He was built like him too, broad, thick. There were bigger guys on the field, and though this guy was leaner, he still had a solid definition that distributed through his body in a way that made him just as intimidating as even the biggest guy. I mean, the boy's thigh made mine look bird-like, and that said something considering I wasn't the smallest girl. I fluctuated, but most days the labels in my pants said size sixteen more than they did fourteen.

"What's going on?" the player questioned. The rogue curls beneath his helmet made him appear only more beast-like. He took the helmet off and all those curls spilled out like an angry sea. They shrouded his dark eyes, his skin a light honey tone. His complexion was a natural tan where most had to bake in the sun to get that color.

Why are you looking that hard?

That might have had to do with the fact that he was looking at me. The guy was, well, gorgeous. I definitely had eyes and could see that. His irises were dusky and borderline black. He used them to peer over me, his jawline perfect, his nose straight and eyes deep-set. They flashed a couple times in my direction, and when he stepped forward, the ref put a hand on his chest.

"Get back on the field, Mallick," the ref barked and snapped the player, Mallick, out of whatever trance he'd been in when he'd been looking at me. I didn't know why he'd been so focused in my direction, but I found myself suddenly grateful considering the way he currently sneered down at the ref.

The guy appeared to grow three sizes, like *legit*, and he was already tall. He pressed that broad chest against the ref's, his finger up. "You looked like you were about to put hands on that girl."

I blinked. What the fuck?

I exchanged a glance between the two, this Mallick guy literally up on this ref, and I definitely noticed when he took a step back. The ref did, a grown fucking man before he brought his whistle to his mouth. "Back on the field or I'm throwing you out of the game."

"I fucking dare you, bro."

The whistle blew, and the ref called it, throwing him out with a wave of his hand, and my jaw dropped. Mallick's did too, then suddenly, a few more guys from his team were sprinting toward the sidelines. The game was still going, by the way, but the three additional players totally left the field.

"What's going on?" one of them called, the first to get to the sidelines, and the other two Windsor Prep players flanked behind him. One of the two was leaner like Mallick and the other was one of the more bigger guys on their team. Actually, he was easily the biggest guy on this whole damn field and literally looked like a man-boy. What did they feed these dudes, steroids? The guy who got here first gripped his helmet, his hair blond behind it. "Wolf, why aren't you on the field?"

"This shitbag just threw me out of the game," Mallick barked. His name was Wolf, apparently. I found that unusual, but as I was in the middle of this shit, I just continued to keep my mouth fucking shut.

"And you will be too, Prinze, if you, Reed, and Ambrose don't get back on that field," the ref yelled to the guy who spoke to Mallick. He did this quick, and needless to say, he didn't stick around. The ref blew the whistle, then headed back toward the game. The two guys behind Prinze yelled "bullshit." Mallick obviously felt the same way, but he didn't fight it when he stormed off the field. He flew past me, but I noticed that he glanced my way before he did.

I wanted to say sorry for... well, I really didn't know what I did. He didn't have to go to bat for me, and I definitely hadn't asked him.

Instead, I held my camera, watching on as he severed his gaze from me. He shook his head before heading toward the track and had to pass our fans in the stands to do so. A few of them yelled at him while he did, the crowd amped.

"You think your shit don't stink, Mallick! Why the fuck would you disrespect the ref like that and on *our* turf," one of them called before throwing a bottle at him. It hit Mallick's helmet, glass exploding, and Mallick immediately cut a look in that direction.

My breath stopped, everything stopped, and even a lot of shouting in the crowd. It was like time had stopped in that moment, that long, *agonizing* moment.

I wished it would have lasted.

Because time moved too quickly after that, Mallick throwing his helmet...

Mallick disappearing in the stands.

The dude scaled the bleachers, actually scaled them, and my heart ceased to function when the crowd screamed as a boy the size of a lion grabbed hold of the guy who'd thrown a bottle at him.

No, not a lion... a wolf.

Nothing but pure unadulterated rage could be described as Wolf brought the guy up and drove his fist down so hard the man's head jerked back. A woman in the crowd shrieked, the stands exploding, and Wolf's teammates (who'd returned to the field) doubled back. Prinze, Ambrose, and Reed ran toward the stands. They ran to Wolf who was clocking that guy who'd assaulted him over and over.

Oh my God.

It was like I was frozen, ice freezing both my limbs and body. Wolf's three teammates entered the stands too, and one of them managed to get Wolf under his arms. The name Prinze on his back, he held him while Ambrose and Reed tried to keep the fans away. With the three boys coming onto the scene and stopping Wolf, I thought this was over. It should have been over.

It may have been had someone not hit Prinze.

The guy, a fan, had come out of nowhere, and he punched Prinze right in the arm. It was the only hit the guy got before Prinze let go of Wolf and started pummeling the guy who hit him. Prinze socked the guy over and over, and unrestrained, Wolf continued to wail on the guy who'd thrown the bottle.

That guy *wasn't* moving, clearly passed out but the blind rage hurled Wolf's fists. He didn't stop, and Ambrose and Reed found themselves in a similar fight. Fans were tackling them, and my hair blew across my face as orange and navy uniforms suddenly zipped past me.

The boys' teammates.

They came… in droves—all of them. The entire Windsor Prep team had left the field to aid their teammates, and once they did, that gave license for our guys. Our team's red and black uniforms zoomed past me too, and the ice bath hit again. Chaos literally happened in front of my eyes.

The bleachers, the *goddamn world*, exploded in what had to be only a few minutes, seconds. There were players fighting players, players fighting fans, and my camera hung deftly from my fingers. I nearly dropped the most important thing in my entire goddamn life. My father's camera was irreplaceable, literally the most important thing to me.

Knowing that, I lifted it, nutting the fuck up. This wasn't the story I came for, but it was here and…

My shutter flicked quickly, anger and rage in front of my lens. I had no problem capturing the fight, nor the story's central focus. I stayed on Wolf Mallick.

And I didn't let go.

CHAPTER
ONE

Fawn - the present

"I have to say, Ms. Greenfield, I'm very happy with what I've both seen and heard from you today. You have a very good chance at this internship. A real good chance."

Sitting across from Kurt Ackerman, Kurt *from the New York Times* Ackerman I had to say, I felt what he said. The interview had gone well, and I'd provided my best work for him today.

Even still, I played that off, sitting professionally before him. "Thank you, Mr. Ackerman."

"Call me Kurt," he passed off before picking up my portfolio. He grinned. "Quite a body of work for someone so young. In fact, it feels like you've lived a thousand lifetimes in only a summer."

He was speaking about what I'd provided for him today, of course. I'd spent the summer of my senior year traveling cross-country. My camera and a bus ticket had taken me to some of the most impoverished communities in the country, many of them forgotten about and neglected. I wanted to show their stories, show the people, and most of my focus had resided on those who couldn't even call those communities a home. They were the ones living off the beaten path and trying to get by from shelter to shelter. Before I knew it, I found myself immersed in their stories, my camera the looking glass on those who truly were passed over. They had a story too, and my body of work reflected that.

I folded my fingers. "Thank you, Kurt."

"No, thank you. It's extraordinary to see," he said, closing the portfolio I'd provided. I had to say I was still in shock by this meeting. I mean, I was confident about my work but never expected to be given the opportunity for an internship in photojournalism this soon. Let alone my freshman year of college.

And my dream internship at that.

That'd been the plan upon enrolling at Pembroke University and getting into their prestigious photojournalism program. It'd been the only plan, and one I'd set course on years ago. I'd had some speed bumps along the way, but I'd ended up getting there.

We're almost there, Dad.

A position at the *New York Times* was the real goal, the main goal. My dad used to grace those halls, and I planned to do the same.

"And definitely not expected from the photographer who had so much buzz her sophomore year of high school." Kurt lounged back, folding his fingers. "I, of course, looked into you and definitely assumed the young woman who took the photos of the *Chaos in the Heartland* story would be providing me a completely different body of work."

He was speaking about what I was known for and probably one of the big reasons he'd reached out to me. When Kurt had emailed me about the internship, he'd said my name was on a short list of applicants the school had provided, and needless to say, when someone googled Fawn Greenfield, only one thing came up.

I tried not to shift in the secondhand suit I'd purchased literally for today. I typically wore things that were unrestricted, comfortable. I traveled a lot taking photos, and comfort was key. "Uh, yeah. Had a lot of excitement in high school."

Too much excitement, and I definitely didn't want to talk about it. I happened to be the only one who got decent pictures of the fight that broke out, and so much so, the local and national papers reached out to me after seeing my photos in my high school gazette. I was Fawn Greenfield, the high school sophomore who happened to have her camera that day and had been the only one not swept up in the fight enough to capture it.

There was some irony in that, my mouth dry as I thought about how the fight had occurred. It'd been weird, crazy, and something I'd fought hard to forget in the time that had passed. Even still, it had opened up a lot of opportunities for me, and one hundred percent bulked up my Pembroke University application. This was definitely something I'd needed. At the beginning of my high school career, there'd been more than a fair bit of truancy on my part.

I shifted again, and Kurt smoothed my portfolio across the conference table. He'd flown all the way from New York to be here at Pembroke's school of journalism today, my name on a short list like he'd emailed. I could imagine when his office had inquired, the school had told him about me and the *Chaos* story. Again, it opened a lot of doors. Kurt nodded. "Well, what you've done since has definitely shined."

"Thank you, sir."

"Again, Kurt."

"Kurt."

"And Fawn Greenfield. Any relation to a Jack Greenfield?" He leaned back. "I didn't know him personally, but he used to work at the Times. Quite prolific."

I hesitated for a moment briefly but only because it still took me a beat whenever people mentioned my dad. I wasn't sure that would ever change. I nodded. "That was my father, yes."

"Ah, a lot's making more sense now. Sense about you and your already expansive body of work. From what I understand, Jack was hitting the pavement hard as a young lad, and probably one of the youngest to ever work for the Times."

I smiled, definitely knowing this. "That was my dad. Never could turn down an opportunity to lift his camera."

"And he was great at it." Kurt's smile faltered a little. "I was very sad to hear about his passing. The world definitely misses him and his work."

My mouth dry, I could simply nod at what Kurt said. Again, it took a second when talking about my father, and though his passing wasn't exactly fresh, it wasn't like it'd been a million years ago.

Nor how it had happened.

Kurt gratefully moved on from that part of the conversation, and I was happy when the conversation got back to the internship. He told me I had a good chance at it, a great one actually.

"We're still in the middle of the selection process, Ms. Greenfield, but I don't think it's too early to let you know you'll be getting a second interview." He reached over, shaking my hand. "You've already made so many great contributions to the medium, and I can definitely see a bright future ahead of you. You're one hundred percent Jack Greenfield's daughter, and that shows all over your work."

He had no idea the compliment he gave me, truly. I strengthened my shake. "Thank you, Kurt. Just... thank you." He didn't know what this meant, meant to me. A lot of times these internships led to actual jobs, and to be offered something like this my freshman year was crazy.

Is this life right now? Really?

It was like I had an angel looking out for me, my dad certainly present. Outside of my work over the summer, I'd done other human-interest projects and had very little roadblocks along the way. People allowed me to capture their stories, and in general, doors just seemed to open for me when I needed them. Doors like this internship and getting into Pembroke with a less than desirable GPA.

Thanks, Dad.

He was definitely in here, and even though Kurt and I had wrapped up, he still entertained all the probing questions I had about the Times and his own work. He let his assistant outside the room know we were done, but he still stayed to chat with me. I really appreciated it as I was excited to hear about the Times and my dad's old stomping grounds. This was certainly the dream for me, and it was seeming closer and closer to being fulfilled. Kurt was actually telling me about some work he'd done in Australia recently when the door opened and his assistant came inside the room.

"He said he's all wrapped up if you want to head in," she said, followed by someone who had to dip their head to enter the room. The conference room had a wide door, a long door, but even still, the guy with curly dark hair had to lower his head to make his way inside.

He took up most of the width too, shoulder to shoulder nearly touching wood, and I just about dropped my portfolio.

But that had nothing to do with his size.

Those eyes, dark and dusky like a buck's fur, I'd captured behind the lens of my camera once. They'd been rage-filled and extremely violent, and his fist was covered in blood in the end.

He'd been beating a man near to death.

That had been what the byline said. Though, I had

nothing to do with that. I couldn't do anything about what the papers said once they got one of my photos. I was just there to tell a story visually, and that was what the reporters had said about him. This guy. This...

"Ares," Kurt exclaimed, calling him by a different name. He waltzed over to the guy, shaking his hand and his basically disappeared in this guy's. Lengthy digits completely covered Kurt's, but it wasn't the guy's hands that captured my attention.

Well, much.

He had a strong jaw, a tight jaw that was well defined. His thick curls waved just below it, and he had a gold hoop looped around his left nostril. He had two actually, close together and pressed tight to his flesh. I rocked a silver one myself but mine looked more like a piece of metal in my nose where his was an accessory. It caused him to look even edgier in the all-black ensemble he wore. A black hoodie hugged his broad shoulders, his dark jeans low on his hips. He rocked solid-black high-tops below them, expensive-looking like the rest of him, and that said something considering he was wearing *jeans and a hoodie*.

And he was looking at me, his eyes on me while he shook Kurt's hand, and my entire body sweated, pits and under-boobs first. The double-Ds were definitely catching perspiration, and I had good reason. I'd captured photos of this guy who'd taken a fan toward the brink of death, and though that should have been the worst part, it wasn't. The worst was what had come after, and something I'd definitely noticed since I had provided the photos for all those news stories about this guy my sophomore year. He'd been one of the best players in the state at the time.

And I had cost him his junior season.

———

CHAPTER
TWO

Ares

Well, that was the reaction I was hoping for.

Yeah, I remember you, Red.

I shook Kurt Ackerman's hand, a family friend. Meanwhile, Red stood behind him, shell-shocked in a poorly fitted suit, her hair up and out of her face.

Her face flushed…

Blasted in color, her freckled cheeks matched her hair. I obviously remembered that well, the red, and she was different from that girl on the field. The suit was way too big for her, hiding her. This girl had curves, and she hadn't been afraid to show them in the pair of cutoff shorts and crop top she'd worn that day.

Trying to impress today, Red?

I supposed she was. She did have this interview with Kurt today. Kurt's assistant had explained all about it before I came in.

Smirking, I let go of Kurt's hand, the man all grins before me. He cuffed my arm. "Good to see you, my man."

"Good to see you," I returned, though it was better to see Red. She still hadn't said anything, her hands working together. She shifted in a pair of heels and a flash of a tattoo on the front of her foot captured my attention. That and the fact that she'd taken the nose ring she had out, her attempt at an obvious professionalism. She was trying to stack the deck here with old Kurt and attempting to play off who she really was.

And what she was capable of.

Red, Red, Red...

This girl was as cutthroat as she was ruthless, and when Kurt let go of my arm, he gestured to her. "Ms. Greenfield and I were just finishing up," he said, and though Red jolted, she came over.

I fought my smirk again, pulling my hands out of my hoodie. I could imagine she hadn't expected to see me today, and that had been the point.

Let the games begin, Red.

"Fawn is one of my internship candidates," Kurt explained. Meanwhile, Red's eyes were on me. They were hazel and filled with an innocence she didn't dare place in my direction. This girl wasn't innocent *at all*, and each and every second she tried to play that shit in my direction had my fingers knuckling.

I returned them to my hoodie for safekeeping, and Kurt Ackerman was completely oblivious. If he wasn't, he'd realize he just introduced the girl who had ruined my fucking junior year, or I guess he was aware. I just allowed him to believe I didn't care. The topic came up in conversation when my father and I ran into Kurt this morning. We'd all made a lunch date for later today.

And we'd laughed about all that shit concerning Fawn.

Water under the bridge, I'd told them both, and my dad had looked at me like I was crazy. I supposed he had good reason. That shit wasn't water under the bridge, not by a goddamn long shot.

Even still, I had made it seem that way, and I had to say, my dad had been pretty proud of me. He called me the bigger man, responsible.

Yes, that was me.

I was all kinds of responsible and forgiving. I lifted my hand in Fawn's direction. "I'm pretty sure we know who each other is, Kurt," I said, nodding. "After all, she did write that article about me."

"Actually, I just took the pictures." Brave this fucking girl, ballsy. She stood tall. "But yes, we know who the other is."

My fists knuckled again, but I didn't lose my smile in her direction. "Was actually just talking to my dad and Kurt about that article." I faced Kurt. "We had a laugh about it. Didn't we, Kurt?"

Well, this shocked Ms. Fawn Greenfield like nothing else. She shifted in those heels again, her attention making a beeline for Kurt, and when he nodded, her brow flicked up.

Kurt braced my arm. "Sure did, and can't wait to catch up more over lunch."

Enter my father stage right. Dad was directed in by Kurt's very helpful assistant, and to watch that shit play out all over Fawn's face…

You scared now, Red? You should be.

My father and Kurt Ackerman were very good friends, as Kurt had covered a lot of the community work my dad had done over the years. Dad was very active in the art world, had several galleries and his charity work by far exceeded the most generous man. My dad and my parents in general liked to give back, and that had gotten the attention of the papers. Kurt was one of the first Dad called to take photos for events he hosted, and the papers loved splashing what he did for others across their pages.

Fawn was seeing that now, that connection. Dad grabbed

Kurt's hand before hugging him. My dad and I were very similar. At least, physically. Dad was slightly taller and broader, but our facial features resembled way more similarly than my mom and me. My twin, Sloane, looked more like my mother, but when it came to similarities anywhere else, my sister was more like my dad. They had a kindness about them and an overall forgiving nature.

Yeah, she was definitely more like him.

I grinned watching Kurt and Dad together. Kurt braced Dad's arm.

"Speak of the devil," Kurt said to Dad. "Your morning meeting go okay?"

This was another nod to my dad. He'd been cutting checks all morning. He and my mom donated a ton of shit to this university. Dad was actually in town today to do that, which was how Kurt had collided with the pair of us this morning in the first place. And of course, we'd made that lunch date.

And what a coincidence that all happened to be on the very day Kurt had his meeting with Red, happenstance a crazy thing, wild...

I studied Ms. Greenfield, as Dad and Kurt chatted. The two were wrapped up, and I took the initiative to close the distance.

She noticed, her head shooting way, *way* up. I had well over a foot on her like I did most people, and she wasn't short, average. Her freckled jaw moved a little. "You know Kurt Ackerman."

She had those same freckles on her lips, and I think I only noticed due to her lack of makeup. *Again*, she'd been trying to be a chameleon for today. Her lips had been painted bloodred the last time I'd seen her, this girl faker than shit. My eyes narrowed. "He and Dad are old friends."

"Old friends?"

"Yeah." I lifted my head about the same time something sweet touched my nose, sugar or honey or some shit. Whatever it was, I didn't like it. I wet my lips. "He's covered a lot of events my dad's done. Charity work." I looked at the pair. "We all ran into each other on campus this morning. Dad's in town to donate money to the school."

She looked at them too, and I noticed a visible jump hit her throat. I wondered if I'd feel her pulse if I grabbed it, squeezed...

This was probably a sick thought, but at the moment, I didn't give a shit. This girl had crossed me, and here we were now in the thick of it.

"And he donates money because you go to school here," she said, putting two and two together. Smart. She chewed her freckled lip. "We both go to school here."

We do, little red. I angled in. "Fancy that."

"Yeah, fancy." She analyzed me, a full tilt down my face and across my shoulders. I was a foot away from this girl, and she didn't step back. Like stated before, ballsy... She folded her arms. "Too much to request an olive branch?"

Intrigued, I cocked my head, and she lifted her eyes.

"For the pictures and all that. The media coverage?" She raised and dropped her hands. "I can imagine that sucked, but I didn't do it maliciously or anything. I saw a story, and I captured it."

She really was cold this one, ruthless.

A little fucking opportunist.

She was lucky I didn't care about it, over it. The school had decided to make an example out of me that year, which was the only reason I'd lost football my junior year. I'd been a minor, and since that asswipe with the bottle had technically struck first, he couldn't press charges. *He* had actually faced charges for assaulting me, and my family had made sure of that. They'd made the whole thing go away, and the football stuff could have been the same had my parents not backed the school up on the decision. They'd wanted me to learn a lesson, and though yeah, that shit fucking sucked, I was beyond it.

I had much bigger plans for Red, my look passive about her proposal. "You want to forgive and forget?" I questioned, leaning even more into her personal space. "A peaceful truce."

"If we could, yeah." A raspiness touched her voice, one deeper and edgier than her already rich tone. *Am I affecting you, Red?* Her eyebrows narrowed. "We're adults. We can act like it. Not to mention, this was three years ago. Now, I'm not saying you should just forget it, but—"

"No, you're right," I stated, surprise flicking her brow up. I nodded. "Completely right. It all should be water under the bridge, and I'm not even playing football anymore anyway."

"You're not?"

"No, I'm not." I passed that off, as Kurt and Dad made their way toward us. "Like I said, water under the bridge."

I couldn't see how that statement played on her face, as Dad and Kurt cut the conversation off when they entered our space. Kurt introduced Fawn to Dad as one of his internship applicants, and Fawn was definitely visibly different as she shook my father's hand. She was well aware now of my family's position to this place and Kurt Ackerman, but the earlier intimidation on her face dissipated. She relaxed before my father and me, and that sick thrill hit again. She was letting her guard down, her sins forgiven, forgotten.

Round one, I guess, went to me.

CHAPTER
THREE

Fawn

My roommate Heath wanted to go to a party tonight, and I think the only reason I agreed was because I was trying to put that confrontation with Ares "Wolf" Mallick out of my mind.

I mean, what were the odds?

Out of all the schools in the state, we ended up at the same one, and maybe my thoughts about previous luck were overzealous. There was absolutely nothing lucky about running into that guy, and the fact he seemed to have some clout when it came to this school wasn't great. I mean, he did say his dad donated money, so there might be some influence there.

At least, we buried the hatchet.

He seemed quick to want to do so, and maybe he was more mature than I might have assumed he was. I might have pegged him as a typical jock, but maybe since he wasn't playing football anymore, he really didn't care about what I'd done to him.

Like stated, big of him.

Still, seeing him had been... unnerving. I'd just gotten done meeting with Kurt, and I wasn't too keen on the fact the two seemed to have connections through Mallick's dad. These were thoughts my brain definitely mulled over as Heath got me and a few of the other photojournalism kids drinks. We all ended up at a frat party, my first since attending college since I typically spent my evenings shooting or doing actual homework.

Again, my brain needed a break.

Heath apparently had no problem at all getting us all beers but handed me the club soda I'd asked for. I didn't drink and sipped on my soda while I scrolled through my phone. I'd gotten a text from my mom today asking how my interview had gone. I hadn't answered, but of course hearing from her sent me down the rabbit hole of seeing what she and my stepdad were up to. They liked to travel a lot, and it appeared they were back from their trip to Paris.

My thumb tapped past them grinning in front of historic landmarks like the Louvre and Eiffel Tower, and another text pinged.

Mom: Hey, did you get my text? Hope things went well. Anton and I are back from Paris. I found some cute little chocolates for you at a small cafe there. They're at the house when you come back for break. *smile emoji*

My mother really shouldn't count on it, and clicking out of the text, I stole a drink from my glass. A light chuckle sounded beside me, and I looked up to find Heath waving his beer toward my phone.

"She's the only person I know who ignores her mother more than I do," he announced to our group, nudging me. My roommate thought he was funny, and the only reason we were roommates was because there'd been a mix-up with housing. Guys and girls typically didn't live together, but we gave it a shot and actually didn't hate each other. He was a hard worker too, and since we both got along okay, neither one of us ever alerted housing.

Maybe I should with him telling all my business to everyone. I shook my head. "My mom's a chatter."

She wasn't, not really. But saying so was way easier than telling him and the rest of our group that I just didn't want to talk to my mother. I had my reasons, and that was none of their business.

I got up off the couch, passing off I had to go to the bathroom. I found it quick since there was a million and a half in this place. From what I understood, this was *the* frat on campus. The best parties were thrown here, and the richest and most affluent resided here.

I kind of wondered if someone like Ares would be here, his namesake Wolf on the football field. I found out later people called him that because of how beast-like he operated on the field. The guy killed dudes, not literally but, yeah, he got work done.

I think I'd looked into him a little more than I would have liked back then, hard not to considering the number I'd done on his life. He'd been forced to sit out the rest of the season, and though his team had still gone to state and killed it, I could imagine it was hard watching from the sidelines.

Not to mention, what he did for you.

I hadn't asked him to do what he had with that ref, him coming in on his white horse when I had shit handled. I'd been okay, and I hadn't needed him.

Why did he have to go and do that?

I was haunted more by that day, what he'd done, more than I wanted to admit. And I hadn't been lying to him before that taking those pictures hadn't been malicious. It was simply my job, and what I felt about him and his actions regarding that ref were completely separate.

It had to be.

I chugged down my club soda, stamping the glass down

on a random shelf outside the bathroom. After, I shouldered my way through the thick crowd, and so in my head, I slammed my face into what felt like solid rock. In fact, I hit so hard I jolted back and collided into a similar force behind me.

"Damn, girl. You wasted or something? Shit." The deep words sounded behind me, lightly slurred, and I pivoted to find a guy with a drink in his hand. I followed it up to narrowed eyes, a stark green that flashed, then twitched on me. "The fuck you doing here, you life-wrecking bitch?"

Whiplash could only explain the response from me, and this guy transformed from slightly inebriated to suddenly on and sneering at me. My brow lifted. "Excuse me?"

"You heard me, bitch." He studied me up and down. "The fuck you doing here at my buddy's frat?"

I didn't know this guy—at all, and he might have been a semblance of attractive had he not barked at me. White, bottle-dyed locks swept every which way. The guy looked like an anime character but was seriously jacked. He shot down a heated look from almost a foot above me, and I backed up into the rock again.

"Yo, Wells, what's..." started the rock behind me, a dude who got one look at me, then puffed up like he wasn't already the size of a wall. He had cross earrings in both ears, the pair sharpened at the tips like swords. Between the two, they definitely looked like video game characters. This guy was a dusky brunette, but the size of this guy had him looking like the final boss on a video game I definitely wasn't trying to play. Sapphire-colored eyes cut down harshly on me. He flashed his teeth. "You got some nerve rolling through here, you problematic bitch."

Okay, *what* was with the bitch thing? I raised my hands. "Okay, you guys are obviously drunk."

"He might be, but I'm fucking not." The dark-haired guy gestured toward his friend with his beer bottle. "Now, I'll ask again. Why in the *fuck* are you here at my frat?"

He was completely serious. They both were, and suddenly, these two were up on me *together*.

The room was feeling too small for my liking.

There were others in this room, but these two were crowding me into a corner. I blinked. "Look. I don't know who you two think I am, but I don't know you."

I think I'd remember, the dark brunette just as fuckboy hot as he friend. These two were bang them and leave them, one hundred percent, and that right away told me I didn't know them. I didn't mess around with players. Especially since guys who looked like that only tended to fuck with girls like me as a fetish. It wasn't like I was considered busted, but I had curves, and guys like them? Let's just say, they liked to get their rocks off with girls like me.

Or more liked to get their hands on *tits* and *ass* from girls like me.

Either way, I didn't entertain it, and I definitely didn't know these guys.

Blond dude, Wells his friend called him, hooked his arm around his friend. He was taller than the guy, more slender too. He grinned. "She thinks our memories fail us, bro."

"Yeah, I'm getting that." He gestured the neck of his bottle in my direction. "But it seems it's not our memories that fail us."

I blinked again. "What are you talking about?"

"Wow. You really fuck with people's lives and don't give a shit about it. What are you? A sociopath?" the dark-haired guy growled, and the next thing I knew, he took his beer bottle and threw it against the far wall. Glass exploded in the corner, several people fleeing, screaming, and my ears rang after my own shriek.

What the fuck?

"Everyone out of the room. *Fucking now*," the dark-haired man-beast barked, and people literally jumped over couches to respond to this guy. Beside him, Wells did nothing but laugh... like manically. The bottle-dyed blond actually bounced up and down in gleeful delight, his tongue out like he couldn't fucking wait for what this guy would do next. Right around then, I decided to curb around them both.

"Oh, not you, socio," the large one, the frat boy, said. He got me by the arm, then proceeded to jerk me with so much force I thought he'd rip my arm out of my socket.

"What the f—"

My voice cut off when he slammed a hand to the wall behind me so hard a painting fell off the *damn wall*. This really had Wells bouncing now, both these guys complete psychopaths.

"What are we going to do with her, Thatch?" Wells asked, biting his fist. He peered over me. "I can think of a lot of things."

"Fucking touch me and—"

Dark hair, Thatch, grabbed my face. His fingers bit into my cheeks so hard he forced my jaw to relax and my mouth to open. Cool air hit my tongue until he breathed heat over it.

"I could think of a lot of things too," Thatch said, making my tongue come out more. He bit at it, and I hissed. He laughed. "But since your memory fails you, how about we backtrack." He settled an arm above my head, smelling like whiskey and flesh, sex. Something cool lingered beneath that, aftershave maybe, but this guy had definitely gotten laid sometime before whatever this was. I could literally smell the fuckboy on him. He wet his lips. "Sophomore year. You took a couple pictures of my buddy Wolf."

My heart kicked at my chest, airflow nonexistent, and both boys laughed at this point.

"She remembers now, bro," Wells crooned, and Thatch nodded.

"I see that too." Thatch dragged his finger down my throat, and he didn't stop until he pressed his knuckle into my cleavage. I shot elbows at him, but Wells got them. He then proceeded to grab my throat, and I choked, hacking. I kicked out my legs, but the two locked their hips against me, both boys impenetrable forces.

I gasped at a thought.

"Thatcher Reed," I croaked out, tugging from the far-off spaces of my brain in desperation. My brow shot up at the dark-haired boy. "You're Thatcher Reed," I breathed out before facing the blond. "And you're Wells Ambrose."

I remembered them now, hard since they'd been wearing helmets the day I'd seen them. They'd aided Ares in that fight, two of the first, along with Dorian Prinze. Only their last names had been on their backs that day, but the news coverage that followed had certainly filled in the blanks. These were Ares Mallick's teammates.

Friends.

"And the memory has fully returned." Thatcher gave his leg a short round of applause with one hand. His other was preoccupied considering he still had it gripped on my fucking jaw. He leaned forward, his sharp earring brushing my cheek. "You should know our names before we have you screaming it."

I wriggled, Wells really, *really* bouncing now. I screamed, ramming my elbows into solid muscle, and somewhere above it all, I heard another voice, a throat clear.

It came from the doorframe.

Ares Mallick lounged casually against it, a beer in his hand, his eyes narrowed. He took a sip before pushing off the frame. "What's going on here?"

Though his friends had stopped their pursuit, their hands definitely hadn't left me. Thatcher faced me. "Found a redheaded weasel, Wolfy."

"Yeah, remember this girl?" Wells yanked me forward, displaying me, and Ares came more into the light. He looked different than he had this morning, his curls up, his jaw clear of errant strands. His hairstyle displayed his undercut, and without his casual hoodie and high-tops, he appeared older. I mean, he had already. It'd been three years since I'd seen him, but the white tee and gray jeans he sported tonight hugged every inch of muscular definition through his lengthy body. He somehow managed to become even bigger than the already large boy I'd seen on the field that day, and the way he dominated his space definitely got my attention. His friends hadn't let go but they were listening. Wells pushed me out. "Can you believe this shit? This is the girl who—"

"I remember her." Ares drew off his beer again before tipping his bottle forward. "But I'm kind of wondering why you have your hands on her."

His friends' jaws dropped, both of them. They exchanged a glance with each other before Ares exchanged his beer with me. He got me by the arm while he handed his beer bottle off to Wells.

Wells blanched. "Wolf—"

"I'll take care of it," Ares said, but I noticed his gaze didn't leave me. This was the second time he'd stood up for me, and though, again, he didn't have to, I was certainly grateful for it this time.

I had been the last time, too, despite not having said it and, well, my actions. There were probably a lot of things that could have been different that day, and though I didn't regret taking the pictures, I could have handled the situation a little better.

And maybe said thank you.

I one hundred percent would today, watching as all three boys exchanged a look between them. Wells and Thatcher in particular stared long and hard at Ares before easy grins touched their faces. I wasn't sure what that was about, but soon, both boys placed them on me.

Thatcher tipped his chin at me. "You would have been better off with us, dollface," he stated, then nudged Ares. "Cuz this dude? A fucking animal."

I smirked, shaking my head. "Fuck you."

Thatcher drew forward, his finger out. "I'd be careful, bitch, or I'll take shit out on you after my boy does."

I'd liked to see him try.

Asshole.

In any sense, he was mistaken as Ares and I had already buried the hatchet. This was something I might have been able to mention had he and his friend not had their fucking hands on me.

"Don't go too easy on that ass, Wolfy." Thatcher nudged Ares again, and Ares's expression was stoic. He gave no reaction to his friend at all, and his friend was a fucking idiot. No one would be teaching me anything, and it was clear Ares had far more brain cells than his friends.

Ares cuffed his arms. "Shut the door behind you, please."

"With pleasure, my dude," Wells said this, but not before making a kissing noise at me. *Fucker.* He shoulder-bumped Ares, then bounced along after Thatcher.

The two closed the door.

My body relaxed. "Thank you," I said, long overdue. I was thankful, and though I hadn't shown it that day three years ago, I had been then too. I sighed. "Really, thanks. Don't know what those psychos would have done if you hadn't—"

It happened so quickly, him towering over me...

His hands around my throat.

He backed me up against the door, my head slamming into it. Ringing hit my ears, and when Ares squeezed my throat, I gasped. "What are you—"

His balled fist collided against the door, the sound ricocheting a thunderous wave within my already ringing ears. Choking, I scratched at the hand around my throat but Ares's hold was unrelenting. Using my windpipe, he forced the base of my skull into the door, and the only way I could describe the way he looked at me was manic, psychotic...

Animalistic.

An untamed rage lined his chiseled features, and I didn't understand it. "Ares—"

"It's *Wolf*, Red," he growled, sounding like an actual wolf. He looked it too. The charged gleam that hit his eyes was nothing but deadly, his teeth showing below it. "Cry it out. Breathe it…"

He got so close once he said that, a soft heat over my jaw, and I grabbed his hand on my throat. "What are you doing?"

The words came out struggled, strained. His crazy-ass friends had already done a number on me, and with this now, I barely had a voice. I kicked, and he grabbed my thigh, squeezing that too.

"Careful, Fawn," he crooned, and when his breath touched my ear this time, I smelled him. His prickly jaw hinted with spice. He didn't smell like sex, but something sharper, sweeter. "Because those psychos? I make look like kid shit."

As if to prove the point, he parted my legs, his hand trailing heat up my thigh. My hip thrust because he had my leg, and all that made him do was chuckle.

"You were so quick to think I forgave you," he said, coming forward. He was inches away from my face, his large body craned over me. He studied me. "Like you weren't completely opportunist as shit and deserved that."

"I never asked you to come between me and that ref," I gritted, snapping. He had me in a completely vulnerable position, but I didn't give a shit. He was acting like a bully, a monster. I snarled. "So, I'd be careful, *Wolf*, because your fragile masculinity is showing."

The wrong thing to say, and his fingers literally dug into my neck when his stark-white teeth flashed. His lip curled above, beautifully full lips he used to spout venom, lies. He completely bullshitted me this morning in the conference room. He tilted my head. "I can break you, Red. A fucking *phone call*, and I can end your entire world as you know it."

He kept calling me that, *Red*, and how original. I wondered if I had green hair, he'd call me *Green*. "What are you talking about?"

He didn't tell me at first, scanning my face. He got really close, and I made out every varying shade in his dark eyes. He even had freckles, darker than mine, but they blended into the rich tone of his skin. Ares "Wolf" Mallick was a beautiful guy.

Too bad he was an asshole.

"Your internship, baby," he said, and when I blinked, he grinned. "That's right. Your pretty little internship, and hell, even your enrollment at Pembroke. Gone at the snap of my fucking fingers."

I blanched. "You can't do that."

"Can't I?" He wasn't even holding me now, his hands on the door, his long reach crowding me. I really could smell him now, the thick aroma rich with a hint of smoke.

I wet my lips and God… dammit. I hadn't smoked weed in a while, but I missed it. I *needed* it most days, but I couldn't take the chance. I'd been clean of anything since I was fifteen.

I scanned Wolf's eyes. "So what? You call your daddy? Blackball me?" I recalled his father being friends with Kurt, and Wolf had said his dad donated money to the school. I lifted my head. "Real big of you."

I was acting braver than I really was, making myself. I refused to let this man-child see any weakness.

Even if I was dying inside.

Even if I killed… *bled* at even the thought of losing either. I couldn't lose either and especially that internship.

He had to be bluffing. Had to.

He didn't look like it, his smile shifting into a smirk. It was arrogant, devious, and how stupid I'd been for falling for his *burying the hatchet* shit before. It'd been too easy, and I'd given this guy way too much credit. His head cocked. "Wouldn't even need to call him," he said, peering over my face again.

He did that a lot. Like he was looking for something, digging. He leaned forward. "After all, a background check would do the job just fine."

My heart stopped, and he became translucent before me. He blurred, and I jumped when he touched my face.

His chuckle followed.

He drew a lazy line down my cheek, his thumb brushing over my lower lip. It came away red, my lipstick.

"Thought that'd get your attention," he said, smearing my mouth more. I moved my head away, and he jerked it back with my hair. Tears pricked my eyes, but all that did was make him grip it more.

"Stop it." I tried not to cry, beg, and I think his threats hurt more than his actual hand in my hair. I shook my head. "I'm sorry for what happened. I'm sorry if I hurt you but, *please*, you don't need to—"

He got my jaw, his mouth hovering over mine. He dampened lips, and when he did, my eyes flashed. He looked like he'd kiss me.

Instead, he laughed.

All too quick he let go, his laughter full as if taunting me with the very thought. I gazed away, and he reached into his pocket.

"I'll be texting you a time and a place," he said, acting completely normal as if he hadn't just threatened me. His thumbs tapped his phone casually. "Get your phone out."

I did despite myself. He asked for my number, and though I didn't want to give it, I did.

I wasn't sure I had a choice.

He had so much power, *information* that could ruin my world. This school and that internship I'd been working toward for longer than this guy probably even had any goals for himself beyond masturbation and smoking weed. They were goals I was fighting for. Goals I needed.

Goals we needed.

I saw my life flash before my eyes when his line flashed on my screen. I didn't answer but didn't have to when he hung up.

"And when I do," he said, continuing on with his earlier thoughts. Dark eyebrows narrowed. "You are to show. I don't care where you are. I don't care what you're doing. You show up, and once you do, you might have an actual shot at me not making your life the complete and utter hell you deserve." His expression chilled. "Because I haven't forgotten about that shit you pulled. I won't, but I might have a way to look past it." He folded his arms. "I suppose that's up to you. You show up, and when you do, we talk about a way you can repay your debt."

He made it sound like I owed him something.

I supposed in his sick mind I did, and his friends were right about him. This guy was nothing but an animal, a wolf in sheep's clothing.

And I'd somehow become his next kill.

CHAPTER
FOUR

Ares

Fawn Greenfield showed up on time.

Way to go, Red. You can follow directions.

She'd entered Jax's Burgers with a camera bag on her arm, a thing she most assuredly took everywhere since she was shameless as shit. I'd dealt with my fair share of reporters, photographers. Things were finally starting to get normal in my life.

At least in that regard.

She noticed me right away at the back of the restaurant and hesitated by the door.

I lifted a hand, gesturing her forward. She came but not without slow steps in my direction.

And she actually looked like herself today.

A pair of ripped jeans hugged her thick thighs, her top cropped and displaying a sliver of her waist. She wasn't shy about showing skin, her arms exposed and something different was her tattoos. A sea of blooming flowers trailed down her arm, watercolors. They blended into the scene of a koi fish swimming along her shoulder and reminded me of the tattoo on her foot. She'd had watercolors there too.

It made me wonder how far that piece traveled up her leg. Was she tatted on both, between them... This girl was an enigma to me despite whirlwinding through my fucking life.

She got to my table, a silver hoop looped around her nose. I'd gotten my nose pierced two summers ago, but my dual hoops sat close to my nose. She eyed me. "So—"

I raised a hand. We'd talk but on my terms. "Take a seat, Fawn."

A familiar red hit her entire face, her freckles across her arms and along her chest too. She'd turned red there as well, the swell of her full tits cherry red. *Are you tatted there too, Red? Somewhere...*

She shoved herself into the booth with a huff, but as I didn't want her there, I told her to come around to me. Her head snapped back. "You're kidding."

I wasn't, fighting the grin when I waved a hand again. I wanted her to know she wasn't in charge here. She'd had a mouth last night and needed to know where we stood.

Obviously seeing I wasn't kidding, Fawn forced herself out of the booth, her camera bag in tow. That thing clearly didn't go far from her.

I fought the growl, not giving Fawn much room when she slid in beside me. This wasn't hard to do considering my height. My feet reached the opposite side of the booth as well as the one behind it.

Because of that, Fawn had to tuck those full hips right up against me, and the build of this girl I definitely tried to ignore. I liked chicks I couldn't snap in half with my dick. I was big everywhere, tall, and with the mouth she had on her, the fucker in my pants couldn't help but be a little hard. Girls with a little lip got the freak shit inside me flying like nothing else.

Mostly because they were so very fun to break.

Ms. Fawn Greenfield would definitely be a project and something else I ignored was that sweet syrupy shit she wore. Reminded me of the flowers on her arm, which made me think about the other tats that *weren't* on her arm. Where they might all be…

I got the menu. Eating food was better than fucking thinking. "Hungry?"

"What?"

I fought the lift of my eyes. Might as well get used to this shit with her.

"Hungry?" I asked again, my eyes peering over her. Like the rest of her, she had freckles on her mouth, and I noticed them again today because she didn't wear her lipstick. No doubt because I smeared the shit out of it last night. I smirked. "You hungry? If you haven't noticed, it's breakfast time."

I was fucking famished. It took a lot to fill this fucker up known as my body, and it'd been known to betray me when I didn't take care of it.

Fawn rocked back after what I said and hadn't been shy when she flipped her hair out and hit me with it. A noise left my chest, and I noticed the slow smile on her lips.

That's your last one of those, Red. I hope you enjoyed that shit.

She was testing me too, and I told myself this was a good thing. This was a great thing actually. She needed to be a certain personality type for what I needed.

I made myself believe it, simmering beside her.

"Actually, I'd like to get on with whatever the fuck this is." Folding her arms, she faced me. "Why I'm here?"

She knew exactly what this was as I'd threatened her ass last night.

Her loss on food, I guess.

The call button had a guy out here. Jax's was a fast-food restaurant but they did tableside service. My buddy's dad owned it, culinary stuff the man's specialty. Because he did, I got free shit whenever I wanted at any of the chains across the country.

I put in for two full stacks, and when Fawn gave me a look, I added a third set of pancakes. Like stated, this fucking body needed food.

"You're free to share if you change your mind," I told Fawn after the guy left with my order, and Fawn sneered.

"Hard pass." She eyed me, feeling like she had the right, and I had to say, it did surprise me she was so mouthy. I thought getting her to see the light last night would have been a little easier, and something told me I could have waited a little longer with Thatcher and Wells. I'd watched them for a second with her before coming in, and she might have been able to hold her own.

At least for a few seconds.

I'd never given her the opportunity, of course, a smirk on my face when I folded my hands. "So, I take it Pembroke doesn't know about your history with drug and alcohol abuse," I stated, her kryptonite, and I knew that immediately.

Her whole body was red now.

That flush touched her ears, my smile widening.

My head cocked. "Or your little criminal activity."

This girl had a history, not a long one, but way more shit than someone her age should have.

And all before her eighteenth birthday.

I honestly had been surprised to find it all, but I'd been delighted. It gave me what I needed, fuel and some shit on her I could definitely use.

Fawn recovered quickly, fluffing her hair out again, but I observed she didn't hit me with it this time. "I wasn't required to disclose that when applying," she said, and though she tried to sound calm, she wasn't fucking fooling anyone. Hazel irises blazed at me. "And I don't appreciate you just putting that out here like that."

I was sure she didn't, sitting back. My food came in, and

she watched as I popped pancakes into my mouth.

"And they can't kick me out for that anyway." She stated this, but I had to say, she didn't sound so sure.

I laughed, adding a second round of syrup to my plate. "Nah, but I'm sure you know Pembroke has a standard." I peered over her again, and the look she shot me could have killed my ass. *Hate me already, Red?* I grinned. "They don't like bullshit, and they don't like drama."

Her little lips puckered like she sucked a lemon. "I'm not drama."

"Oh, you're drama." Chuckling, I pointed my fork at her. "And you've also caught on to the radar of one of the Legacy families."

"Legacy families?"

I swear to God for a girl who reported news she was living under a rock. "Yeah. *Legacy.* My friends and I own this campus, baby." She winced after I said that, no doubt because of what I called her, but I didn't give a shit. My head tilted. "Let's just say, we come from a long line of influence. You bother one of us. You bother all of us."

"I haven't bothered," she started, but then she stopped. She knew good and well she bothered me. I mean, we were fucking here, weren't we?

I nodded. "This university doesn't want drama, and by crossing one of their most influential families, you've created it. Pembroke value us. They value *me*, so if I got a problem with someone attending their school, they don't ask questions." I got close, studying that flush across the bridge of her nose. "They just bow."

They served me, *mine*, and the same went for this girl in the booth with me. The minute Fawn Greenfield had decided to snap her little pictures my junior year, she'd made an enemy out of me. She'd become *mine*. She was mine.

And she owed me.

Her life and everything she held valuable belonged to me,

and I knew that just as well as her reaction to me threatening her yesterday. This school and that internship meant something to her, and her mistake was letting me find out about that.

I really had to give it to Fawn in that moment. Because despite my threats, my proximity, all she did was hold her little camera bag, her hands knuckle-white on it.

Pushing her, I looped a finger around that red hair. Right away, she lodged a shoulder into me, but all that did was force my fingers into her scalp. She screeched, but that cut off when I made her look at me. "You're out of this school with a call, and the same goes for your internship."

Letting her go, I allowed my finger to follow a strand down from her scalp, and the hate that returned to her eyes sent that thrill through my dick again. That really was some freak shit, dangerous…

I forced myself to let go, sitting back. "I think we both know Kurt's not going to want anything to do with you. You're dead in the water with the school, but there's always other schools." I forked a piece of pancake. "I suppose there are other internships too, but Kurt knows people. Word will get around. I mean those pictures…"

Fawn froze, her eyes completely expanded. She knew what pictures I meant.

After all, she was there.

She'd seen in full detail what she'd done. She touched the table. "Wolf…"

"And what's ironic about it all is you made the shit *I did* in high school look like a school yard fight. At least, the dude whose ass I kicked could kind of walk after the stadium fight."

"Wolf—"

"You put that girl in intensive care for *weeks*," I stated, smiling. "I mean, her face didn't even look right after you—"

She tried to slap me in that moment.

I got her wrist.

Her body huffing, she hissed at me. "You don't know anything about that. You don't..." She scanned away before shooting back. She jerked her hand from mine. "You know nothing. *Nothing* about that day and what happened."

She was right. I didn't, and honestly, before I'd found out, I never would have thought this girl would be prone to such violence. She'd been so quick to capture me in the act, caught after I helped her.

And here she had her own dirty laundry, her own sins and a story tucked away in the deep. It had taken some manpower to even find the dirt, but once I had, gold.

"And there were no charges," Fawn continued, swallowing. It definitely sounded like she was talking to herself. "She and her family didn't file any."

I saw that too, very unusual considering she'd left that girl black and completely blue. I hooked an arm behind the booth. "You aired my dirty laundry once, Red. You did, but fortunately for you, I'm about to give you a way to ensure I keep a lock on yours." I leaned in. "I need a favor from you. You do that, and I'll make sure you and I part ways amicably. Your drama stays shut, and you and I will spend the remainder of our college experiences doing our own things."

I.e., away from each other. Though, she definitely didn't deserve it.

Maybe I had more of my father in me than I thought. Forgiveness was certainly a stretch, but I supposed I could forget.

"What could I possibly do for you?" she asked me, really listening now and good. Her arms folded. "What could you need that I could give you?"

More than she knew actually, and righting my fork, I ate the last few bites. "I want you to be my girlfriend," I said between chews, her jaw dropping. I nodded. "The whole semester and all is forgiven."

CHAPTER
FIVE

Fawn

He had to be crazy.

And he was ordering more food.

I watched as he added bacon, sausage, and a round of eggs to what he'd already consumed. Meanwhile, I had no fucking words for what he just said.

"Uh…" Maybe I had just the one, blinking. In any sense, Ares "Wolf" Mallick didn't seem to care. His fast food arrived, and he proceeded to pile it all on his syrup-filled plate. Large guy meant large appetite, I guess. I pulled back my hair. "What are you talking about?"

I felt like I was on some hidden camera show. This guy literally moments ago said he wanted to ruin my life.

And now this?

My internal *what the fuck* was fitting, and Ares—er, Wolf sat casually. He even lounged his big body back, and with as much animal product as he was currently consuming, I supposed that was fitting. He angled a look in my direction. "Did I stutter?"

No, he hadn't, the asshole. I growled. "I mean, what do you mean by what you just said?"

He knew exactly what I meant, and if this guy still didn't manage to look completely fucking hot while he shoveled food into his mouth. His wild curls were up again today, a few of them hanging lazily over his eyes. The style never ceased to do anything but display that perfect jawline of his, chiseled, strong. The guy looked like a model, and something told me he one hundred percent knew it. He caught me looking at his full lips at one point, syrup on them, and when he did, he tipped his chin at me.

Ugh!

He then proceeded to run his tongue over them, and I had to look away at that point. That guy on the bleachers was right that day before he started the fight. Wolf didn't believe his shit stunk. The arrogance off this guy reeked to high heaven.

I wished it did hold an actual aroma, something different than whatever spicy aftershave he wore. It reminded me of apple pie and the woods and shit. He didn't smell like apple pie per se, but whatever it was gave that feeling. Like homey or familiar.

Like comfortable.

That didn't make sense, and I wasn't comfortable in the slightest. Especially in a booth with this guy. He was a man-god, his exceedingly long limbs taking up this entire booth. He was basically elbowing me every bite he took, and his hip touching mine had my own surging beside him. I told myself that was just because he made me uncomfortable by sitting so close.

I told myself.

I brought my camera bag in close. I had a class after this but also had some time to shoot in the park nearby. Whenever I could get some extra shooting in, I did, good practice. Wolf cocked his head. "I want you to be my girlfriend, Fawn. You and me in a relationship." He waved his fork between us. "Not sure I can be clearer on that."

"Yeah, I got that part, but why are you saying you need a girlfriend at all?" Let alone with *me*. "That doesn't make sense."

This guy could ask anyone to be his girlfriend. So why was he asking me instead of some leggy blond follower bitch?

"Fake girlfriend actually," he said, then stretched his wingspan out. The motion hiked his shirt, revealing what had to be an eight-pack. I counted a few sections before they disappeared into his jeans.

I shifted, hugging my bag closer. Without missing a beat, Wolf was right back in his food. He faced me. "I need a fake girlfriend for appearances. A smokescreen as I get back into things after last year."

"Last year?"

"You know, for someone who reports the news, you're really fucking unaware about shit," he stated, annoyance gruff in his voice, and I considered that a win. I liked that I got to him. He got to me, so yes, I liked that. He pointed his fork at me. "You didn't know about Legacy, and now you're telling me you don't know I was out of school most of last year."

That was because my entire world didn't revolve around him. And why would it? I'd been in high school when he'd been here, and I didn't report the news. At least, not in the way he was saying. "Why on earth would I know that you weren't here last year?"

"Because it's news. Stuff regarding my friends and me relevant." His brow lifted slow. "Everyone in this fucking campus is in our business. Everyone talks, and you, as a new freshman, have a job to make yourself aware."

"Why?"

"For starters, to keep yourself out of trouble." His fork

touched the plate, his eyebrows narrowed. "You step on the wrong toes in this place, you get hurt."

Something I was figuring out now. Though, I obviously hadn't known it.

Wolf had had coffee come with his meal, and he got a fill-up when the guy came around. The server called him Mr. Mallick before he left this time, and he was a college kid like us. What the fuck? My eyes shifted to Wolf. "Why were you out?"

"Personal reasons," he said, scarfing another bite of food. He ate quicker for some reason, barely taking a breath before shoveling in more. He swallowed. "And before you ask, nah. They aren't your business."

Well, sorry.

"Just know I wasn't here. Left in the middle of fall semester." Finally finishing what was on his plate, he sat back. "It was rather abrupt, and like I said, people talk. It was bad then, but it's even worse now that I'm back. I got people and *bitches* all over me all the time."

Again, arrogant much. I shrugged. "Yeah, no idea what that has to do with me."

"I told you why. I need a smokescreen. I take school seriously, and with me being behind, I don't need any distractions this year. Needless to say, pussy hasn't been hard to come by since I've been back. It never is, but that shit's basically breaking down my fucking door these days."

Jesus, this dude.

"I don't need any of that shit right now, and a fake girlfriend will alleviate the problem."

Smirking, I shook my head at him. "You're a piece of work."

"And you got a mouth." He got in my face, woods and apple pie hitting me again. I followed those freckles along his nose once more, real close but I wasn't backing down. This guy liked to push but I did too. His expression darkened. "But also fortunately for you that's what I'm looking for. I can't have a weak girlfriend. Wouldn't be believable, so you fit the bill."

Surely, though, a follower bitch could take some direction. I mean, if he was as popular as he said, that shouldn't be a problem. Not to mention, they'd actually look like they belonged together. Wolf and I couldn't look any more different. He was taller than me by well over a foot. Maybe even two and looked like he should be modeling on a beach somewhere in the Southern Hemisphere. I wasn't quite sure of his ethnicity, and the ambiguity certainly had him ticking all the boxes regarding the universal standard of beauty.

He might have even invented it.

Needless to say, that wasn't me, nor did I desire that. I was just me, and I liked me. I was average, but I was okay with that.

Because I was, though, that certainly set off some red flags here. I folded my arms. "What's your angle?"

"Angle?" This guy really didn't like to be questioned, the word snipped, terse. "What are you talking about?"

"I mean, *why me.*" I gestured between us. "We don't exactly look like we belong together."

That much was obvious and his look of confusion had me agitated now. He lounged back. "Not sure why you'd say that."

Why wasn't he saying it? I laughed. "Come on, Wolf. I'm not some idiot."

"Actually, *Fawn.* I'm beginning to question that," he stated, pissing me off more. He folded his hands. "And what the fuck would you know about the kind of girls I hang with? Especially since you've clearly been living in a fucking cave since you got here."

"I know they probably all look like models," I shot, and rather than be insulted, I stood up. I shouldered my camera bag. "So, until you stop taking me for that idiot, I think we're done here."

Leaving was probably pretty stupid considering what he had on me, but I'd always been hotheaded.

I guess he knew that.

My stomach twisting, I started to go, but Wolf whipped me back so fast my head spun. He jerked me into the booth, then pressed his hard body against mine.

"Girls like that I fuck," he gritted, snarling. Harsh heat moved over my face, his nostrils flaring. "They're *ass*, and considering they use me for the same due to my clout, I don't feel fucking bad about that."

My heart beat swiftly, the thuds quickened, constant.

He wet his lips. "You aren't ass, and to everyone around me, you wouldn't look it."

He was trying to compliment me... I think, but he basically called me average. He did call me average, and for some reason thinking that about myself seemed different, felt different. I swallowed. "Okay."

"In addition," he continued, and this time his hand moved to my throat. Lengthy digits completely encased my windpipe, but this time he didn't squeeze. "I need something I own, Fawn Greenfield. Something that bows to me, and if you haven't noticed, that's you as of late."

I winced, my throat tight, but not because he had a hand around it.

I gazed around in that moment, hoping this position he had me in might draw some attention. I refused to believe this guy had as much power as he stated, and though there were others around, I noticed something rather quick.

No one was doing anything. At least to help me. In fact, the minute I locked eyes with someone, they averted theirs.

My throat jumped once more, a familiar ringing in my ears. I looked up to find Wolf's grin, his thumb tapping my pulse point.

"I own every inch of you," he said, my body twitching, trembling. He cast his dark shadow over me, his hard chest solid against my tight nipples. I was scared by this just as much as the ringing he'd inflicted upon my ears, the tops of them hot, surging. His digit pressed into my neck. "I own what you do, and as you can see, no one cares about that. No one cares about you. I told you. This campus is my bitch, and even the booth you're sitting in is ours, Legacy's. My buddy's dad owns this restaurant chain."

Power and influence all around.

"You're mine, Red." Wolf brought me to him by the neck, squeezing. "My loyal, dutiful girlfriend. She shows up when I want. She acts how I want, and she'll be what I want."

Basically, he wanted a slave, me. "Another bitch for you, then?"

"An equal as long as you behave." His smile widened. "I can make this as painful or as easy as you want it to be. You act right, you'll be off the hook this time come Christmas. I'll leave you alone, and all will be right in the world. Just gotta be my good girl…"

I cringed at that. This fucker really believed I owed him something. I had a debt to pay, his slave for showing the world what kind of darkness lingered inside him. This wolf was completely fucked, crazy.

I grabbed his hand around my neck in that moment, my nails digging into his skin. He didn't care, merely smiling, and it took all I had not to spit at him.

I had a feeling it'd make this all so much worse.

CHAPTER
SIX

Fawn

Wolf never explained the details of his little arrangement. He said he had a class, but once again, would be in contact. I had no idea what his plans were for this, and though he said the arrangement was fake, I didn't know how real he wanted this to look to the outside world. I didn't know how much of his "girlfriend" I actually had to be. Did he just want the illusion of it?

Or did he want the physical too?

He seemed like the type of fucked-up bastard who, if he had his cake, he'd want to eat it too, but I wasn't that kind of girl. I may be his girlfriend to the world—for a semester—but he wasn't getting that part of me.

Hell fucking no.

I bided my time waiting for his next Wolfy contact. Meanwhile, I was doing my own research on a guy I should have investigated from the beginning. With as much power and influence as he and his friends seemed to have, he was right, I needed to know.

Needless to say, I found a lot.

For starters, Legacy was actually a thing. I asked around and not only did everyone on this campus know about them, but that was how the crew had been regarded in high school. There was Thatcher Reed, Wells Ambrose, Wolf himself, of course, and their other friend Dorian Prinze. I recalled Dorian from the fight that day too, and though I hadn't seen him yet since then, his name was around just as much as the other boys'. They apparently had been friends since grade school and maybe even before. Their parents had a long history of being in each other's lives. At least, businesswise. Many deals came up with the names Reed, Ambrose, Mallick, and Prinze, their families connected.

This campus was also littered with buildings named after all of them, so this only cemented the fact that these boys meant something to this campus. Two of them had sisters too. Thatcher's sister, Rainbow Reed, was still in high school, but I was surprised to see Wolf had a sister.

Mostly because of what came up when I looked.

A lot of dark stuff surfaced, *a lot* of dark stuff, and come to find out, the two hadn't even always been in each other's lives. Actually, they'd reconnected their senior year in high school, twins.

Wolf was a twin.

My journalist/investigative hat really on now, the majority of my searches surrounded them and the fucked-up shit they'd both gone through before coming here to Pembroke. The two had gone through a lot, an understatement, and honestly, some of how messed up Wolf seemed to be was really starting to make sense. He and his sister, he and his family really seemed to have been given a shit bag when it came to life. Of course, that didn't give him license to treat people the way he did, but yeah, I got it.

I kind of wished I didn't, though. I didn't want to sympathize with him, and I definitely didn't want to be obsessing the way I had. I was on my belly googling for what felt like the umpteenth morning, searching about him, when Heath knocked on my open door. He had his camera bag on his arm, his school one on the other.

"Uh, so Ares Mallick is at our door."

I froze, the pencil literally falling from my mouth. I'd been searching on my laptop while jotting notes on my Steno pad.

He said he'd text.

This wasn't a text, or a call. The fucker had left me on read the last time I'd asked if we could, I don't know, maybe hammer out what I was supposed to be doing regarding this girlfriend shit. He'd been completely silent since that day at Jax's Burgers.

Heath's eyebrow arched. "Actually, he's on our couch now." His shoulder touched the door. "Want to let me know why a member of Legacy is in our dorm right now?"

Okay, so even Heath knew about that shit?

I really must have been living under a rock because, like me, Heath spent most of his time doing schoolwork or shooting. I started to get up, and Heath lifted his hand.

"You're going to have to explain it to me later," he said, shouldering his bag. "Late for class, but like I said, he's on the couch. Told him to make himself at home."

And I was sure he would, knowing him.

After eyeing me again, Heath pushed himself off the door-frame, and I proceeded to get a bra on my suddenly sweating boobs. That was always the first place the sweat went, and I shoved Kleenex under them, blotting them. Once dry, I aired out my freaking pits.

Why the fuck does this fucker make me so nervous??

He made me more on edge than anything, and I didn't like that he was in my dorm—at all. This was my personal space, and he had no right being here.

Let alone going through my purse.

And that was what I found him doing the moment I

entered the common area Heath and I shared. We had a nicer dorm than most, a shared living space and separate bathrooms. The place had a waiting list like a bitch, and now I was watching the subject of my nightmares going through my bag on a couch that barely held the length of him. Actually, it didn't, his legs crossed over the arm while he lounged on the sofa. The purse was on his stomach while he went through it, and when I ripped it away, he smirked at me.

"Got something to hide, Red?" he asked me, situating that big body on the couch the right way now. He still took up most of it, his bent knees well above our coffee table's height. Dark eyebrows drew inward. "And who the fuck was that dude who let me in here?"

Uh, yeah, he had no right to ask that question. I crossed my arms. "Why are you here and going through my purse?"

I was well aware I answered his question with a question, and he was too, that stupid smile of his back. It made his dusky eyes twinkle, and I certainly didn't like that I noticed that.

Or how well those dark jeans of his hugged his thick legs. He had boots on below them, and his Henley was tight and fitted over his lean muscles. No, I certainly didn't like how good he looked today, or how every time he wore his hair down, I wondered what it'd be like to put my hands through it. This guy had a curl pattern for days.

He also had far too much control over my life, and I knew that as I actually waited for him to answer me instead of demanding he leave. He was in my dorm, and I didn't want him to be. His grin hiked. "Guess I need to know who I'm dealing with, and all that shit you girls keep in there says a lot."

How ironic he wanted to know more about *me*. "Why are you here?"

"Nah, I answered a question. You answer mine." He

draped that eagle-length wingspan of his behind the couch. "Who was that guy?"

"My roommate," I said, not that that was any of his business, and the moment I said the words, any trace of a smile left his lips. Next thing I knew, he was getting out his phone, and I cocked my head. "What are you—"

"Yeah, I got a student in need of new housing," he said, getting up, and a noise left my throat. He studied me. "Yeah, it's an emergency."

What the hell?

"Wolf?" I stepped over to him, and he raised his hand, his words clipped on the line of whoever he spoke to. I heard the words *today* and *whatever you got*. Meanwhile, I was jumping at him trying to get in his face. I might have gotten the phone too had he not had like two frickin' feet on me. "Wolf—"

His hand shot out again, the guy in my face this time. He sneered. "Her name's Fawn Greenfield, and she can meet with you today. No problem."

I couldn't believe this was happening and what the fuck? He hung up, and in the next moments, he was grabbing my camera bag. I shrieked, grabbing for it, and he got my schoolbag too.

"What? You got class, right?" he said, as I managed to work my stuff away from him. His lips turned down. "You trying to be late for it? You do have a class."

I did, but how did he know? "What? You know my schedule too?"

"Amongst other things," he stated, cocking his head at me. "But I somehow missed how you were in here living with some dude. By the way, someone from housing will be contacting you about that. You're not living with a guy. Not when you're with me."

I couldn't believe this guy. I pushed my hair back. "I'm not moving."

"You are, and now you're going to class." He took my

stuff again, *my stuff,* and he was so quick, I barely had a chance to get my purse and lock the door before trailing after him. He grumbled. "Also, Red, shit like that will have you making an enemy out of me, and I'm sure you already know what a bad idea that is. I told you this can be as easy... *painless* as you want it to be."

This guy was psycho, crazy. "This is fake. This arrangement?"

"It's real to the fucking world, and believe me, no one in my life would believe I'd allow the girl I'm dating to be living with some guy."

We were outside now, me taking like three strides for every one of his. The guy wasn't even walking quick, and I was out of breath. Not to mention, fake or not, there really was no threat when it came to him and this stupid arrangement. Heath was bi, but his dating preference edged more toward guys. He said he hadn't dated a girl since middle school, but something told me that wouldn't matter to this big bad Wolf.

"Really fragile, aren't you, Wolfy," I said, and he got my arm. He hiked me up, and I jerked in his hold. "Let go."

He didn't, all up in my face, and he really was good about that. He sneered. "Fragility has nothing to do with it. You're something I own. My property. And no one touches my things. Point-blank."

My flesh buzzed, my arm where he touched me. My throat flicked. "You don't own me."

"You know I do. At least, until the end of the semester." He didn't let go, hiking me up farther. I was on my tiptoes now. His eyes narrowed. "Which can be extended if you don't play by our little game."

Heat surged my face, a wash of anger, fear, and something else I certainly didn't want to touch with a ten-foot pole. My flesh still tingled from where his fingers had embedded themselves in my arm, and I wanted to sock myself for it. It wasn't unknown to me that I was attracted to him, but my hate should balance out the scale.

It should tip it.

My head clouded in weird ways because I did hate him. I hated everything he stood for. This guy believed he was a god among men, and that definitely extended to me.

Releasing me, Wolf moved again, and I didn't have a choice but to follow him since he had my camera bag. I could lose anything else, but that he couldn't have.

I started to tell him that, but slowed down when he strode toward a Hummer truck.

"You coming?" he barked behind him, opening the door of that same truck. The dread hit me when I noticed the hood.

A silver wolf scrolled into the paint. This behemoth of a machine was obviously his. I shook my head. "I usually take the bus."

Ignoring me, he cracked opened the back, and I watched with horror as he placed my stuff inside. I ran up on the truck then, ducking under his arm. I grabbed my things, and he frowned.

"Well, you're not today," he stated, hitching his hip against his ride. The thing was completely obnoxious with its size and definitely like him. I mean, he had a damn wolf painted on the front. He nodded. "Anyway, isn't your class like history? That department is on the other side of campus, and it'll take you at least an hour to get there."

I knew how long it took. I did the trek every day after all, and it'd bother me more that he really did know my schedule if I wasn't trying to put some distance between me and getting in a vehicle with this guy.

Swallowing, I started to back up, and Wolf pushed off his truck.

I didn't give him a chance to do more than that.

I ran, knowing the way well to the bus stop. My bags slammed against my sides, as I heard Wolf calling after me.

"Fawn, what the fuck?"

I didn't gaze back, knowing this guy was way faster than me. Even outside of his long legs, he had a history of playing sports, and though I had an active history myself, it didn't travel beyond the steps I took in order to snap a photo. He'd snatch me in a second, and the only chance I had to get away came when I cut my way through a bunch of photography students. My dorm happened to be in the general area of the photography department, a big reason I took up residency there since many of my classes were photography related.

"Fawn!"

I chanced a look back, as Wolf was pushing his way through students. He shoved around people a full head beneath him. Meanwhile, I made it to the bus stop with exactly no breath.

And at not a moment too soon.

The door of the latest bus started to close as I made my way to the stop. I rushed on, hoping to God the driver would close the doors before Wolf got a chance to catch up with me.

But of course, I wasn't that lucky.

My luck really did seem to end. Wolf was suddenly at the stop and making his way onto the same bus as myself. He paid fare right around the time I found a seat at the back of the bus.

And the look he gave me...

Ares "Wolf" Mallick had shared a lot of looks with me, the majority of them rage-based, anger. This look, though, seeped enough venom to alter the chemical properties of the compact space we were in. He found me. He sat with me, and when he did, he simmered beside me—heatedly.

And the bus was looking at us.

Everyone inside the vehicle was gazing our way, his way. I had a feeling a member of Legacy taking a bus wasn't common.

"That was your *one* of those," he stated, placing an arm

around me. It more so landed on the back of our seat, but people definitely noticed. He faced me. "Your one allowance. Pull something like that again, Red, and I swear I'll take it out on your ass."

The words had been low and so obviously for me. I shifted, playing them off. "I told you I usually take the bus."

He made a noise then, also low. It hit somewhere within the confines of his big chest, and I shifted again.

"Like I said, your last. Defy me again, and it's over. Your little life... Your entire existence as you know it—mine, and that won't stop at your internship or your place here."

He was so good, almost looking at me like he hadn't just threatened my entire life in front of a busload of people. A hint of a smile even returned to his face as he threatened me. Maybe even because he threatened me. I gazed forward. "I can't just change things. I take the bus to school. I have a routine. I..." I fought another shift, fingers bracing my bags. "I can't just *move out*. I'm Heath's roommate. I can't just—"

"He'll have another by the end of the week," he said, casually. He shifted this time, but I figured that was more so because he'd folded himself into bus seats. "As far as what you tell him, I don't give a shit."

"You're unbelievable, and why did you even show up at my dorm out of the blue? You said you'd text." I found it unnerving, that and all these *eyes on us*. People weren't being shy about looking, and a dude had even dropped the burrito he was eating in his lap.

"I did say that, but last I checked, I don't answer to you." He tossed me a look. "And I actually came to take your ass to school this morning."

"Why?"

Another look, like it was obvious or something when it wasn't. His lips turned down. "Because that's what a guy dating a girl would do. That's what we're doing, by the way, and consider us in the early stages." He glanced toward the front of the bus. People were still watching on, but since we were at the back, we did have a semblance of privacy. At least in our hushed conversation. Wolf adjusted in his small seat. "I'll make the announcement when we're official. We do it too quick and people will know something's up."

Wolf flicked his chin then at some dudes at the front of the bus. I recognized them as football players, something I only knew because they lived in my dorm too. I hugged my stuff. "So, what are the logistics of this?"

"Logistics?"

I nodded. "Yes, what's involved with this assignment? How often should I expect you around and have to play this game?"

And what did he expect out of me while I played?

I leaned off his arm then, easy to do. My hair up today, he was starting to touch my skin, and I didn't like that. He made me uncomfortable in more than one way, and like he knew, his arm returned to the place behind my neck.

"You don't expect me around, Red. In this arrangement, this *relationship* you answer to me." His lengthy digits folded around the back of my neck, his finger tracing lazily at the short hairs at the nape. Lava coated my skin again, and when I shot away from his hold, he grinned. "Which means I get to touch you, and when I do, you don't recoil from my fucking touch."

"Well, that would require some pretty good acting," I said, laughing. He sneered and a little flutter of pleasure burst in my chest. I smiled. "Anyway, you touch me and—"

He hooked his arm around me, and not just on my chair. Face inches from mine, he scanned me like he always tended to do, and I shivered.

He noticed.

"Yeah, real hard acting, Red," he crooned, tipping my chin. He pinched, and I angled away. His breath touched my ear. "I get to touch you. You're my girl, so I get to do that, and something tells me that won't be so bad for you."

God, he was arrogant, cocky. He basically had me in indentured servitude, but I wouldn't be his sex slave. I looked at him, face on. "I'm not having sex with you."

"You're right. You're not."

I blinked he said it so quick, a grin touching his full lips.

His thumb tilted my chin down. "So, don't get any ideas about that. At least, not until I put them in your head."

He shook my chin, and I jerked away, the *audacity* of this guy. Like I'd be the one who'd be honored to sleep with him.

And to think I'd felt bad for him.

I had upon learning all the stuff I had about him. What happened to him and his sister not even two years ago sucked, and their tragedy had started even before that. Them not being in each other's lives hadn't been by choice, and I'd had empathy for him.

I found myself hard-pressed to do that now as Wolf was in my space, my face. He dropped his arms on the seats surrounding us. "Anyway, you just take my lead regarding any of that. The physical stuff, I mean. Like I said at Jax's, this arrangement is for the public, which means when I take your hand, you let me. I put my arm around you the same."

"Kissing?"

His smile widened, and I scoffed. He shrugged. "If I see fit."

God, this *guy*.

He was pompous enough to think I'd let him too. Again, he probably thought he was doing me a favor. I growled. "And what if my acting isn't so good that day?" I arched an eyebrow. "What if I slip and decide to give you cheek when you lean in?"

Which I would. This guy *wasn't* kissing me, and at this point, the thought of him even taking my hand made me cringe.

Mostly.

My heart kicked up when Wolf gave little to no reaction to my threat. If anything, his grin just turned more wolfish. Two fingers got my chin again. "For your sake, you better hope you don't have bad acting days because the moment you do, this little game of ours stops being friendly."

A wickedness touched his eyes with his latest threat. This game wasn't friendly at all.

"And I have your first assignment tonight." His arm returned around me, and my breath expelled. My chin prickling, it took all I had not to lodge my camera bag at his pretty face. He gazed out the window. "A party. Think of it as our coming out."

My eyes narrowed. "What time?"

"Ten. I'll pick you up," he said, his curls brushing over his shoulders when he faced me. "That a problem?"

Shit, I must have looked it.

Playing it off, I shrugged. "Actually, I have some shooting to do tonight. Just give me the address, and I can get myself there."

Please let me get myself there.

I waited for what felt like eons for his response, a millennium, but I was sure the time that had passed was only a few moments.

"Night shooting. I'm sure that will be real nice." His brow flicked up, but I kept my retort at bay. He got out his phone. "I'll text you the address."

Thank God.

"And be there *on time.* I'm not joking, Red."

I definitely would be. Especially because he was letting me get there myself.

I nodded, my transfer coming up. I tugged the chord, but when I stood up, Wolf got my shirt.

He tugged me back.

"You forgot something, babe," he said, lounging back, and

when I looked around, he turned his cheek. He tapped it. "You can't leave me hanging."

He had to be joking with this.

And people were looking at us again.

They hadn't stopped honestly, but they were really looking at us now. That dark twinkle hit Wolf's eyes once more, and I know I pleaded with mine. "Wolf..."

He said nothing, his cheek still in my direction. If I didn't kiss him, something bad would definitely be happening.

This son of a bitch.

I fought myself from cringing when I pitched forward, and though I brushed a kiss on his stubbled cheek, I kept my lips tight. I made it quick too, and I probably could have broken a record.

"Have a nice day," he said, those dark eyes doing their familiar dance. He'd won today, and the audience with their jaws dropped around us told both of us that. He got me to submit to him in public, put on a show for his loyal followers. He tipped his chin. "Remember, ten o'clock. It's a pool party, so wear that suit I like."

The *looks* hit double time then, my stomach twisting, tightening. I rushed off the bus, but the next thing I knew, I was catching the next. I'd be skipping history class today.

I had a bathing suit to shop for.

CHAPTER
SEVEN

Ares

"The fuck you going on about?"

My best friend Dorian sat back after what he said, our other two best friends Thatcher and Wells nearby. Thatch and Wells had been preoccupied by their dates before what D said, but the moment the tone changed, they looked at us.

"Out." Thatcher basically pushed his blonde off his lap, the chick in a string bikini and really playing up tonight's angels and demons theme. Her little halo bounced when her head cocked, her pouty lips tsking at my boy. Thatch rolled his eyes. "I won't tell your ass again. I said out, so get the fuck out."

The sad thing was this girl would probably still end up sucking my buddy's dick tonight. He just had it like that, and though he was a freshman, he owned this mother fucking frat we were currently partying in.

This was Legacy's party house, ours by association with Thatch. We all did what we wanted on this campus, Thatcher's frat house included.

The girl Thatch pushed off his lap huffed, and Wells directed his dude to head off in the same way.

"You too," he'd said, dismissive about it before drawing off his beer. Bro was savage considering he'd already let the guy fist his cock tonight.

But these hookups were a dime a dozen to us, and odds were, that guy would be back quicker than the blonde. Wells was certainly a love-them-and-leave-them type guy, and since he hooked up with both guys and girls, they often fought each other over him.

And that was this kid in his freshman year.

The guy Wells had been entertaining was dressed as a demon tonight, and Wells definitely didn't move his feet to let him pass. Again, savage. Wells frowned at me. "Yeah, what the fuck are you talking about?"

I may have been more intimidated by my friends ganging up on me had they all not been wearing fucking costumes. The "angels and demons" thing had been decided last minute for the pool party's theme. It was something I'd texted Fawn about, and Wells asked his question with a set of wings strapped to his fucking back. He'd gone full white with them to match his hair, his swim trunks black like the rest of ours, and needless to say, we'd all laughed our fucking asses off at him. Fucker actually thought himself angelic, and though D and I were dressed as angels too, there wasn't anything pure about us. I had black wings pinned down by a harness, and D's looked like they'd been razor-bladed off. My sister, Sloane, had helped him with that, using charcoal to create haggard lines on his back. The illusion had ended up being pretty sick, and I wished Thatcher had taken a few tips. Dude showed up like a demon, and his horns basically reached the ceiling of any room he entered.

They were extra as fuck, like him, and Dorian, Wells, and I took every opportunity we could to hang shit off of them. Socks, condoms, the whole nine yards, but the laughter of all that was obviously over. I flicked a card from a deck I'd shuffled at a trash can, bored with this conversation. "I said I'm seeing someone."

"And again, I say, *the fuck* you going on about?" D gritted, my sister on his lap. The two of them were dating, something I was still getting used to, but that was only the second thing considering I had a sister now. I mean, I'd always had one. My parents never lied about me having a twin, but the topic had definitely been a sore spot for a long time. It always had been until she'd come back. Things were better now, great now. Dorian barked a noise. "Since fucking when?"

"Dorian?"

I glanced to find my sister calming my buddy down, my twin defiant. She'd come as a demon tonight, whereas most girls bopped around this bitch looking like angel whores. Little horns on her head, my sister complemented D's fallen angel quite well, and I'd been relieved to see she fought the status quo even more by wearing a full T-shirt on over her swimsuit. She'd arrived in that and her kicks, which meant the boys and I didn't have to keep putting towels on her all night. I mean, that was my sister and D's girl. She rubbed Dorian's arm. "Relax."

She was the only one who could say that to him. Fuck, even Wells, Thatch, and I couldn't say shit like that, and we were his boys. Dorian, like the rest of us, was a hothead, all of us holding our fair share of rage and toxic shit. Back in the day, we had tended to bond over it, but recently, it'd been changing. Sloane was a big part of that. Especially when it came to D and me. The trauma and pain in both our families we could bottle, but when Sloane came around, it was like the world was handing us something. Good shit was happening instead of so much bad.

I guess that had been my first problem, getting complacent and shit. I got too used to good things happening to me as of late.

I tossed another card and smirked at the shallow breath Dorian took in. Sloane had him meditating, and that shit was funny as fuck when I'd walked in on them both doing that in D's and my dorm. The two of us shared a space like Wells and Thatcher did, but we all eventually planned to get a house together. D wanted Sloane to move in, but she'd only do that if she wasn't cheating Dorian out of an experience of living with his friends in college. She'd actually said that, my twin.

Like stated, she made things better.

"I'm sure he'll explain what he's talking about if you give him a chance." Sloane crossed her legs, the pair of us very similar. She was taller than shit for a girl, lanky, and I think I only had the latter part on her because I worked out like fucking crazy. She also kept her dark hair straight where I didn't give a shit, the mess of it bunched up on her head. She faced me. "It's a surprise, but I'm sure there's a reason for that."

My fingers dug into the cards, the tone of her voice putting me off. Another thing I liked about my twin was that, like my boys, she gave zero fucks about handling me with kid gloves. She gave that shit to me just as hard, but she wasn't today, hadn't for a while now.

Knowing the reason why, I distracted myself, tossing more cards into the can. "Nothing to explain. Like I said, I'm dating someone." I swung my sight over to my friends. I shrugged. "I'm only telling you because I wanted to give you a warning before she gets here. So you guys act right and don't embarrass me."

I'd told Fawn to come at ten for a reason. I needed time to explain this all to them.

Putting my cards down, I let silence fill the air, and considering who my friends were, there was a lot of it.

"Act right. Ah, okay." Dorian pushed dusky blond hair out of his face before cutting a look at me, and dude was fucking jacked to hell these days. He was quarterback for

Pembroke's team just like he'd been in high school. Because of that, the guy had just about doubled in size, and Thatcher and Wells weren't far behind. Especially Thatcher with his giant ass. I didn't think that dude could have gotten any bigger since high school, but he was starting to break the legs of couches he sat on with his weight. Football training was obviously going well for all of them, and in high school, the four of us used to compete against each other for the best gains.

Those days were gone at the present since I didn't play, but I still joined them for workouts off the field. I needed to keep my body in shape, strong.

Dorian grumbled. "Well, who the fuck is this girl?"

"Dorian?" Sloane questioned, and D sighed.

"I'm sorry, little fighter, but this dude don't date people."

He wasn't wrong about that, and actually, I held a record amongst us. I didn't date. I fucked, casually, and though my boys had a track record too, they'd all at least had a partner on their arm for longer than a month.

I didn't even do that.

D hooked his arm around my sister after what he said, *little fighter* his nickname for her. He shook his head. "It just doesn't make sense."

"Yeah, suspect as hell." Wells's lips pinched together, and I swear to God, if he didn't pull that halo off his fucking head. He crossed his arms. "You said her name's Fawn?"

"Greenfield, yeah," I stated, and when I said that, Thatcher shot up. The guy had been listening too, but it wasn't uncommon for him to be slow on the pickup.

He certainly wasn't now, ramrod straight. He directed a finger at me. "Wait. That bitch who got you kicked out of football?"

Fuck.

Thatch's eyes expanded. "No fucking away—"

"Wait. She was here the other night." Wells's head whipped in my direction. "Right? Wolf, what the fuck?"

"The fuck's going on?" D sat back, his eyebrows pinched together. His hand lifted. "Someone slow the fuck down and explain."

"Oh, I'll explain it." Thatcher was laughing now, and he was lucky I was waiting for the appropriate time to come in. I'd prepared for this, to check his ass, but he was testing me to keep my cool right now while I waited. He flicked a digit in my direction. "This guy had me dig up all kinds of shit on that girl who took pictures of him and got him kicked off the football team your junior year. I'm talking her social media accounts, her class schedule, housing, and enrollment information." He slapped the back of his hand against his palm. "Basically, anything Pembroke had or didn't have on her I was to find out. I got information on her family and what she *and them* are into." His gaze flicked to me. "He pretty much had me find this girl's entire life, and I figured he was using it to ruin her. Especially after she came here the other night."

The room was real quiet now. Though I had prepared for this, it wasn't fucking awesome to be at the center of it.

Sloane's feet touched the floor, and since she didn't know about the football thing, I could imagine she was confused. This was before her, not long before but before. Her eyebrows narrowed. "You got kicked off football, big?" she asked, calling me by her nickname for me. She called me *big* and I called her *little*. Something I'd started. Her head cocked. "How?"

I supposed I shouldn't be surprised she shared more concern for me and less about the latter part of what Thatch had said. She was a special breed, my twin, and was just as protective as the rest of us. She wanted to know about what happened to me and didn't give a shit about anything else. I pressed my hair back. "It was nothing."

"Hardly. There was a fight, and this Fawn Greenfield's

pictures provided evidence of it." Dorian's look could kill, not so different from Thatcher's and Wells's in that moment. He settled a hand on Sloane's waist. "Got this fucking guy kicked off the field for an entire season, and now you say you're dating her?"

"And how does that happen exactly?" Wells draped his long arms over his knees, his hands opening. "And how is this you taking care of the situation?"

He was mentioning the party from the other night, and though I really didn't have time to go over this shit with them, I knew it was necessary. They'd never let go of this if I didn't.

They'd never be convinced.

I knew my friends, *my family*. These boys weren't just my buddies. They were my brothers, and because they were, they knew me. They knew my MO, so I had to work this angle just right with them. Knowing exactly what to say (because I knew them too), I sat up. "Thatch is right. I did ask for all that shit on her. I saw her on campus and asked him to dig up all he could find on her."

Most of that was true. I mean, I did see Fawn on campus before I had him look anything up. I saw her a lot of times.

I nodded. "And also right, I had every intention of ruining her life."

That was a part of the plan for him to think that, assume that. He was the only one I knew who could get the kind of information I needed on her. My boy Thatch was a computer hacker, and I needed everything he could find, necessary.

I also knew I'd need to give him a reason to look up the information, though, and her destruction would only make sense. It was something we'd all do, again, darkness in our nature. If people crossed Legacy, we came for them, and that was actually how D and Sloane had met. She'd gotten in his way once, and immediately, he'd gone for her neck. Of course, that was before we knew who she was. Her being my sister came later.

That year had been difficult for all of us on so many levels, but I'd take a million of them to have her back. Sloane had been taken from my parents when we were babies, and though the transition back had been rocky, I didn't think any of us would change it. She and my adoptive brother, Bruno (her brother), made our family fucking whole. Bru was actually away at college himself. He'd chosen to go to a fancy school overseas, on his own journey, and was a freshman like Wells and Thatch.

Sloane sighed after what I said, and though I didn't like her disappointment, I expected it. Out of all of us, she was the purest. She had a soul still, a heart. She pressed her hands together. "Big—"

"But that was until I talked to her." I faced the room, a show I was putting on. I didn't like lying to my family, but it was necessary. They only didn't see it now because they couldn't, but they would. They had to. "I talked to her that day at the frat, and we had breakfast not long after that."

"Breakfast?" Thatch barked, and I nodded.

"Yeah, dude, and through it, I realized she was human. Did she screw me over? Hell yeah, she fucking did, but she's also a person. Flawed?" I watched Thatch's jaw drop along with the rest of the room. I shrugged. "I decided to forgive her, and once I did, we talked and connected. I got out of my own way and saw she was pretty kickass."

This was an Academy Award–winning performance I was giving, but in all honesty, this was the only way these people would ever believe I'd date anyone. If Dorian dating my sister taught me anything, it was that we guys attracted a certain type. We liked the challenge, sick like that. I'd want Fawn because I wanted to ruin her, break her.

"Holy shit. Holy shit. Okay."

This came from Thatcher, his head nodding. I really did

know these guys because Wells's nod wasn't far behind. Wells's head shook. "Well, that's good... then."

I laughed. "Thanks."

"Nah, man. Seriously." Wells pounded my fist. "That's great."

"Real great, big," Sloane said, and I was relieved to hear that. I thought she'd be harder to convince. She nudged D's leg. "Isn't that great?"

Dorian wasn't saying anything, a harder sell, but I expected that too. We were the closest out of all of us. His shoulders lifted. "Yeah, great."

I wasn't convinced by that, but considering I had my hands full with Thatcher and Wells, I let it go at the present. The two fuckers proceeded to throw fake punches at me in congratulations, and shaking my head, I let them.

"Hope it works out, my dude. Legit." The crosses in Thatch's ears danced, his head nodding. He shook my shoulders. "I mean, after the year you had, you deserve that shit. A fresh start?"

Well aware of the year I'd had, I bobbed my head twice in acknowledgment, and that got a slap from both Thatch and Wells. They fed me their congratulations again before heading back to the party, but only after they made me promise to reintroduce Fawn to them. They said they wanted to apologize to her for the other night.

Feeling some kind of way about that, I scrubbed into my hair.

My sister came out of nowhere with her hugs.

I was still getting used to *that*, never much of a hugger, but whenever she gave them, I didn't fight her off. They felt like home and shit, so no, I didn't fight.

"This really is so great. You here and just... ah!" Her shout in excitement had me laughing, and she nudged me. "Shut up. I'm just happy you're back. Thatcher was right. Your year was bullshit, and you need this. Need something like this."

I didn't know what to say to that, so instead of choosing the wrong thing, I just tapped her shoulder. "Thanks."

In my periphery stood D, and I assumed him waiting around meant the real challenge was coming. This kid and I knew each other, the first of our clique to come into the world. A year older than Thatch and Wells, we connected on that, but in general we were just really freaking close. Because of that, his bullshit radar wasn't an easy one to work over.

So imagine my surprise when he put his fist out for mine.

"Sorry about my reaction before," he said, tapping it. His arm went around my sister. "I was just shocked, but I am happy for you. I hope this works out, and Sloane's right. You do deserve this. A break."

I was sure that was the only reason for the fist bump, him being easy about this. I wasn't quite sure he believed me, but other factors here were obviously edging him the other way.

Ignoring the locking in my chest, I nodded at him, surprised when Wells and Thatch made their way back.

"Eh, uh. Wolf, you should probably get out there." Wells had his hands tucked under his arms, Thatch beside him. "It's your girl, so…"

My girl…

Fawn.

Not sure what this shit was about, I cut around them both, and the guys shouted out I needed to get to the pool.

The commotion outside the room was already leading me there.

The frat house was loud with the party, but the general chaos definitely bled from outside. Most people were out there with the pool and DJ, but many were pumping their fists in a completely different direction.

"Out of the fucking way!" I barked, pushing through. I cut through the sea easily and didn't have to fight far through it. Fawn was up on a goddamn picnic table.

And she was shaking her hips.

Thick thighs swayed in a white bathing suit, a one-piece but that didn't mean shit. Her hips danced her ass cheeks in my face, in *everyone's* fucking faces since the suit left nothing to the imagination in the back. It exposed every inch of her full ass, and when she swiveled her hips forward, I saw exactly how far those tats chased up.

Heat surged my mother fucking neck, watercolor tattoos decorating her leg from hip to high heel. Some even graced her inner thigh, but I was too busy focusing on how her tits were out just as much as her ass. A deep V flashed her flushed chest, freckled and just as generous as what she teased in the back.

There was no tease here, her game blatant, defiant. The slap in the face was the halo and wings she wore, white, pure.

Licking my lips, I shoved a fucker to his ass to get to her, and she didn't see me because she was too busy being a loud, *stupid* bitch.

She wouldn't after tonight.

CHAPTER
EIGHT

Fawn

I screeched, picked up by my hips…

Tossed over a shoulder.

Okay, so shit like this never happened. At least not to me. The last time I'd been picked up like this was probably infancy. I wasn't a tiny girl, but that didn't stop whoever from picking my ass up. My hair hung in a curtain over a set of black wings. They gave the illusion they were folded, the whole thing held back by a harness over this guy's back. It was a pretty killer costume really.

Jesus, this guy's ass.

Perfect and solid, the only thing taking my attention more was the whole package, his golden thighs tight, body hard. My fingers physically itched to touch it, but I resisted as each and every step resulted in this guy's shoulder ramming into my stomach. My body flopped, and I caught a whiff of him, spicy, and the potency made my mouth water.

Wolf.

I kicked, and he grabbed my ass, growling.

"Get the fuck out!" he roared, and swinging me around, Wolf shot a finger at the people in front of us. I realized now Wolf had taken us into a crowded room, and needless to say, that shit cleared the moment he howled.

People moved in double time, dodging the massive guy and his mood swing. He obviously hadn't liked my little dance on the table, but that had been the point. He told me what to do and embarrassed me on the fucking bus.

"Put me down, Wolf—"

I flopped on the couch, dropped from an unknown height. My hair whipped around my face from sheer velocity, and I sat up to find Wolf ripping the curtains closed. A fireplace roared in the room, and of course, it spotlighted him.

Beautiful, gorgeous. He wore absolutely nothing but a pair of black swim trunks, and the harness that held those fake wings. Honestly, he looked kind of like a sub in a sex club, hotter than fuck but there was nothing submissive about this man. He hadn't dressed like a demon, but the angel he portrayed was dark and warrior-esque. Black paint smeared across his muscular chest and torso, an eight-pack there like I guessed.

I wet my lips, that same paint delving into the lines of his perfect hip bones. He had his hair down too, war paint on his perfect cheekbones, and a necklace flashed as he approached me.

"Get the fuck up," he said, the thing around his neck twinkling. I couldn't really make out what it was, as he reached for me, and my head shot up.

I backed up, snarling. "No."

"I said *get the fuck up*," he gritted, getting a hand under my arm. I shrieked this time, but he ignored that. His hold released the same way it had on the couch, but this time, I hit the floor.

A dagger of pain shot directly into my kneecaps, white hot and enough to send tears pricking my eyes.

I fought them, moving to my hip. My teeth lodged into my lip. "You bastard."

"And you're a stupid bitch."

My head shot his way again, the guy towering over me. He got my arm once more and put himself inches from my face. "The fuck was that shit out there, huh?" Stark-white teeth flashed, his nose rings glinting from the fireplace's flame. "And why in the actual fuck did you think any of that *at all* would be good for you? Good for me?"

That had been the point. I smiled through the pain warming my knees. "You told me to wear the suit you liked," I said, glancing down at my chest, my breasts. I basically had two straps of fabric holding up my double-Ds. I smirked. "I was only doing what you said."

Like stated, he'd embarrassed me on that fucking bus.

"Think you're cute, don't you?" His hold did nothing to loosen, his fingers pinching into my skin. His dark eyes radiated like hot coals, and the moment they flicked down, my nipples tightened. Like actually fucking hard and a flush of warmth moved over my chest. My cleavage charged beet red, and Wolf dampened his full lips.

My core buzzed then, my stupid fucking body reacting to him. I didn't know why. I wasn't sure I'd be able to walk after he threw me on the floor.

"Up on your knees, and when you do, I want you to take your top down," he said, my eyes launching wide. He had to be joking, but it didn't seem like he was, considering the way his attention didn't leave my boobs. He glanced up. "I want to see your tits."

What the fuck?

"Fuck no." I ripped my arm away, my skin still warm from where he'd grabbed me. I wished it was just because what he'd done hurt, but honestly, he hadn't grabbed me that hard.

What's wrong with you? He asked you to take your top down.

Disgust curled my lip. "Have you lost your fucking mind?"

"No, but you have." He stood to full height, godlike. Or I guess, in this case, an angel considering his outfit. His chiseled arms folded, biceps lean, cut. "You did the moment you decided to flash your fucking tits and ass out there. You obviously wanted a certain amount of attention."

I'd been playing a game then, a game with him.

"So, show me those tits," he said, eyes darkening, and my clit buzzed. What the fuck? "Show them to me or our deal is off, and I call Kurt right fucking now."

He wouldn't, crazy. "You're bluffing."

Honest to fuck, he didn't grace me with a response. He merely reached into his harness, a strap of material there. It looked like maybe it was supposed to hold some kind of weapon for his costume, but out of it, he pulled his cell phone.

My heart leaped when he pressed a single button. Like he was ready for this moment.

Maybe he was.

"Hello?" sounded from the phone. Wolf had it on speaker. "Ares, is that you? It's late, son."

My stomach twisted, my heart hammering. I crawled on pulsating knees toward Wolf, but he stepped out of reached.

A grin touched his full lips, as he brought the phone to his mouth. Kurt was on the other line. I recognized his voice easily. "I know it's late, Kurt, and I'm sorry about that." Studying me pathetically on the floor, Wolf's grin hiked. "I guess I just wanted to talk to you about something. Something important that I feel you need to know."

He'd warned me about this. He'd *warned* me, but once again, I'd let my temper get the better of me. I reacted like I always did. I shook my head. "Wolf, please…"

"Oh?" Kurt came in with, but before he could say another word, I guided the straps of my bathing suit down. Tears pricked my eyes for another reason this time, and Wolf's attention directed away from his call.

"Actually, Kurt," he said, watching as I exposed my breasts. I almost got the material down to my nipples when Wolf took my hand.

Lengthy fingers folded around my wrist, his thumb brushing the flush across my chest. My nipples pebbled again, and the sensation physically made me ill.

It was like Wolf knew my body's physical response, his digit lazily outlining the eye of my koi tattoo. I shivered, and that wolfish grin of his hiked once more.

"I might be mistaken," he stated, quick. "I'll call you back later."

He wanted to see if I'd actually do it, submit to him. My gut churning, I got on my knees, and the look he gave me...

Fascination. A wide array of it hit his eyes, and something dark and equally disturbing lingered beneath. He gripped my hair, exposing my neck.

"I want this up," he said before giving me the hair tie from around his wrist. He might have used it earlier since his hair was down. His thick curls grazed his cut cheekbones.

I did what he said, and he stood back, watching me. More of that fascination touched his dark eyes again, and when his irises flared, my stomach fluttered.

Was this... turning him on? Me? I mean, he said I didn't know anything about the girls he dated so...

I turned the thought away, making myself. Nothing about this was flattering. Nor what he was making me do. This was purely sexual for Wolf, which made me the object.

His plaything.

He wanted to see tits, and whether they were mine or anyone else's didn't matter. He was a dude and thought purely with his dick.

My arms lowered, my hair up aside from a few loose

hairs. Hooking a finger, Wolf tipped my chin, and my jaw tightened when he moved a thumb over my lip.

"What's wrong, Red? This is what you wanted, right? Attention?"

I didn't want humiliation, this. I tugged my chin away. "And here I thought you wanted a girl who wasn't weak. One who stood up to you, so this was believable."

That'd obviously been bullshit. He wanted a submissive, someone to bow to him. He didn't want an equal.

A smirk touched his mouth. "That's not why you did what you did tonight," he growled, hunkering down. "You did what you did because you were in your feelings and wanted to test shit."

I hissed, and he grabbed my jaw, hard.

"And because we were in public, you thought you could get away with it."

"You were being a bastard on the bus today." I fought his hand on me, but he wasn't letting go. My eyes narrowed. "You don't have to embarrass me for this to work."

"Maybe I don't, but it does make it more fun."

God, he was gross, sick.

He let go of my face, beckoning me to work down my straps again. I did, but once more, he told me to stop before I flashed him tits.

"Good enough," he said, then rose above me. So close, I could make out each and every hair across his sculpted legs. Strong, powerful, he brought them forward, and though his trunks were black, the outline of his dick was easily made out.

He was hard, thick, and...

"Want to see it, Red?" he questioned, then out of nowhere started stroking himself through his trunks. I looked away, and he chuckled. "Don't be shy now. I mean, you were looking at the guy like you couldn't wait to taste him."

Fuck, why was he so filthily, nasty. I faced him. "I was looking because you had it in my face."

I was proud of myself in that moment. I didn't look away despite him fisting himself in front of me. Nor did I have a waver in my voice when I said it.

"You'd know when I have it in your face." He gripped himself, lengthy digits smoothing up and down dark material. He was long under there. That was a given, and judging by the thick outline, this guy was definitely packing.

He probably thought that made him something, more of that god complex he clearly had. He brought himself forward again, and my fists knuckled, resisting the urge to move away, flinch. I wouldn't let him win.

"So, here's what's going to happen," he said, so beautiful above me, handsome. He was kick-in-the-face gorgeous, and I wondered what kind of sick game the universe was playing. To make someone that visually striking completely demented. His chin lifted. "You're going to let me come on your tits…"

My head shot his way, the reaction out of me making his eyes dance. I cursed internally, and all Wolf did was fist himself more.

I watched despite myself, my own fascination there. A part of me *did* want to see, and God did I fucking hate myself for that.

"And you're not going to move an inch," he continued, his voice rough, gruff. His hand moved, and I closed my eyes when his digit traced lazily down my breast. "Not a goddamn one until those beautiful tits of yours are completely *soaked* with my cum."

A tingle hit between my legs, one I fought before I opened my eyes. Of course, he found my boobs beautiful. Again, he was a dude. My jaw shifted. "So, what are you waiting for, then?"

My response surprised him, his eyes widening. He tempered the reaction, and his next move was to pull himself out. His heady scent hit the air, and I swallowed at the visual force suddenly in his hand. He pumped what was probably the biggest dick I'd ever seen, thick, veiny. Pumping lazily, Wolf studied my reaction to it, but I didn't give him one.

I stayed there on knee caps that pulsed tight with pain, my thighs squeezing together to resist the surge between my legs. I wouldn't react to this guy, mentally, physically…

"Look at me, Red."

I did, saliva lining my mouth. I could *taste* him he was so close, the head of his cock dotted in pre-cum. My thighs hugged tight once more, my body shutting down in complete refusal. I sweated everywhere, my brow damp, my breasts. I kept envisioning him sliding his dick between them, and I wasn't even *in*to that stuff.

What's wrong with you?

I'd always been attracted to Wolf. I mean, he was fucking hot, but I hated him too. I *despised* him, and that should be enough to resist whatever this shit was I felt. He was degrading me right now, the humiliation worse than it'd been on the bus.

His hand encased my throat then, something weird hitting his eyes as his fist picked up on his cock. An anger laced his dark eyes, and though I'd seen it before, I didn't understand it now. It was like he was mad at me or something, like this was my fault and I was making him do this. His strokes got more aggressive, and that rage only rose its dark fury.

Mine matched as I watched him, hate and resentment buzzing my entire body. This beast of a man had me on my knees, and when those first jets of cum hit my chest, I closed my eyes. Thick streams splashed my breasts, dotting my neck…

My chin.

I sucked back any emotion, physically swallowing it down. My hands knuckled at my sides, and when I opened my eyes, Wolf was tucking himself away.

"You can go now," he said, glancing away, *dismissing* me.

His curls shrouded his face, and I didn't give him a second to actually look at me.

I got up with shaking legs, weak from the floor, my knees burning. My steps wobbly, I forced assured steps, ignoring the shake in my legs yes, but also something else.

The dampness between my thighs, my own wetness I was definitely aware of, but I refused to think about it. I *refused* to believe it was nothing more than a physical response. I wasn't sick like him. I wasn't *him*.

"Fawn."

Wolf's voice sounded different. Softer than before, lighter. I didn't turn around, but it was closer.

He sighed. "Fawn…"

"Fuck you, Wolf." I'd stopped at the door, my chin lifted. "Just… fuck you."

Maybe he had remorse for what he'd done, but I highly doubted that.

This guy was the devil.

Continuing my steps, I pushed myself out of the door. I needed to find the nearest bathroom.

I had cum all over me.

———

CHAPTER NINE

Fawn

Noa Sloane-Mallick was in my class...

And she definitely didn't have this class.

I'd notice, I think. The girl was a goddess. Her long legs crossed, she sat at the front row of my lecture, and I passed her.

Maybe she's just in the wrong room...

Hoping for that, I treaded to the top row. Up there wasn't my usual seat, but I'd take one today.

She moved.

Casually, Noa picked up her things, trekking toward the back in a pair of worn kicks and a hoodie that cut off just above her knees. I assumed she wore shorts beneath, her dark hair up in a messy bun. She definitely wasn't as flashy as her twin brother, and I tried to ignore her when she sat in the back with me.

When she sat *next to me.*

Literally, her butt housed the seat to my right, and she completely ignored college etiquette. One always left at least one seat between yourself and a stranger. I mean, any other way was just weird.

Well, Noa didn't give a fuck, right up next to me, and the resemblance between her and Wolf was uncanny. Obviously, she was his twin, but sitting this close tripped me out. They held the same striking features as each other, hers soft, feminine. She faced me with the most perfectly smooth complexion and was just as gloriously tan as her brother.

I faced away, caught looking at her. I fought the curse in my mouth and the shift in my seat. I had hips, and she did sit next to me.

"I take it you know who I am."

Fuck.

I sat back, this shit more than awkward. I was still getting over the trauma of her brother. "Hi."

I mean, what the fuck else did I say? Hello, I'm faking dating your asshole brother who came all over my boobs the other night? I hadn't heard from him since then, but I hadn't questioned small favors.

I *still* felt his cum on me, that hot sticky cum I scrubbed off in a fucking bathroom. His heady scent lingered on me, though, aromatic, potent. The cruel wolf had claimed me, and when I finally did get home, I hadn't even been able to shower in a place familiar to me. Wolf's call from housing had landed me in a new dorm that day, a layout similar to my own but sans roommate. Two bedrooms, I figured that new roommate was coming, and according to Heath, he had a new one by the end of the day.

He hadn't even questioned my excuse that housing found out we'd been living together, the coed thing a fluke. We'd known it'd been a mistake from the jump, so me using that as an excuse had been easy.

In actuality, his text messages surrounded Wolf. He'd heard rumors about us going together, but I wasn't trying to talk about that shit. *Not* after what Wolf had done to me at the party.

Noa Sloane-Mallick being here now reminded me of the deal with the devil I'd made, her smile a faint one in my direction after my small greeting. I did know who she was, and because I did, I knew why her name was hyphened. She hadn't always had Wolf's last name. That had come later when she'd entered their family. An entire website could be made with all the information Wolf, his family, and even the rest of Legacy had on the internet. These people were like the Kardashians but managed to have way more drama.

Noa put out her hand. "We haven't been formally introduced. I'm Sloane."

A necklace flicked across her hoodie, an emblem on a chain, and I recognized it. Wolf had worn the same one at the party. Perhaps a family thing, a twin thing. She also had a thick ring on the chain in the form of a gorilla. It had ruby eyes.

Not letting myself care enough to ask about either, I shook Sloane's hand. Her brother was still very much in my head, so no, I wasn't going to ask. I nodded. "Fawn."

It was weird shaking her hand, weird seeing her. She really did look so much like her brother, like the girl version or something.

A curious look flashed across Sloane's face as she shook my hand, and she kept it short. She started to say something, but my professor started class.

I got my stuff out like everyone else, but Sloane didn't. She simply sat there. "So, um, you new to this class or…"

"No."

My attention flicked in her direction. "You're not?"

"Nope."

She hadn't bothered to keep her voice down. Though, I supposed she didn't have to. This class sat two hundred, the class at half capacity, and the hall we were in was large. We also sat in the back row, and since my professor lectured with a mic, we probably could converse at a decent volume without disrupting anyone or anything.

That didn't mean we should, though, and Sloane's *eyes* were still on me. She had a worse stare than her brother, and I one hundred percent felt it.

"Can I help you with something, then?" I asked. She'd obviously followed me up here and had sat where I'd see her at the door.

"Actually, yes. I came to say you can take your *good time* somewhere else. Specifically, somewhere else and *away* from my brother."

I froze, my fingers mid-type on my laptop. I'd been setting up my doc to take notes. "Sorry?"

Sloane's legs crossed, her high-tops in my direction. She looked pissed, royally. Her dark eyes narrowed. "Just what I said. You seem like the type of girl who likes to have a good time if the frat party was any indication. And that's fine, but my brother, Ares, doesn't need the distraction. Not right now and after the year he just had."

I was kind of at a loss for words here. I mean, for a few reasons.

The year he had...

Out of everything, I found myself more caught up on that. I didn't want to be, but yeah, that got my attention.

Sloane's head tilted. "He lost a year of his life. It was a hard year, and he's doing everything he can to catch up."

"I—"

"So, yeah. You can do me that favor." She grabbed her bag. "I'm not an idiot. I know this is college, but a *good time* and *the life of the party* is the last thing Ares Mallick needs right now. So, if you're that, I'm going to kindly ask you to bow gracefully out of his life. You're wasting his time and, honestly, your own. These days, he's definitely not the life of the party. He isn't because he's trying to focus on school and get his fucking life back."

I blanched. Again, for a few reasons.

Her lips turned down. "Just please. Don't waste his time or yours."

Her chair snapped up after she stood, and I took back what I said about us being able to be loud.

The entire hall gazed back at us as Sloane traipsed down the stairs. My professor had even stopped talking.

The door slammed shut after Sloane exited, and only after the sound bounced off the room for a beat did the professor redirect everyone's attention forward.

He restarted his lecture, but once more, I just sat there. Apparently, Wolf's sister didn't want me with him because she believed I was a party girl.

And, also apparently, he'd had a hell of a year.

CHAPTER
TEN

Ares

Fawn: So, your sister came to see me today.

   Fawn: Showed up in my class and basically looked like she wanted to kick my ass.

   Fawn: She also pretty much called me a party girl and told me I was wasting your time and distracting you.

   Fawn: Anyway, thought you should know.

   I dropped my deadlift. Barbell literally slipped from my fingers. It hit the floor with a clank, and I picked up my phone.

   Fuck.

   "Dude? The hell? You okay?"

   The boys rushed over, D first. He'd spoken, but Thatch and Wells flanked him. Apparently, I wasn't the only one who'd stopped lifts.

   Christ almighty.

   Ignoring my friends, I took a seat on a weight bench, but that didn't stop my buddies. They crowded the fuck around me, and the shadows dimmed my phone's backlight. I growled. "Space?"

"Fuck you. Are you okay, bro?" An insult and a question about my well-being in the same sentence. Leave that to Thatcher Reed. He flung back his dark hair. "I told you guys he was lifting too much."

My eyes rolled, my thumbs hovering over my phone. I couldn't focus on a text with them surrounding me and shit.

"Space, *please*," I requested, nicer this time. I even showed fucking teeth. "I'm fine. You didn't need to come over."

They did this shit. *All the fucking time*, they did this shit. I thought since I was lifting more than them these days, they'd stop, but they hadn't.

My friends hovered around, their eyes on me. We'd been all working out for a couple hours now. We'd all come back home for the weekend following final classes. Weekends at home were something we often did since Maywood Heights, our small city, wasn't far away from Pembroke U. Wells and Thatcher were lazy fucks and came back to get laundry done, which I was sure their parents both loved. They had staff at their houses to do it, but still.

Dorian and I weren't that lazy, and our reasons were far better. He liked to spend time with his folks, and since Sloane and I came home every weekend to see ours anyway, he often tagged along. Sloane and I hadn't gotten a lot of time as a family with our parents before graduation. Because of that, we did come home, and when all the boys traveled back to Maywood Heights too, we usually hit up the local gym.

I was starting to regret that the way they hovered over me. It'd been terrible since school had started. They did this at Pembroke too when we were working out together.

I sighed. "I'm good. I swear."

They liked to check in. I got that, and the only reason I didn't completely lose my shit was because I'd probably do that too. I cared about these fuckers.

And they cared about me.

Dorian huffed, the shirt he'd sweated out tucked in the back of his shorts. He used it to wipe his head before pulling it behind his neck. "You say something if you need us. And don't be deadlifting shit you don't need to be. This isn't a competition."

My buddies had obviously noticed the extra weight, and I admit I'd pushed myself. I didn't do it for them, though, never for them.

I waved them off, and Dorian gave me the finger. He and Thatch headed to the weight bench. One spotted the other, but Wells lingered.

He patted my shoulder. "Take it easy, all right?"

He didn't wait for my response, heading over to his own weight bench. He started curls, and before I could think about my friends' little intervention, I picked up my phone.

I just… held it. It'd been more than a week since I'd talked to Fawn, and the last time I'd seen her, she'd had my cum all over her tits.

I wet my lips.

Me: I'll handle it.

I kept that shit quick too, my text. I had no room for thoughts in my head. She and that stupid shit she'd pulled had me in the gym every day this last fucking week, and it was good the boys had been too busy with football to join me. The kind of weight I was lifting would have given them a coronary.

Let's not even talk about my fucking *runs*.

I was up at the crack of dawn, every fucking day. I came from a family of runners, but the shit I'd been doing lately was ridiculous, the miles never ending.

Fawn and her stupid shit.

All she'd had to do was listen. Fucking listen, and things wouldn't have gone as far as they had. Honest to fuck, she'd been lucky I hadn't nutted off between her tits, the swell hugging my cock, my seed between them... I wasn't even sure I had hands big enough to hold them, and I had huge fucking hands.

Grunting, I adjusted my shit in my shorts before heading to the weight wall. D had moved over there, and I raised my phone. "You know anything about Sloane talking to Fawn?"

I was sure he did. She may have been my sister, but she was his girl.

Eyes were on us both, Thatcher and Wells. They were spotting each other on the weight bench now and were smart enough to keep doing that shit.

"I'm aware," D said, the heat rising on my neck. I had full intentions of talking to my sister about this, but the fact she'd already discussed this with my best friend wasn't fucking right. He definitely should have talked to me about this. Dorian docked a weight. "Said she was going to talk to her. She was worried Fawn would be a distraction for you, and I agree with her."

"So, you two are my mom and dad now." I tucked hands under my arms. "How in the fuck did she even know where to find her? Fawn said she targeted her in class."

A lot of silence came from my friend, but he did glance over to Thatcher and Wells. Thatcher in particular scrubbed into spiky blades, and I barked out a laugh.

"You're fucking kidding." I laughed again, but this shit wasn't fucking funny. "What happened to you were all happy for me?"

My friends remained silent but these three were loud fuckers. Thatcher started to get up, but Dorian put out a hand.

"Thatcher didn't do anything but get her schedule, and though Sloane is the one who wanted to confront Fawn, I completely backed her up." D picked up another weight, grunting with his curl. He glanced at me. "We all saw her at the frat, man. We get you wanting to have fun, but something serious? With her? She just seems a little wild."

"Yeah. Because you fucking know her." I got in my friend's face, the only thing between us his weight, and Wells and Thatcher did get up then. Thatcher stood on standby, but Wells put a hand on me.

"Let's just all calm down, yeah?" Wells's words were for no one but me because Dorian did appear calm. My face fucking hot, I was the only one who was heated, and I really didn't know why. Fawn and I weren't real or anything, and what we had was even less.

My jaw shifting, I didn't move, and Dorian sighed.

He put his weight down. "We just want what's best for you."

"Yeah, you guys are real good about that lately. Your hover shit?" I stared at them all. "I mean, I can't even go to the gym without a fucking babysitter."

I'd literally had to dodge them all week, going at odd hours when I was at the gym every day. They stalked me. Always texting and calling with their fucking check-ins. It was driving me insane and not necessary.

I put my hands together. "I'll give you the gym, but respectfully, you need to back off this stuff with Fawn and me."

Again, I didn't know why I was getting my back up and all this with her was suddenly making things a lot harder than they should be. It shouldn't be this. Not the point.

I gazed away, but glanced up when D placed his hand on my shoulder.

"Of course, we'll give all this a chance, and like I said, we're just looking out for you." He tapped my fist, a little relief there when he did. "But you can do us a solid and not give us any more reasons to worry. Last year was shit, and none of us want a repeat."

No, we didn't, which was why I was laboring as much as I was lately. That was the last thing he'd ever know, though, him and the guys. We couldn't have any more shit years.

It might just break us this time.

CHAPTER
ELEVEN

Ares

"So, Ares is seeing someone. Someone at school…"

The roll flew down the wrong pipe at dinner that night.

Coughing that shit back into the right one, I hit my chest, and my mom dropped her fork from across the dinner table. She started to get up, she and my dad both, but they stopped when I raised my hand.

"I'm good. *Fine*," I cut before facing my twin. Despite me about to fucking die over here, she appeared completely calm. As if she'd said nothing really. My eyes narrowed. "Sloane…"

"What?" Sloane folded her fingers. "You weren't going to tell them?"

I wasn't. That wasn't a part of the plan. School stuff and Fawn were definitely staying at school. My jaw moved. "Hadn't planned on it since we *just* started seeing each other…"

"So, it's true, then?"

Fuck.

Mom's attention pinned to me. Dad's too after what Mom said.

Between the pair, my sister and I were basically their clones. My dad was Middle Eastern and white and Mom was Latinx and white. Mom was fairer than Dad, her hair straight and darker, and both could easily pass for models. Being a mix of the two, I one hundred percent took advantage of that shit every waking day of my life. It was easy, so yeah, I took advantage of it.

Mom's brow lifted. "Ares?"

My gaze on my sister, I gripped my goddamn fork. "Yes."

"Honey…" I honestly wished my mom's word followed some kind of curiosity, judgment even. Like why in the fuck her twenty-year-old kid—who'd never *ever* spoke words about dating anyone—was suddenly seeing someone only weeks after being back at school.

It would have been better than her smile.

Her finding this weird would have been so much better than being *pleased*, and my dad grinned to the nines with her.

"Ares…" he said, his head cocked, eyes bright. My dad was a naturally happy person, but lately, he hadn't had a whole lot of things to be happy about.

Knowing I'd been the reason for that, I kept my mouth shut. To the right of me, Sloane lifted her head. "Her name's Fawn Greenfield—"

"Sloane." I didn't know what game she was playing here, but she needed to stop playing it. "What are you doing?"

The question held a double meaning, my eyes on her. The gym had held me up, so I hadn't gotten a chance to talk to her about her contacting Fawn. I'd gotten home and dinner was ready.

Normally, this table would hold more people. My brother, Bru, obviously couldn't be here since he was overseas, but sometimes the guys would join us or even Thatcher's sister, Bow. They all opted to have dinner with their own families tonight, a rare occurrence since Sloane and D were always all over each other. With as tense as things had been at the gym, I knew he only wasn't around so I'd have an opportunity to talk to my sister.

A silent exchange passed between my twin and me, her eyebrow arched as if to say, "What?"

I shook my head, our parents all smiles.

"Well, I don't know why you wouldn't say anything." Mom shook my arm, squeezing. "This is, well, great."

"Yeah, it is." Dad folded his long wingspan. Sloane and I got our heights from him. He nodded. "You said this is new?"

"Yes, real new." I forked peas. "That's why I didn't say anything. Didn't want to make a big deal about it."

I fought myself from snarling at Sloane, something definitely going on here. I was obviously hard-pressed to confront her about it now, our parents around.

"Sounds like you're really getting back into the swing of things. Living life again?" Dad's smile reached his eyes. "Glad to hear it, and you deserve that."

Sloane had said something similar, and instead of appearing all aloof, her plate took her attention. Her fork tines guided around peas, leaving me to our folks.

"Trying to get back into things," I said, swallowing. I waved. "We're just talking, and things have been good."

The ease with which lies flew from my lips these days unsettled me, but now that Sloane had mentioned Fawn, I couldn't very well back down.

This is what you wanted.

I tried to remember that, making myself smile when Mom knocked my leg.

"You should bring her home sometime," she said, taking my dad's hand. He nodded, and Mom tilted her head. She smiled at me. "God knows we have plenty of room. Maybe she can come down with you and Sloane one of these weekends."

Sloane really had left me to the wolves here, and she wasn't even eating anymore. She had her hands folded, her stare completely away from everything regarding the conversation. I sat back. "Sure."

Of course, that would never fucking happen, and if my parents pressured me, I could just tell them Fawn and I broke up. We would eventually. That was the plan.

Shifting, I tried to make Sloane look at me, but she wasn't having it. We would talk, and when I volunteered us both for dish duty that night, I set out for that goal. Our parents sat back and let us, and I had a nice stack when my mom called my name.

"Before I forget, honey, I ran into Dr. Sturm at the grocery store," Mom said, and the grip on my dishes increased. She gestured to me. "Said to remind you to reschedule that appointment you had. Something about your class schedule getting in the way?"

I schooled my features, forcing myself to ease my grip on the dishes. I nodded. "Yeah, just figuring out when. Plan to call him soon."

And I would... eventually.

"Good. And don't forget, please?" Mom took Dad's hand. Or more so he took hers. He squeezed it, and she let him before facing me. "You know, it's, um, taking a lot for us to let you go back to school."

"Don't give us a reason to worry, bud," Dad finished for her, nodding. "So, call him. This week?"

Twice in one day, the people in my life were saying things like this to me.

I bobbed my head once in acknowledgment, quickly leaving the room. Sloane had already dipped out, again leaving me to the wolves. She had her arms elbow-deep in bubbles by the time I got into the kitchen, and she had a few moments that way before I got to her side.

I stayed at the door for a beat. What my parents said

threw me. I would call Dr. Sturm, but I couldn't just yet. I needed a plan first, some time…

I edged in beside Sloane, and it was easy to put the previous conversation away when I thought about what she'd just done out there. Not to mention, that stuff with Fawn. I got low. "What was that out there? Why would you ever say something to Mom and Dad? And talking to Fawn too? Dropping in her class and shit? I mean, have you lost your entire mind, little, or just some of it?"

That was the only thing that could explain what she'd done on both counts, and it was by the grace of God Bru hadn't been at the table too tonight. The kid and I definitely had our fair share of handling each other, and odds were, he would have completely backed Sloane up out there. If anything, just to piss me off since that was how we were.

"I mean, why didn't you say anything?" she countered, and my head snapped back. Her shoulders lifted. "Shouldn't you be, I don't know, *proud* about someone you're seeing?"

I couldn't help it. I laughed.

But then I sneered.

"You don't know *anything* about Fawn, and you definitely don't know anything about me and Fawn." *I* didn't know anything about Fawn and me, but I couldn't tell her that. I gripped the sink. "And you're doing all this judgy shit when you have no right."

I felt my pulse racing, spiking. Again, I was getting all amped up about this shit, which didn't make sense. Fawn and I were fake, but I didn't like people talking shit about her.

Especially since it wasn't true.

She'd done what she had to get back at me, but even outside of all that, D, the guys, and Sloane had no right to pass any type of judgment. Not when it came to my life. I didn't care who the fuck I was dating. They needed to accept it and respect it, my choices. Not theirs.

Calm the fuck down.

My twin was making it hard, and though I loved the shit out of her, she was *annoying the hell* out of me right now with this. She lifted her hands out of the water. "All I did was use my eyes. And also, all I did was let her know you're at a place where you're not trying to do the party shit. And, if that's who she is, she needs to bow out and not waste your time."

She was making what she did sound completely sane. My eyes narrowed. "And you had the right to do that because..."

"I don't know, big, because you're my brother, and I care about you!" she whisper-shouted. We both were, which I'd find funny if we weren't so goddamn heated. She raised and dropped her arms. "I do, and I'm not going to let someone drag you down."

Because even though we hadn't grown up together... years apart, miles apart, she was still like my brothers, Bow, and me. We were family, *Legacy*, and we took care of each other.

We protected each other even without the biology.

But Sloane and I, we did have the biology. We were bonded in an intricate way that was just as strong as the others and myself, but it was different. We were twins.

So, yeah, that made it different.

I sighed. "I care about you too, and though I appreciate it, you don't have anything to worry about." I couldn't have them worrying. None of them. I gripped the sink. "I'm tired of everyone worrying about me. Mom. Dad. The guys... I'm just tired, Sloane."

I'd probably said more than I should have, but I needed her in my corner most of all. Her coming around meant D would, then Wells and Thatcher by proxy. Dorian was the one we all looked to in order to be okay, so yeah, if he came around, Wells and Thatch would too.

It all started with Sloane, though, the catalyst and pulse of our group. She did make things better all around.

She sighed too. "I know you are, and I'm sorry for overstepping. I just…" Her eyes closed. "Last year was real hard, Ares. Not just for you. I mean…"

Her voice broke, but I kept my composure, making myself. I rubbed her arm. "Eh. No more of that. We don't have time for it, right?"

That was a promise we'd made. Just her and me. We'd shown strength together, strength for Mom and Dad. Strength for the guys and their families who were like family. We'd shown strength for Bru who hadn't even wanted to start his freshman year of college. The kid would have stayed home, home for me…

That was how bad it had gotten, people worrying, and fuck if I'd ever be the central focus of it again. I'd seen what worry does firsthand.

I'd seen what I'd done to people firsthand.

It was Sloane's and my strength that had gotten our family and friends to get back on track. We'd gotten everyone to move on, be normal.

She nodded, and when she hugged me, another one of her hugs, I didn't fight her. I also wouldn't let myself feel guilt, guilt for tricking my twin along with everyone else. This relationship with Fawn was necessary and strictly business for me.

And I'd make it work at all costs.

CHAPTER
TWELVE

Fawn

I entered what should have been an empty dorm room.

Not one filled with football players.

I knew this because they wore hoodies and T-shirts exclaiming *Pembroke Football* and other things across their large chests.

What the hell...

The guys had my door open, moving boxes in and over the chaos, and a male voice directed them to the where.

A male voice I recognized.

Wolf sprawled out on the sofa that came with the dorm, his cell phone in hand and thumbs dashing across the screen. He waved a hand. "You guys can put things wherever."

Wherever consisted of his friends putting boxes on my stuff. I'd been working at the kitchen table, the kitchen connected to the communal living space. My computer and research articles were out and all those boxes stacked on top of everything but my laptop. My bag dropped from my arm, and Wolf glanced up from his phone.

Dark eyes pinned me in place. Especially when he placed his high-tops on the floor. He hadn't really fit on the couch, his legs too long…

He rose in a pair of tight jeans, his curls chunky like he'd just taken a shower, damp. He fingered through them while looking at me, and I shouldered my bag.

"What's going on?" I hadn't been prepared to see him. He'd gone radio silent for like ever, and it wasn't like I wanted to see him. The last time we were in the same room together, he'd violated me.

"Was texting you just now," he said, stepping over a box, and I realized he somehow had access to my dorm. Did housing give him the keys?

I wouldn't put it past them with the power he had, and suddenly, he was ushering his friends out of the dorm. Large football guys pounded his fists, snapping their fingers at him after.

"Can't wait to see you back out on the field," one of them said, and Wolf lifted his chin.

"Maybe next season. Gotta get caught up with school and stuff first," Wolf stated, and I maneuvered my way over to my stuff. Shoving boxes around, I cleared my space.

"What the *hell* is this, Wolf?" I shot, and my head snapped up when he came over. Suddenly, we weren't in a dorm filled with other people. Suddenly, he was just with me, and I didn't like that shit.

My hands left my computer, backing up, and when Wolf noticed, he placed his large hands on the table. His head cocked. "What? You scared of me now or something, Red?"

I realized now that I hated that stupid nickname of his. I hated everything about him. My jaw moved. "Wasn't that the point of the other night, Wolf?"

He'd done what he had at the party to show power, point-blank, and though I didn't want to be scared of him, I was. He could do anything he wanted. Anything he wanted *to me*.

His lips wet, his expression hard. He pushed off the table. "I never wanted you to be scared of me. I just wanted you to listen."

And so he taught me a lesson that night, right? "It's nice to know what happens when you don't get what you want, and why are you in here? What is all this—"

"I'm moving in."

My head darted in his direction, my hands curling on my bag. "What?"

"Just what I said. I'm moving in, and if you'd let me explain, I'll tell you why."

I didn't want to know *why*. I wanted him out of my life.

I wanted to be free of him.

"Fawn."

He called my name as I headed to my room. I had to pass the empty bedroom on the way, which wasn't empty. A ton of boxes filled the space, and the nausea hit.

He really is moving in.

Well, he could do that, but I wouldn't be living here with him. I got into my room and immediately started packing my stuff.

"What are you doing?"

"If you're moving in here, I'm moving out." I didn't know where I'd go. Heath had another roommate, and according to him, things were really working out. We'd had lunch the other day. "Have you lost your fucking mind?"

Was this a new clause to the plan? Him and me together and not just for show. Would he force me to sleep with him? Be with him in all the ways a girlfriend was with a boyfriend?

My hands were shaking at this point, and it took a second for me to realize Wolf had entered the room and closed the door. Of course, when he had, I backed up, and if we were on the first floor, I definitely would have headed out the window.

"Stop freaking out. Fuck," he gritted and started to

approach, but I pressed myself against the wall. His hands lifted. "I'm not going to touch you. Jesus. I'd never do that. Not unless…"

Not unless what? To put his cum on me? I braced my arms, and he pinched the bridge of his nose.

"Would you just sit down? I want to talk to you, and you're making this shit fucking hard right now."

What the fuck did I care how hard I was making things for him? I bared teeth. "You made me get on my knees and *show you my tits* while you came all over me, and you want me to listen to you right now?"

He really had lost his mind, his expression blanching like what I said had been a shock, and not what he'd actually done.

His arms dropped to his sides. "I know that. I do."

"Well, it's nice that you know." My body rose and dropped, heavy breaths forcing themselves through my lungs.

God, I really am scared.

This guy terrified me. He really was capable of anything.

He drew his curls back, bunching them with his fingers. "I didn't want that to happen. Things got out of fucking hand that night, and it shouldn't have happened."

"It's nice that you know that too." Fuck, he was unbelievable. I laughed, dry. "And if that's your way of apologizing—"

"It's not an apology," he stated, his voice hard, eyes narrowed. "You had a simple assignment that night. Act right. Be my girl." His expression cooled. "That could have been an easy night. Cake for both of us, but you decided to flash your tits and shit happened."

I shook my head. "You're an asshole."

"Well, asshole or not, we had an agreement. I'm not sorry about what happened, but I am sorry it happened. Like I said, it shouldn't have, and I am sorry about that."

What an ass-backwards apology. I lifted a finger. "Get out."

"I will not, and I'm sorry about that too."

I raised and dropped my arms. "I guess we're at a stalemate, then." I started to get my things, but he put a hand on my luggage. He was a foot away from my face, maybe even inches, and as they disappeared, I didn't move.

"You and I still have an agreement, Red," he said, and though he didn't touch me, he didn't have to. I felt every second of his proximity, the air charged with his heat and scent. It reminded me of his cum on my chest, so brazenly *him*, and my thighs hugged, my face flushing like a psychopath. I wanted to move away, but all I did was study those dark freckles across his nose.

"I don't want to be anywhere near you," I stated, huffing. That woodsy smell of his warmed my blood, but instead of fleeing, I got closer. Something about it felt so familiar, comfortable, and I recalled the feeling before. It was so fucking weird. I mean, the guy terrified me as much as he drew me to him.

"I don't care what you want." The words breathed across my face, spicy. He had gum in his mouth today, cinnamon. "But I am conscious of that, so today, I'm offering you a way out."

"What?"

"Being with you is becoming more of a pain in the ass for me than it's been helpful. Because of that, I'd like to see this end sooner rather than later, and since you obviously feel the same, I think you should listen to what I'm thinking."

I was listening now, less clouded.

And he finally pulled out of my space.

I blinked upon having clear air, my oxygen free of him.

"What are you proposing?" I really couldn't believe I was listening to this, my fingers clawing through red strands. I stood, and Wolf was analyzing my things. I had articles on the wall, stuff my dad took. I pasted them there as motivation and sought comfort in the shots. I connected with my dad through photography. Always had.

I didn't know how I felt about watching Wolf study the photos, and though I was fully clothed, I felt naked for some reason, vulnerable.

"You see this through. *The right way,*" he said, scanning the photos. "No more antics. You and I are together, and because we are so serious, we've moved in together. That's the story, and you follow through with it completely."

I laughed. That definitely wasn't ending the relationship. I came over. "How is that ending all this sooner rather than later?"

"Because instead of a semester with me, you'll have weeks. Possibly days. I haven't figured that out yet, but moving in together will be the catalyst of a smooth separation." His gaze finally left my dad's photos, and I could breathe. He pocketed his hands. "You and I rushed into things. Got too hot too quick. We moved in together because we were so drunk in love, and it all fell apart quickly."

I blinked and at more than one thing. Him throwing around the L-word had something to do with that. "You want us to move in together so the world can see why we broke up so fast?"

"Essentially, yeah."

"Why?" My shoulders shrugged. "Why do you care? I mean, your own sister came at me about being with you."

"Yeah, and that was your fucking fault." He lounged against my dresser, his hands bracing it. "Sloane never would have talked to you had you not been flashing your fucking tits, and you made this shit way more complicated for me. You had her ready to put your head on a goddamn spike, and my friends aren't too excited about you either."

I twitched, again about more than one of those statements.

"Why would you even lie to them? I thought this was all to keep girls off your dick."

"It is to a degree." His gaze analyzed the floor. His head lifted. "But it's more for them."

But *why* and why had his sister said what she had in my class that day? She'd said Wolf had a hard year, and he did say he'd been out most of last. I put my hand on my bag. "Why are you pushing this so hard? If they're people you care about, why would you lie?"

I doubted he'd tell me. I mean, he'd certainly told me none of this was my business before, so I definitely didn't expect anything but a bark in my direction.

"Because above all else, I need them to believe this." His hands gripped the dresser now, fidgeting. He both tucked and re-tucked his hands under his arms before ultimately pushing off of it. "They have to. Last year had them worried sick about me, and even though I'm back and things are okay now, they haven't stopped. They hover and are completely in my business."

He scrubbed his face, his admittance giving me pause. I sat on the bed. "What had them worried?"

Again, I didn't think he'd tell me, but then he was looking at me. My heart did something, a slight jump, flip. Especially when he squeezed the bridge of his nose again.

"I had a health scare," he said, and my gut churned then, tight. His tongue darted across his lips. "And it freaked everyone out. It was bad."

"Well, are you okay now?" *Why are you asking?*

Why do you care?

It was like that stuff with his sister again, all the trauma he seemed to have in his life. He did have so much, and my heart couldn't help but go out to him.

A small smile took his lips, smoky eyes drifting to me. He tipped his chin. "You care about me now, Red?"

I didn't, but I had a heart.

He approached the bed. "I'm fine. Like I mentioned, things are better now, but that hasn't stopped their worry. They're all over me, and I do need to focus on school."

"Why didn't you just say that at Jax's?"

"Because I'm a private person, and no offense, but you aren't. You air people's shit all over, and I really don't need the world knowing my business."

My head shot back. "I wouldn't have shared all this."

"Yeah, because I know that?" He was in my face again, breaths away when he leaned in. "I don't know you, so no, I wasn't going to tell you all this."

My gaze hardened. "What happened in high school was a job."

"Yeah, well, now I'm your job." He pushed away. "And this time, it won't be what it was. This shit is for my fucking family. It is, and they fucking mean the world to me."

It was rare I heard emotion from Wolf, but when talking about his family, I heard it.

His head dipped a little, dusky waves shrouding his face. "They need to know I'm okay. That I've moved on from last year, and things are better. They need to know that I'm good and not just physically. That will give them peace of mind, and I fucking need that for them."

But it didn't seem like he was good, better. I mean, I didn't know him either but *better people* didn't do stuff like this. Lie to their family? "Wouldn't us just suddenly living together, I don't know, set off red flags? Create worry?" I huffed. "I mean, that's the reason you didn't jump into telling people we were official yet."

"Correct, but the story I've told my sister and the guys is you needed a roommate. You were hard up, and I'm helping you out."

My jaw dropped. "You've already told them."

"Yes. I explained you left your old roommate situation for

personal reasons, and rather than go through the roommate process again, I'm taking the spot. I wanted them to think I was crazy about you. Not crazy." He flopped some of his hair forward. "They didn't like it, but they got over it. My sister ended up being the harder sell, but once I had the guys on board, I got her. My buddies weren't that hard to convince, and if you knew anything about my brothers, you'd understand."

"Brothers?"

"Yeah. My friends Dorian, Wells, and Thatcher are like brothers to me. They are brothers, and when we get passionate about shit, we go all in. They understood me wanting to help you out. Even if that would sound crazy to most. That's just who we are. Once we get invested, we show up for who needs us."

That was all great, except this was a lie. "All this does is buy you time, though. This arrangement? If it's only temporary, what's the point?"

"True, but those weeks are relief for both me and them. They are hovering, and I need to focus on school. That's why I'm leaning more toward this being weeks instead of days. We'll see how it goes."

Regardless, I didn't like either. "I can't live with you, Wolf."

"You can and you are. Like I said, your sentence goes from months to weeks. It puts a time clock on us, and I know you want that."

I did want that, but I couldn't live with this guy. He was so angry, crazy, and I did ridiculous things around him. Things like agree to get in a fake relationship in the goddamn first place.

Things like get on my knees for him.

It was hard for me to admit the real truth about that night. How only part of me hadn't wanted to do what he'd asked. It was true, though, facts, and because I didn't know how big that part was, the whole thing freaked the shit out of me. Perhaps, I was just as psycho as him, a freak.

I swallowed. "We'd kill each other, and you'd definitely want to kill me if we lived together." I wouldn't let him push me around. Hadn't before, and I wouldn't now. I braced my arms. "This is a bad idea."

"That's the point." He sat next to me on the bed, and the thing screeched under his weight. He sat close too, and I forced myself to ignore that and look at his face. "We'll be a beautiful disaster, and my family will definitely know why we broke up. It's perfect. It'll be perfect."

"Except for the fact I don't want you anywhere near me." I moved away to make the point. My eyes narrowed. "You don't respect me, and I definitely don't respect you."

"I will."

My lashes fluttered.

He nodded. "One hundred percent. You do this for me? You make this *real* for the people in my life, then you will one hundred percent have that from me." He put his hand out. "You have my word, and that shit's my bond."

But what did I know about that? His word.

This once again felt like a deal with the devil, and I simply stared at his hand.

"Weeks?" I questioned, swallowing hard. "Then you're gone, and I never see you again."

His mouth closed, but his hand didn't lower. He put it closer to me. "You won't even know we're on the same campus."

CHAPTER
THIRTEEN

Fawn

Wolf had a plan this time, and gratefully, it didn't involve toting me around like a trophy. Not that I was his trophy, but he was trying to make a declaration to his family and friends.

Which was wild.

He'd obviously lied that this was for the public more than the people closest in his life. I still didn't get why he'd lie to them. This was a temporary situation, but that seemed not to matter to him.

When it came to friends and family in general, I was so far removed. I cared about my mom. I loved my mom, but we hadn't been close in years.

Not since Dad anyway.

Dad had always been the glue in our family. He'd been my person and hers, so when he'd passed? Yeah, things had gotten weird, different. We'd only drifted apart further when my stepdad came into the picture, and I wasn't proud that I hadn't gotten to know the guy over the years. It wasn't because I didn't want to. I was just busy, so yeah.

Anyway, this Wolf thing was crazy, and I guess I did get him wanting to give his family comfort. Even still, he certainly was going to extremes, but I supposed I didn't know the extent of his health scare. Must have been pretty bad if he was going through all this for a temporary situation.

Of course, he didn't talk about that, going right into his plan. The guy was a brick wall when it came to emotions. Probably even more so than myself, so I didn't push him any more than he pushed to give. We were two people trying to rid ourselves of the other, and that was something he had us start the next day.

I agreed to let him take me to coffee every day between my first and second classes, and also, to hang out in the afternoon before my last lecture. I had a full course load, and since he did too, the timing worked out great for us. There was also no more of him trying to get me into his car, which I was grateful about. He was often up and running before I even got up, which left me to my own devices.

Again, I was grateful.

And by running, I meant actually running. He said he'd jog in the mornings and probably would miss me, and honestly, that first week, I didn't really see him at the dorm. Again, he had a full course load, so it was often I didn't even know I had a roommate. It'd only be when I caught him sneaking back inside when I was pulling an all-nighter that I noticed him. I never knew where he went, but he always came in before midnight.

"Night, Red," he'd say before depositing his bag on the table. He'd leave for his room after that, closing the door. His fingernails would always be dirty when he dropped the bag, but that was something I never commented on before going back to work. It wasn't my business, and two weeks went by with him coming and going like this. We saw each other on our coffee dates and strolls, but outside of that, we had little to no interactions with each other.

It'd been nice.

Wolf proved to make good on his promise of being respectful. The purpose of the strolls and coffee, of course, was to let the world know we were together, but he really didn't make me ham it up too much. Occasionally, he'd put his arm behind my seat at a cafe, but he never made me hold his hand or anything. He didn't even put his arm around me, and there were certainly no kisses. Honestly, we basically looked just like two people hanging out, and I never did see his family and friends, Legacy.

But something told me they definitely knew about us. Well, besides the obvious of us being roommates. Our public appearances garnered plenty of whispers and stares, enough to certainly get back to them. Ares "Wolf" Mallick tended to have an aura around him that received way more attention than I liked, but it fit the purpose for what he was trying to achieve, I guess. He wanted talk about us.

He wanted awareness of us.

Really, the arrangement was way easier than I thought it'd be, and it made me wonder why I'd fought it so much. This all really was painless like he'd said but still. He had me in a situation I didn't want to be in, and I could never ever forget that.

I wouldn't.

"Red?"

A knock hit my door that afternoon, Wolf's voice behind it.

Son of a gun.

Again, being respectful, and he didn't even come in until I announced he could. Of course, I got my shit together first, and I was totally aware I looked in the mirror before hopping on the bed and trying to look casual.

You're stupid.

No, stupid was the butterflies that hit my stomach, anticipation of him opening the door. I ignored it, repositioning my laptop on my legs. I'd been editing some photos before he knocked, and my stomach made another stupid flip when Wolf opened the door and grinned at me from the frame.

You can't forget who he is, what he's done...

This was a constant game I was playing with myself because he was being so decent. I had to remember this guy was a wolf just like his namesake, and the fact he could turn it on and off so seamlessly set off more than alarm bells. They were more like alarm gongs. His muscled shoulder hit the doorframe. "You busy?"

Trying to be. I shrugged. "Just editing some photos."

"Mmm. For business or pleasure?" He pushed off the frame, and immediately filled up the space, my space. "For school or fun, I mean."

"Both." I studied him, watching as he shameless guided my laptop around. "Don't recall giving you permission to do that."

"What? You already have it open." He waggled his eyebrows, being playful. Something else about Wolf? He also had charisma when he wasn't being an asshole. This made him even more dangerous since who knew when an over-step could force his brawny back up. "You being shy about it?"

I had nothing to hide, and since there was no fighting this guy, I let him peer over my shoulder. That spicy, oak smell of his still reminded me of apple pie, log cabins, and open air. I shifted on the bed. "I had to shoot some scenic stuff."

Specifically, I was doing a story on greenhouse gasses. The horticulture department gave me access to some rare plant species that were dying out due to them, so I took some photos of that.

"Should have known you were a flower girl," he said, eyeing the tatted wild flowers on my arm. I started getting tattoos after my dad died, the prick of the needle my latest vice, a safer vice.

I tugged my sleeve up, my skin flushing. I certainly felt Wolf's eyes on me.

His gaze flicked to my face. "Anyway, you busy? Sloane's here, and she wants your feedback on something."

I nearly dropped the computer. "Sloane?"

"Yeah. Told her you take photos," he said, his voice far off. He'd found my flowers again. His rough jawline pierced his skin before his attention lifted. "She's an artist too. Not photography, but she had to take some photos for a project she's working on. She's an art major. Anyway, I tried to help her, but I'm not great at that shit either. Sketch work and designs are mostly my thing..."

"Wait a second." My lashes flashed. "You do art?"

"Uh, yeah." He made it sound like common knowledge, and finally backed up out of my space. He passed a hand over his head. "So, um, she'd love your feedback. She already knew you took pictures, but when I mentioned it again, we both thought your eye would be better than ours."

She probably did know I took them if he'd explained how we initially met.

Another point in my direction for his sister liking me.

Of course, I shouldn't care one way or the other, but no one liked not being liked. "Uh, sure..."

I started to clean my stuff up, and he waited by the door. I headed through it once I got up, but he cut me off with an arm.

"Be natural." The last words he stated before sliding an arm around me. This obviously gave me pause since he didn't really touch me. During coffee and stuff, we kept decent proximity.

My fingers wrestled, damp from the weight on my shoulders. This wasn't acting natural, but I fixed my face and stance by the time Wolf and I entered the common area we shared. His sister was on her knees, a collage of photos in front of her. She had the whole thing arranged in a bigger picture, abstract, but the overall image appeared very birdlike.

Upon closer observation, I observed birds in the photos, but I cut off from that when his sister directed her attention to us.

"Sloane, this is Red," Wolf stated, and though his hand moved from my shoulders, it landed in mine. This somehow managed to be worse since my hands were wet, but if he noticed, he didn't say anything. If anything, he held my hand even more, his lengthy digits interweaving with mine. He brought me closer. "I know you guys have met, but it wasn't official, so…"

Yeah, it'd been fucking weird, but I'd give it to him that wouldn't have happened had I not acted like I had. I wouldn't apologize for it, but his sister had nothing to do with our rivalry.

She got up. "Red. Cute." A restless hand touched her neck, and something told me her brother had probably set up this interaction more than she did. Sure, she probably did want my opinion, but she probably would have been fine without it. She lifted a hand. "Nice to meet you again."

"Same."

Sloane rocked on her high-tops. "So, I see you guys haven't killed each other."

"Not yet, but give Red a bit." Wolf used our woven hands to tuck me into his side, and I fit more naturally than expected. He was a big guy, but he didn't dwarf me, his hard body enveloping my curves. He glanced down. "She definitely likes to humble my ass. You saw that shit at the party. That was her trying to teach me a lesson about telling her what to wear that night."

I was surprised he mentioned that, the truth?

"Really?" Sloane appeared surprised by that too, her hands cuffing her arms. Her sweatshirt hit the midpoint of her thighs again, her dark hair up and messy. She smiled a little. "Reminds me of Dorian and me. Don't know if Ares mentioned it, but I'm dating his friend. His name is Dorian."

He hadn't, but I was aware of Dorian. I remembered him.

She eyed Wolf. "What's with you guys thinking you can tell us what to do?"

She shoved her brother after she said it, and I definitely realized Wolf painted me in a better light by saying what he had.

"Not that y'all listen," Wolf said before releasing me. "Anyway, that's what happened, so yeah. Fawn's never been one to back down."

"You could stand some humbling," I stated, playing along. I fake-nudged him, and when he smiled, something warm hit my stomach. *Stop that.* I tucked my hair behind my ear. "Anyway, you guys wanted my opinion on something."

They showed me, her collage in front of me. Sloane pointed out what she was trying to do, and it was kind of obvious with the bird pictures and the overall image she'd created with them. All pinned together, she'd made a bigger work of art based on the images in the photos.

"We have to make a piece out of unconventional tools for one of my art classes, but I suck at taking photos." She frowned. "I took these with my phone and the lighting's crap since I didn't know what I was doing."

"Actually, these are really good."

"Yeah?" She faced the piece. "You're not just saying that?"

I wasn't, getting down on my knees. She could stand to reposition herself when it came to the sun, and since she was new at taking photos, she should probably only take them early in the day. Some of the photos were at dusk, and I told her that.

"You can always edit the photos in post op if you're trying to go for a particular look," I said, and she nodded. "Some think that's cheating, but it's all a part of the process."

I could hear my dad's words coming out of my mouth.

He'd taught me everything he knew when it came to lighting and everything.

I chewed my lip, and Sloane had gotten on the floor with me sometime during my advice. I didn't see Wolf, and I realized now he was in the kitchen.

He had a cereal bowl in his hands, chewing, and I wondered how long he'd left me with his sister. He was making it look like he wasn't paying attention, but I certainly noticed a subtle smile on his lips when he devoured whatever he had in his bowl.

For some reason, that had me facing his sister with a smile too, and I didn't know why. I shook my head. "So, yeah. Do that and there's a ton of photo editing apps. Also, camera phones are completely fine. There's this stigma you have to get the latest and greatest camera for a decent photo, but that's not true. Cameras on phones have gotten a lot better over the years."

"Yeah, that was a concern too. Thanks. Really, that gives me way more confidence."

"No problem." I smiled, and she did too.

Wolf returned then as if he never left, and when he offered some of his Captain Crunch, I did shove at him, getting up. "Ew. No."

"Like you mind my spit," he said, drawing in close. My insides buzzed, and he lifted his spoon, milking dripping from it. "Sure you don't want a taste?"

The utensil hovered between us, his cereal waiting. It entered his mouth before I could do something stupid like say yes, and his long tongue licked it clean.

"Too bad cuz I'm not sharing," he continued, his voice suddenly gruff, low. A flash of heat hit me directly between the legs, and his sister's throat clearing was the only thing blinking me out of something else stupid.

"On that note," she said, quickly gathering her things. Her artwork was one solid piece but the extra photos she put in her bag. She got up. "And never again will I give you a hard time about me and Dorian because yeesh…"

She shuddered, and Wolf, who'd also just blinked, raised his hand at her.

"Whatever," he passed off, his cereal now his fascination. He took two big heaping bites. "This is what I get for letting you in my place and trying to help your ass."

Her eyes lifted, and though his did too, he offered to help with her art piece.

"No, I got it. You do you." She eyed him, laughing, and when her brother flipped her off, spoon in hand, she just chuckled again. "See you later."

"Yeah, see you." Wolf was certainly moody, and I'd say something if I wasn't trying to stop seeing the image of him *licking a spoon*. What had just happened was definitely too real for me.

Busying myself, I sat on the couch, and after Wolf saw his sister out, he joined me.

"Good job." He said this around more bites, a sheen on his full lips every time he removed milk.

I glanced away. "Well, that went well." Talking, yes. Talking was good. Great. "She doesn't seem to hate me now."

That was because of him and his save, which I hadn't missed.

Wolf was still chomping on cereal bites at this point, rigid. He merely nodded after the words, and I wondered if what had just happened affected him in the same way it had me.

Probably not. You're just an idiot.

I swear to God I wasn't one who self-deprecated, but I'd been doing nothing but that since he entered my life. He rattled my confidence, and that alone had me shifting to the other side of the couch.

"Yeah, you did well," he reaffirmed, and I'd give him a hard time about that cereal shit if I still wasn't *thinking about it*. His bowl hit the table with a clank, empty. Dude even drank the milk before running the back of his hand over his mouth. His arms draped behind the couch. "She was the hard sell, so yeah, good."

His fingers clenched and unclenched, and since his arm was behind the couch, I noticed. He had a ring below one of his knuckles, and I recognized it. "Your sister wears one of those. On her neck?"

I hadn't noticed she'd been wearing it today, but she had worn a bulky sweatshirt.

Wolf lifted his hand, his ring slightly different. It was still one of those gorillas, but the eyes weren't red like Sloane's. He had white diamonds in his.

"Uh, yeah. It's a home thing," he said, before returning his arm back. He brushed my neck this time, and I eased forward. His gaze flicked my way. "It's for a society we're in, a club in our small town. It's called the Court, and the guys and I are all in it. Sloane too. It's mostly high school shit, though, so we don't wear our rings. The one around Sloane's neck is Dorian's. He gave it to her since they're dating and all that." He released a breath. "I'm only wearing mine because I was cleaning."

I studied him, his chest rising and falling. He'd also said that really quick, which had a smile tugging at my lips. I didn't know why. I brought my legs up. "So, when am I going to see your art?"

"What?"

God, his chest was big, massive. My fingers itched to touch it, but I resisted. I leaned on my arm. "You said you do art. I'm assuming like your sister." I shrugged. "When can I see it?"

Oh my God... was I flirting? That couldn't be possible. No way.

But my face was hot.

Still, it was hot from that cereal thing. I glanced off, and Wolf huffed.

"You won't."

"Why?"

"Because it's private." His body shifted in my direction. "So, you get whatever thoughts out of your pretty little red head about that."

My gaze flicked up, shot up. Did he just call me... *pretty*? *Fuck, is he flirting too?*

He couldn't be, and I was crazy. My feet touched the floor. I started to get up when I noticed his necklace. That emblem sat on his chest, and when I asked him about it, he touched it.

"My sister and I wear them, a gift from our parents." He let it go. "She lost hers for a while, but we found it when she came back."

I studied it. "I read about how you both weren't always together."

"You finally looking into me, Red?" His hands came together, his big shoulders lifting, shifting. "Tell me. What did you find?"

That playful tone returned to his voice, his eyes dancing, and my skin flushed that he knew I'd looked into him.

I just didn't *know why*, or why this conversation was seeming so intimate. I tucked a leg under my knees. "Might have looked into some things when I realized I had a stalker."

His chest bumped a laugh. "Hardly." He said this though his attention shifted to the table. "And yeah. We weren't always together, which was bullshit. For me. Her. Our parents." Restless, he weaved fingers through his wavy locks. "Anyway, things are better now."

Still, must be hard. I studied the necklace once more, and he let me. For a long time, he did and that itch ticked at my fingers again. He watched as I reached forward, and when he didn't draw back, that gave me permission to run my fingers along the emblem.

An instant heat pulsed my digits, and Wolf pulled his hair out of his face. That cleared the way for me to really look at the necklace since his hair was so long, but that also meant his face was like right next to mine.

His lips.

They parted, a flush running over them. It matched my fingers. I was a terrible blusher, no doubt red everywhere.

"Red?" His voice was husky, a warning in it, but I didn't pull back.

"I'm sorry that happened to your family," I said, head clouded. My breath stuttered from my lips, but laughter had me stopping.

"Sure." He tucked his necklace away, taking it from me. Rigid again, he shifted in his seat. "Anyway, I'm going to need you again tonight. There's another party at my buddy Thatch's frat, and we need to make an appearance. He and the other guys have been asking about you, and I've been putting it off long enough."

I blanched he transformed so quickly. It was like that wicked wolf had returned, and I hooked an arm over my leg. "Well, I can't."

"Why?"

Besides not actually wanting to, I had a social life. One I'd been neglecting no matter how little it was. Heath and some our other photojournalism friends planned to do some shooting tonight, and after, we'd made arrangements to do some studying. I shrugged. "I have a study session."

Wolf smirked. Actually *smirked* at me, the arrogant fuck. "Well, cancel because you're going, and it's not like I've been making you go to anything. *Do* anything."

"No, just mandatory coffee and strolls every goddamn day." They hadn't been bad, but still, they hadn't been optional. "I don't want to go to that party."

"Funny how that's not really your decision." Things had been playful before, almost fun even in a way.

Almost different.

Wolf and I hadn't had any push and pull lately, and I realized now that was because we weren't interacting on the regular. Whenever we did, we were *this*, and I couldn't believe I'd actually been flirting with him moments ago.

You really are as dumb as this arrangement.

I started to get up, but he got my arm. His eyes narrowed. "This party is not optional, and neither is your attendance." He let go. "So, I expect you there, and I don't want to hear another word about it."

He sounded like my dad, and last I checked, I didn't have one of those. I'd lost that, gone. My jaw clenched. "Wolf..."

"You asked for respect, right?" He got in my face. "Well, I've been respecting you. I also haven't been making you go anywhere, so it's time to respect me and our agreement."

A familiar anger rose like a heavy devil inside me. It was one I was too familiar with because I did go off the handle sometimes. It was exactly that, and those images he had that bound me to him in the first place. I didn't consider myself an angry person.

But even calm people could be pushed too far.

We were in a stand-off, he and I, one where I knew he was right, and I unfortunately was wrong. "Fine."

His casual look only angered me more. He knew he'd get his way, always did. "It's at the same time, and I'll take you. Just be here and be ready."

So that wasn't happening. I shook my head, and when he started to open his mouth, I did first. "I do have plans with friends, but I can meet you after. I don't know how late we'll be studying, but I'll be there on time. I promise."

He appeared as if he wanted to contest that, but he sat back in the end. He lifted a hand. "Whatever."

"And can I bring a friend so I at least, well, know someone this time?" I needed a buffer. From him and all this.

"You'll be with me, so I can't see why you'd need to."

I gave him a look, and he sighed.

"Fine. Just be there."

I nodded and couldn't help slamming my door that afternoon. I had no idea how we were actually going to make this work for even a few weeks because his sister was totally right. This guy and I would kill each other.

It was just a matter of who drew first blood.

CHAPTER
FOURTEEN

Ares

Fawn never said her guest would be her goddamn roommate. But that was exactly who I caught her bopping around with moments after I properly introduced her to my friends. Thatcher and Wells had just gotten their apologies out to her. They'd been serious about that, and Fawn had seemed appreciative of it.

At least, for the few moments she'd been there.

She'd claimed she'd gotten a text from her friend, and not thinking much about it, I let her go. I had told her she could bring someone even though that shit put my back up. I'd been in front of the guys and Sloane, though, so I hadn't wanted to seem too possessive.

You're playing with fire, Red…

I watched her now, the little fucking firecracker. Her jean-clad hips touched the bar, thick, full. She swayed them a little to the music in the room, her tattoos out and on display on her arms and shoulders. This girl just might have an addiction with as many as she had. I'd no doubt seen the majority at the pool party, and the memory made me click my tongue.

I ran it over my lip before taking a sip of my beer. Fawn's tits weren't out today but that didn't matter in her *fucking top*. That bountiful chest of hers had a nice fucking swell, and currently she was allowing that ex-roommate fucker to get a full view. She stood right next to him, laughing with him, and I think the only reason I wasn't going over there right now was because Sloane was chaperoning the situation. She'd seen Fawn enter with the guy and wanted to meet Fawn's friend. My sister had been trying too, to be nice and accommodating as Wells and Thatcher had been.

Sniffing, I stole another drink, wondering why in the actual fuck this dude came to a college party looking like some nerdy-ass dark academia fuck. He'd dressed like he'd come out of the '30s, all formal and shit with his button-up shirt and pants. Then there were his fucking glasses that took up half his face, actual spectacles like some uppity goober. The things probably were symmetrical to his face, but the fact that he'd come up in this bitch all pretentious and shit just worked me the wrong way.

Not to mention he was too close to Fawn.

The growl stayed low in my chest but it was there. I put my beer on a bookshelf. "I need a refill."

"Yours is full."

I swung my gaze over to Dorian who'd spoken. He bumped a laugh. "Relax. Sloane's over there. She's fine."

"What are you talking about?"

Dorian, Wells, and Thatcher, who I'd been drinking with across the room, exchanged a glance. The three of them busted out in laughter, *audibly*. D slapped my chest. "Sorry. It's just fun watching you this way is all."

My eyes narrowed. "What way?"

"Completely strung the fuck up." Wells angled back, his

elbows hitting the bookshelf. "Please tell me that shit's not catching."

"Right? I ain't got time for that shit." Thatch sucked back some beer, wiping his lips. His earrings danced. "It is fun seeing Wolfy this way, though."

"Yeah, I mean we figured this shit was serious considering you moved in with the girl. Even though you did pass that shit off as just wanting to help her." Dorian eyed me. "But still, this is killing me. You jealous? I never thought I would have seen it."

"I'm not fucking jealous," I barked. I started to walk off to go break that shit across the room up, but Dorian caught my arm.

He chuckled. "Hold up—"

"D..." I kept my warning low, but I wouldn't if he didn't step the fuck off. I jerked my arm away, and my buddy lifted his hands.

"Dude, tell him before he loses even more of his shit than he already has," D said, slapping Wells's chest, and I frowned.

My brow lifted. "Tell me what?"

"That you ain't got anything to worry about with that guy." Wells's lips tipped up. "My guy over there? He's bisexual, but I know for a fact he doesn't hit up girls. Not since like grade school anyway."

"How do you know that?"

"Because we travel in some of the same circles." His head cocked. He hooked an arm over my shoulder. "In which he's made it very apparent he wouldn't mind a casual hookup situation. I haven't yet but I might tonight if I feel like it."

I'd lift my eyes at my friend, but I used to be that fucking way too. Conquests were objects, ass.

I studied the pretentious fuck with my girl. "You sure?"

"One hundred percent. So relax," Wells said, but then I shoved him.

I lifted a finger. "I owe you an ass-kicking for keeping that shit quiet." He let me eye daggers at the dude half the night before saying something. Not to mention, he'd clearly told D and Thatcher. They'd all been laughing and shit at me.

My chest pressed into Wells, and even more when the dude couldn't stop fucking smiling. Dorian came between us. "I thought you weren't jealous?"

I wasn't.

At least, I shouldn't be.

Fawn and I were real for the world, but we weren't real.

My eyes narrowed. "Fuck all of you."

"Aww, you know you love us." Thatcher made kissing noises, and I shot a shoulder into him so hard he hit the bookshelf. A few books fell off but the fucker didn't stop laughing.

I lifted my hands, not fucking jealous. Red and I just had an arrangement, and it was one I obviously had to remind her of again. I'd seen her on the couch today. How she'd looked at me...

She'd been fucking stupid and needed to not forget what this shit was. We weren't serious. We weren't real, but she did need to play that off for the world.

Behind closed doors, though, she needed to check herself. She'd actually looked like she wanted me to fucking kiss her today.

My jaw moving, I clipped someone on the way. I barked sorry, but then a hand came on my arm. "Wolf. Hey. It's been a while."

Yeah, I didn't remember this chick at all, her dark hair and wearing way too much makeup for her face. She also was barely wearing a dress, and her lack of curves reminded me of what I'd had in my life as of late. Of what I'd had up against me on the couch today, her hip burning solid into my jeans, warm...

I forced myself to look at this girl. "Hi."

Staring at her, I think her name was Alexa. Maybe Ava? I

didn't fucking know. Nor did I care. Pretentious fuck was laughing at something Fawn was saying now, but this girl crossed in front of me when I tried to move in that direction.

"Glad to see you at a party again," she said, trying to press what she thought appealed to me in my face. The girl had tits, but they weren't like Fawn's.

Why the fuck do you keep thinking about her tits?

"Can I help you with something?" I grunted. I only asked to not be an asshole, and I noticed something when I passed a look in Fawn's general direction. She'd gotten really close to uppity fuck. In fact, so close she had her arm hooked on his shoulder.

And she was also looking at me.

Full on, her eyes narrowed, a harsh cut to them before smiling at the pretentious fucker. Her hand cuffed his arm, and it took me a second to realize someone else cuffed mine. This dark-haired chick was being too much, and she was squeezing me at this point.

I redirected my attention from her hand over to Fawn who was now squeezing *this guy's*. She grinned at him, all that red hair falling back with her laughter.

What are you doing, Red?

Seemed something stupid at the present. She kept getting closer to that guy, who, from what Wells had said, wasn't even hitting what she was selling. At least, in a while. The whole thing made me smirk, but that left at what this chick said next to me.

"I hear you're with some chubby girl."

The fuck did this bitch just say?

"Is that her?" She angled around me, bold, and she was lucky in that moment. Fawn happened to still be cozying up to pretentious douche, and if Red had seen this chick staring at her, judging her...

"The fuck you just say about my girlfriend?"

The dark-haired bitch's lashes jerked up, her brow flicking. "Girlfriend? So, it's true?"

I paused, wetting my lips. I hadn't called Fawn my girlfriend officially, but as far as this campus knew, it was true. We had moved into together, were seen together.

I hovered over this cunt, leaning in real close so she could hear my words. "I hear you say shit about my girlfriend again..." I paused, muscles tightening, surging. I physically felt my body locking up, the urge to ring this cunt's fucking neck in my hands. "I swear to fucking God—"

A force hit my shoulder, clipped. My gaze jerked up to bark at someone else, but the flash of red hair gave me pause.

And the smell.

It was floral and light like daisies in a summer sun. The scent glided in my nose and over my tongue, as Fawn's hips strutted in the opposition direction of me. I let go of this girl because apparently, I'd grabbed her.

I didn't know what I was going to do to her as I was too busy watching Fawn leave.

I started to go after her, but this bitch grabbed me.

"Wolf, I didn't mean to offend—"

I flashed teeth, enough to get her the fuck off me. She backed up like a coward, and nearly ran into my sister who'd been walking over to me.

"What's going on?" Sloane asked, and she hadn't come alone. Pretentious douche came with her, Fawn's friend. Sloane eyed me. "Everything okay?"

"Where'd Fawn just go?" I lost her, my sister in the way now.

Sloane shook her head. "I don't know. She just walked off. Heath and I were just talking with her and some others, and she said she needed air."

I bit into my cheek, *air* code for she was pissed. I did just have my hands on some chick. Not to mention, that flirty shit she'd been doing with a guy who wasn't even rocking with chicks.

Said guy actually had his hand out to me, his grin wide. "Hey, I'm Heath. Fawn's friend—"

"That's nice." I left, zero fucks given. If Fawn needed air, she was getting it with me.

CHAPTER
FIFTEEN

Fawn

I groaned into the mirror, steaming as I applied a fresh coat of lipstick.

The nerve of that fucker.

He asked me to show up here as his girlfriend, and he let that girl get all over him. I mean, what the fuck was I even here for?

And why was I so upset about it?

Embarrassment hit me just like on the couch today. I'd been definitely flirting with that idiot like, well, a freaking idiot. If he hadn't been his same douchey self, I may have even pushed things harder, which would have been really stupid.

After fluffing out my hair, I left the bathroom. I didn't return to Wolf. Fuck that. Instead, I looked for Heath, but as I stalked around the frat house, I couldn't find him either.

What the fuck is my life right now?

I was aware I was shouldering folks out of my way and

slamming doors, but I didn't fucking care. I didn't like being made a fool of, and I'd cut my plans short for *him* tonight.

Calm down.

Forcing myself, I attempted to contact Heath, who, of course, had been super jazzed about coming to another one of these frat parties. One of our other friends had gotten us into the first one, and since I was dating someone from Legacy, I'd easily gotten Heath access tonight. He'd walked right in since I'd given his name to the guy at the door, and Heath sure had something to say about that. He'd been all questions tonight at our study session, and though we did have lunch on the regular, I had a tendency of keeping my relationship with Wolf under wraps. I was a very private person anyway, so he didn't make a thing of it.

But still he had questions, all our friends had. I'd met up with them all tonight for the first time in what felt like forever, but again, I'd dodged shit. I'd done that for Wolf since he was a private person too.

That ungrateful fucker.

We were going to have a talk, a serious one about expectations and what I was really here to do. If he was truly trying to make our situation work in front of his family and everyone else, he needed to get his act together and do this properly with me.

What, are you his mom now?

I had to remind myself to calm down, raking my hand through my hair. Eventually, I chilled enough to actually send a text to my ex-roommate.

Me: Where are you at? I want to leave.

It was probably a bad idea, but I had plans to leave with him anyway. Heath, like myself, didn't have a car, so he took buses everywhere around campus. Since I did too, I'd always had plans to go with him. Really, that was the only plan I had. The only possible one. I didn't do cars, so… yeah.

I got clipped in the hallway enough where I entered

another room. It was a lot quieter in there, and I was relieved to find that. What was cool about it was I'd somehow found the library, stacks and stacks of books around.

I eased through the shelves, putting my back to one.

Me: I'm going to be heading to the bus stop with Heath. I'll see you around.

My fingers left the text to Wolf, and I waited a beat. I wanted to see what he had to say about it. I wasn't trying to play games with him. I was just pissed at him. He'd embarrassed me tonight.

Wolf's text message bubble appeared, and for some reason, my heart fucking jumped. I thought at first it might be fear. This dude tended to have a crazy-ass temper, but once the bubble disappeared, something weird hit me. It was relief, yes, but also disappointment. I wanted to hear from him for some reason. I wanted to see if what I said would affect him in some way.

Because you're fucking stupid.

Again, with that self-deprecation. Again, the constant need to test him and be the one doing the testing. The shameless girl inside me liked to get a rise out of him, deep down inside. Like I enjoyed drama when I wasn't that girl. I had enough in my early teens to bottle, so no, the last thing I wanted was drama.

But to see Wolf that way...

Something about when he was unhinged... wild got to me. It did, and I hated that. There's no good reason on God's green earth why I'd want to see his wrath.

You're obsessed with him.

A part of me was, yes. I enjoyed his power, and the fact that *I* was somehow able to make him lose control. It made me all kinds of seriously fucked up, and as I waited for Heath to text me back, I scanned the stacks. I did this for about ten seconds until I heard the moans.

"Give me that dick."

I blinked, immediately moving around a couple books. I peered through the stacks like I was the opposite of someone who enjoyed drama.

Some books hit the floor, multiple ones. Two guys shouldered the shelves, one with his hand down the other's pants.

Holy crap.

The biggest guy bear-hugged the other, his hand pumping and hitting the inside of the guy's jeans. He rocked solid hips into the guy's jean-clad ass before bending him over a library cart, and my eyes flashed.

I recognized both of them. The one standing was an ultra blond with a joker grin. Devastatingly handsome, Wells Ambrose had a guy submitting to him, and when he yanked the guy back by his dark hair to kiss him, I instantly confirmed who his hookup was.

Heath, *my Heath*, grinned below Wells's mouth, and the elation on the guy's face was something more than I'd ever seen. This guy didn't get excited about stuff, way more serious than me, but Wells yanking down my ex-roommate's pants had the delight on the guy's face like nothing else.

You shouldn't be watching this.

I turned away. At least, at first. I didn't consider myself a Peeping Tom, but I wasn't a prude either. I watched my fair share of porn, and it was a necessity considering how single I'd been in the past.

I eased a book over, my heart thudding. Wells had his tongue down Heath's throat and Heath's pants and boxers down to his ankles. My ex-roommate's glasses were skewed, and eventually, he took them off and immersed himself in the kiss.

"You want this cock?" Wells crooned, my lower lips tingling, surging. Wells had his hand down his own pants now, rubbing himself off against Heath through his designer jeans.

"Fuck. Give it to me," Heath gasped out, and something

flashed inside me. I was a complete perv for watching this. Not to mention, doing so was a complete violation of privacy on Heath's part. He was a friend.

I started to back up, but something hard hit my backside.

The aroma followed.

Spicy, woodsy. The air flourished with masculine scent, and my knees weakened at the familiarity.

Don't be stupid.

I tried to back up, but the solid force behind pressed me against the stacks. I jerked but hands fell on either side of me, locking me in when they gripped the shelves.

"Whatcha doing, Red?" Wolf whispered, his dark voice deep, low. Laughter touched it. "You seeing a little something?"

He knew exactly what I'd seen, heard. His friend wasn't trying to be silent with mine, and Wolf totally let that symphony play around us. I shouldered him. "Wolf—"

"*Shh.*" His breath touching my ear zinged my pussy lips. They'd already been buzzing before, but him around me, those sounds around us... "This is a library, Red. You gotta be quiet."

His teeth tugged my ear, and I flattened to the stacks like butter. What the fuck? His arrogant laughter followed, and for some reason, my nipples tightened.

They hurt.

The urge to rub them against the stacks hit me. Especially when Wolf tugged me back by my hair.

"That's my girl," he said, his hand on my stomach, and I quivered, shaky as fuck in my heels.

"What are you doing?" The words left my throat in a shuddered mess, and I realized I had my eyes closed. I opened them to see Wells had his cock out, the guy working his hard length. He was sliding it between the seams of Heath's ass, and I turned away.

"Ah, ah, ah," Wolf chided, his digits folding around my

jaw. He made me face his friend toying with mine. He leaned in. "After all, you came for a show, didn't you?"

"Stop." I said this, but I noticed my breathing was rapid, tense. I also noticed I didn't look away. I swallowed. "Wolf, this is fucked. We shouldn't be here."

But for some reason, I couldn't stop watching, and I was pretty sure that had nothing to do with the fact he was making me look. Wolf pressed his hands to the stacks, and he wasn't even holding me at this point. His face touched my hair. "What was your angle earlier tonight, Red? Tell me..."

His friend was still *playing* with mine and agonizingly so. Begging for Wells to be inside him, Heath gripped the cart, but all Wells did was keep him pinned down. The grin on the blond's face reached his eyes, and the deviousness reminded me so much of the guy behind me. Wells liked games.

And so did Wolf.

Wolf's mouth heated my already tingling strands, my body shaking, convulsing. "What are you talking about?"

"My buddy over there told me a little something about your pal Heath," he said, my eyes flashing wide. We were both whispering over here like two people weren't fucking in front of us. "Said he's bi but doesn't generally date chicks. At least, not lately."

Sobered up, I pushed at him. "Wolf..."

"So, the way I see it." He paused, locking me with his hard body. "That little stunt where you were all over him tonight was you trying to make me jealous. Was that your intention, Red? Seems like it with that last text you sent me about leaving with him."

My face flushed, from anger but also something else. My jaw tightened. "You embarrassed me."

"Embarrassed you?"

"How about that bitch who was all over you?" The words came out before I could stop them, but I couldn't see his reaction to them considering he had me pinned to the stacks. "Get off me."

His hips moved instead, hard length hitting the curve of my back, and I froze.

I gasped.

He leaned in.

"I don't want that bitch," he mouthed over my ear, his hands falling to my hips. He used them to rub me against him, and he was so tall his dick probed my spine. He hiked me up. "What do you think I want?"

I didn't know and wasn't stupid enough to ask. He had embarrassed me today, but that girl had only been the second time. He'd shut my idiocy down so fast today on his couch.

"Wells, please," Heath gasped out ahead of us, sighing. He reached back for Wells, his hand on the guy's hip. "I need it. Fuck…"

Wells entertained Heath, studying him with a grin. Heat touched my ears that maybe he'd just leave Heath like that, dying at his mercy. It'd sure reflect something Wolf would do.

But then Wells spit in his hand.

He worked his dick nice and good, then did nothing more than place a hand on Heath's hip before driving himself to the hilt inside him. Heath's cries ripped through the air, a mixture of pain and pleasure no doubt contorting his face. He gripped the cart while Wells slammed powerful hips into him. Wells's jeans were low on his muscular ass while he thrust his hips.

The burn shot through my body like electricity, and Wolf let me watch for so long before returning to my ear.

"You want that," he breathed, tugging my ear with his teeth again. A noise left my throat and his hand covered it. "You want me to do that to you…"

The cart screeched forward, and Heath cried out while Wells grunted.

"So tight," Wells crooned, his eyes rolling back. He grinned. "So fucking tight. So good, bro…"

Heath's moans followed Wolf's hand to my breasts. I said *hand* because he only had to use one. As big as my tits were, he only needed one to hold them, and the ache bled from my mouth again.

"You want that." A statement in my ear, the rumble deep from his chest. He pressed me into his cock. "Admit the truth. Admit you wanted to make me jealous. Admit you want me to do that to you."

He tweaked my nipple through my shirt and weakness zapped my legs. "I don't want anything to do with you."

Such a lie, completely. Especially as I watched our friends. Wells's grunts and Heath's moans had me fragile, then add Wolf's hands on me…

"You're lying." His voice was aggressive, agitated as his hand left my breasts and shot immediately between my legs. He gripped my pussy. "Let's see how bad you're lying."

He was crazy, insane.

And yet, I wasn't fighting him.

I let him rip down my fly. I *let him* shove his hand down my panties, then brazenly force his fingers against my folds. Rough digits parted them, playing, teasing. His fingers spun in my juices, and I came up on my heels.

"Wolf, stop." It came out in a muted ache, and when he did pull his hand out of my underwear, I sagged. I wondered why he stopped.

His fingers glistened in front of me.

"Your lie," he ground into my hair. He pressed his fingers together, my sticky heat between them. "Now tell the truth."

He seemed hungry for it, and his friend and mine were against the bookshelves now. At some point, Wells had brought Heath up, and he slammed him into the stacks so hard I thought the shelves may fall.

I did want that. I wanted it so bad I bit my lip. "Please…"

"What?"

I closed my eyes. "Please give it to me. I want you to do that. I want that."

Wolf growled, crowding me again. "You want me in your ass."

It sounded insane. Not to mention, I'd never even had my ass played with before. I mean, I'd messed around back there in the past but only with my fingers. I bit my lip. "I was trying to make you jealous."

This sent him over the edge like I knew it would. He seemed to need that even though this was all fake between us. He wanted my submission.

And I guess he got it.

My jeans jerked down, my panties with them. I gasped, and Wolf's hand returned to my sex.

"Buckle up, Red," he said, his fingers swirling in my juices. He took them out, and I shot forward when he forced his digits inside my tiny hole.

Holy shit.

My mouth fell open the same time he clamped his hand over it, my scream silenced, muffled. I bit his palm while he drove me forward, fucking my ass while I gripped the shelves.

"Wells!"

Wells was doing the same thing to Heath, drilling him again and again. His rhythm matched Wolf's fingers in my ass. The two were in sync like they'd done this before.

"Fuck, Red. What you do to me…"

I heard it in my ear, trying to look back, but Wolf wouldn't let me. He had his face in my hair, panting hard, and when his hand left my mouth to finger my clit, I was done for.

I exploded over his fingers, my ass squeezing the ones behind me. I bit my lip so hard I drew blood, and that was about the same time Heath shot his load all over Wells's hand. The platinum blond had been working him, and soon, he too stiffened behind him.

"Fuck, bro. Fuck," Wells said, his snow-white hair fingered through, his brow glistening. His shirt had also risen up and a set of glistening abs told me just how hard he'd been working. He smiled. "Fuck, yeah."

He bent to kiss Heath, but I didn't see it.

I was too busy being righted.

Wolf jerked up my pants and underwear and didn't even close them before picking me up in his arms. I fought the screech in my throat, my walls still vibrating and head still clouded. I saw Wolf through hazy eyes, the first time he'd let me.

He looked wild.

His hair hung thickly over his eyes, his expression tense, aggressive. He looked like he was going to murder someone.

But the only person he had his hands on was me.

CHAPTER
SIXTEEN

Ares

"Get out of the fucking *way*!" I roared, barreling through at least three dudes. Fawn kicked her little feet in my arms, gripping me.

"Wolf, what are you doing?"

I didn't fucking know, my shit hard as fuck and this girl in my arms. I shouldered a guy so hard he almost hit the floor, and the next thing I knew, I was in one of these guys' bedrooms. I didn't know whose, and there were always extras in this place.

There'd be an extra today.

Genuine fear touched Red's eyes the moment we were inside, the girl's cream still on *my hand*. I tossed her on the bed, and she backed up on it.

She was a goddess.

Her heels flashed her toes, her jeans hugging over the flare of her full hips. I hadn't even closed them, anxious, ready and the flash of her underwear reminded me I'd ripped them.

I licked my lips, stalking over to her like a caveman.

Something of a protest left Fawn's lips, but it escaped the moment I grabbed the back of her neck and forced my lips down on hers.

Fuuck.

This was madness, crazy. The growl touched my lips, and I bit down on hers so hard I swear to fuck I tasted blood.

"Wolf. What?" She said this with a trembling mouth, trembling herself when she lay down on the bed. "What are you doing?"

Again, I ignored her question. Just tasting her. Drinking from her. This girl was like a drug, and I couldn't believe that shit I'd said downstairs. But she was doing something to me, something intense. Something…

Once more, the thought was stupid, and I forced her off me so fast her head hit the pillows. The swell of her large tits bounced in her top, and I wanted to rip my goddamn hair out.

What the fuck is happening?

I pulled back my hair, just eyeing her. A haze touched her eyes, all that luscious red hair over her tatted shoulder. My eyes narrowed. "Strip."

It was like I was outside of myself in that moment, a fly on the wall watching me both say and do stupid things.

She didn't move, and a noise rolled in my chest.

"Fucking now, Fawn," I threatened, and she didn't want me to do it for her.

I might tear her in half.

Deft fingers touched her buttons, debate in her eyes as she exposed those big beautiful tits of hers. A chick had called her chubby tonight, this girl the literal opposite of chubby. She had curves, but they were deliberate, like God had a plan and executed that shit for a fucker's wet dream. A fucker like me, and when the buttons fell away, I just about nutted myself.

I'd seen Fawn's breasts before, flushed, freckled but her

lying on the bed with her pants open was doing something to me. My tongue escaped. "More."

Shut the fuck up, you idiot.

I wouldn't let myself, fascinated when the shirt hit the bed, and she went for her bra. I nodded, and she reached behind. The straps eased down her shoulders, the one painted in watercolor flowers even more flushed.

I touched myself through my jeans, an anxious fuck at the sight of her pale, pink nipples. I'd seen all kinds of fucking nipples, but Fawn's shit had me salivating. Big, round.

"Wolf, this is crazy," she said, but she tweaked one, the motion matching my hand on my jeans. I was sure it hadn't been intentional, just a response to me and what I was doing.

But the way that shit had me in chains.

I was angry at myself. *Furious* when I launched at her and didn't bother accounting for the fact I had size on her. I pinned her down under my full weight, her tit in my fucking mouth, and I pressed those things together so fucking fast.

Perfect for my hands, bountiful like a fucking feast. I put my face in them, and she cried out.

"What are we doing?" She was questioning herself now, my teeth biting, tasting. Her claws gripped my back, and I roared. "We should stop."

"Shut the fuck up," I gritted, my mission shifting to sucking. I hoovered the shit out of her tits, and that exchanged her protest to cries.

"Wolf!"

That's it. Scream my fucking name, Red.

I had my hand in my jeans, my fist slamming into my boxers as I stroked the shit out of myself. I bit down on her, hard, and when she called out, I laughed. "That's it, Red. Cry Wolf."

"You shut the fuck up," she ground out, playing our game now. Our push and pull was ridiculous, but that shit had me steel and her wet.

I felt it.

My fingers slid into that space between us, easy with her panties ripped. I got my hand nice and good down her jeans, watching her reaction as I fingered her.

Fawn's head touched the sheets, her mouth open. The urge to ram my dick in it hit me like a motherfucker.

What are you doing? Get off this chick now.

This wasn't part of the plan, zero plan here. I had a mission for this girl, and it wasn't this. This was bad and could honestly jeopardize everything I was trying to accomplish with Fawn Greenfield.

But tell my mind that, tell my dick that, which was now ramming into her heat through my jeans as I played with her. Her face had reddened a million degrees, my teeth touching that. I licked her from cheek to nose ring. "How bad do you need it, Red? How bad do you want me?"

If she said anything else beyond what I wanted to hear, I would split her in half and what the fuck? I needed to turn around right now. It wasn't too late. I could stop this…

"Ares…" The name, my name falling from her lips made the blood rush to other places. The muscle in my chest beat in overdrive. Especially when she placed her hand near it. She braced my pecs. "Ares, make love to me."

Fuck.

Our mouths fused together, quick, hungry…

Intimate.

It was like my name in her mouth. My real name and not a moniker I made her and everyone else call me. The name Wolf had always been a football thing, but until this year, I hadn't gone by it exclusively. It'd only been after I came back and after everything I'd gone through that I started to use it all the time. I was the wolf. Untouchable.

Unbreakable.

My arms cradled above Fawn, easing up on her. She wasn't something I was trying to possess or claim, and that scared me more than what was happening. I didn't want her to be real to me or anything outside of a thought from afar.

Thoughts from the past...

Kissing her harder, I forced out images of her, other thoughts I had of her, connections... This girl and I were bound more than she probably even knew, and I was aware of that.

My hand had hers over my hip, and I turned on my back, letting her get on top of me.

Christ.

Her chest rose and fell, those nipples so tight, pink. I tweaked them before forcing my face between them again, my hand in her hair.

Stop this. Stop this.

I couldn't, really freaking drugged here. This girl had me fucking fragile.

Weak.

"Ares, please." My name again, her hands on my shirt. She wanted me to take it off, but I fought her.

I sucked her harder instead, her pants picking up.

"Ares, I can't... I..."

A sick pleasure came over me as I undid her, played with her. It was like in the library, and Wells had been doing that same shit to her former roommate. I'd like to say my buddies and I never fucked our partners within feet of each other before but that'd be a lie. In high school, we used to take conquests into the computer lab.

Fawn wasn't a conquest. She was a challenge, yes, but that wasn't what went down in the library. It was like I *wanted* to please her, be everything for her, so she did fall apart for me.

A dangerous thought, that. So many dangerous thoughts as I reached between us and rolled my shirt off. My abs worked as I brought her against me, and at the sight of them, Fawn's hands touched down. I thought she'd go for them first. Chicks always did.

I wished she would have.

I wished her hands touched anywhere else but the tat on my hip. It was so small and could only be seen because I did have my jeans low, open.

Her fingers traced the flower there, something she obviously hadn't noticed before when I nutted off on her tits.

I would have noticed.

I would have noticed her studying it, and I'd made sure she hadn't that day. I'd kept my hand strategically placed when I jerked off.

She wasn't supposed to see it.

Well, she had now, and when her hands did move to my abs, her attention away, I released a breath.

I jerked her to me.

My hand in her hair, I kissed the shit out of this girl. All this was nothing more than a casual fuck, a taste. I did this, and I'd get this girl out of my head.

I'd make sure of it.

I forced her jeans down, my hands over her ass, and it took everything in me not to turn her on her stomach and bite that shit. I knew what she had back there from her bathing suit, and that might undo me.

Control. Control.

It felt like it was fleeting. The noises she was making were sending me over the edge, making me crazy. I bit her lip once I had her naked, my jeans the only thing between us.

"Ares, come on. You can't." She laughed a little, my mouth biting her neck. "You can't play with me like this."

She was full-on naked on top of me, rocking those glorious hips. She put a wet spot on my jeans before I stopped her, and she growled. I grinned. "So impatient, Red. You want me to fuck you or not?"

I almost sounded like I needed her to say yes. Like this wasn't just for fun but was real. Like *we were real*, and this wasn't something I needed to simply move forward.

I kissed her before she could come at me with a quip, test me in all her mouthy ways. One day, I would fill that mouth if I could. If I was stupid…

Her hand came between us. It was really dumb letting her do that and even more when I allowed her to pull me out. She fisted me, working me, and my eyes rolled back.

"Red…" The warning in my voice was low, gritted. I bit her jaw. "I won't fuck you. I'll draw this shit fucking out. I swear to God."

That was if I didn't nut myself first, my eyes pinched tight, *my head* going back. I put my fingers in my hair, enjoying all this for a second, and she laughed.

"So, he isn't just a god," she said, bold and even bolder when she put her hand in my hair. She kissed me, and I almost did come, refusing.

I moved her thighs against me, our kiss slow, warm. It did feel real, and I lost myself.

But not for long.

I sobered myself, ripping her back by red locks.

I can't look at her.

I didn't, turning the tables and getting her beneath me. I had her on her knees, ass up but I refused to take note.

I jerked her arms back.

I had her bound, unable to move aside from what I was about to do to her. I wanted her vulnerable this way, nothing but flesh, ass.

Yeah… completely fucked.

I got the condom out of my jeans. My boxers at my hips, I kicked my jeans and shoes off before ripping the foil packet open with my teeth. Fawn waited, perfect and patient like a little submissive.

Don't look at her.

Disconnecting, I angled into her—hard. In fact, I thrust so violently the bed shot forward, and she called out.

I rammed again.

Over and over, as I used her bound hands to drive into her. My hips slapped her ass. It was charged red just like the rest of her.

"Fucking fuck," she groaned out. This girl was into the hard shit. It only made me pick up, and I did something stupid again. I let go of her hands and yanked her to look at me. Starry-eyed, she studied me for only the two moments I let her before my mouth hit hers.

Fucking shit...

I was done, fucking her so hard and fast. The fury built in my cock, my balls heavy and about to explode. "Fawn..."

I bit her lips as I said her name, my dick kicking, pulsating. Her body locking up, her walls closed around me, and as soon as that shit hit, I exploded like a fucking *teen.*

Holy fucking shit.

I watched her, eyes opened while I kissed her, claimed her. I was flooding the condom but all I was doing was studying her while I did it, enamored. A flush touched her face, the ecstasy lining it. She kissed me harder, and I found myself kissing back.

Groaning, I flattened against her, crowding her. She fit right into my body, and I didn't pull out while I moved my hips against her. I just kissed her, her head back while she let me milk her. Neither one of us stopped, and we spent so many moments like this I didn't bother counting. I actually couldn't even say when we ultimately stopped because the last thoughts I had were us in the sheets.

I had my arm around her before everything went dark.

CHAPTER
SEVENTEEN

Fawn

Goddammit…

He was gorgeous.

The sheets cinched at Wolf's chiseled waist, his broad chest moving in and out with each breath. He'd fallen asleep, and I fingered his curls.

I guess you really aren't a god.

As far as I knew, gods didn't sleep, but what did I know about gods?

Absolutely nothing.

Wolf had a hand on his abs, his other arm around me. He had me hooked to him, tight, and when he eased in a short breath, my fingers stilled.

He dampened his lips. A sigh escaped them, but soon, he fell right back into steady slumber. My fingers played again, but the unease didn't leave me. I was quite sure he was only letting me play with his feathered locks because he was sleeping. I'd tried to touch them while we were having sex, but he hadn't let me do that long.

He hadn't let me do a lot of things.

This guy still had me scared of him and for good reason. When he'd brought me in here, I hadn't known what was about to happen.

Wolf shifted.

His muscled arm slid from beneath my neck, and I sighed. I missed the heat immediately like an idiot and missed his hold even more.

I watched with my stupid foolish heart when he gave me his back, but my fascination soon transferred to that. His back was perfect like the rest of him, but that wasn't what stole my attention.

My hand hovered over a line of colorful tattoos, dark, vibrant. A constellation design tatted directly down his spinal cord, and I realized I'd never actually seen his back in full. He'd been wearing that harness before, and the wings covered his spine.

God, he really is gorgeous.

His back was a work of art, the line of planets only enhancing it. Tight, muscular planes moved perfectly beneath tanned skin, this guy a canvas. He'd said he was an artist, and the intricacy of the planets, the beauty...

I wonder if he drew this.

A thick black line tied them all together, and I had to admit I'd snap-judged the asshole. I figured he was just a vapid jock, and he hadn't given me a lot to work with in the past. I definitely didn't think he respected anything regarding any kind of art, but his back piece was telling me something different. If he was an artist, some deliberate thought had gone into this piece. Regardless if he rendered it himself.

And it was lovely.

Putting my arm under my head, I simply stared at it, analyzing every line. I admired it from my own creative brain. I crafted stories through photos, its own art form. Dad had taught me so much about the artistic side of it. The process wasn't just about snapping photos. There was craft to it, art just like what was in front of my eyes now.

I peered down Wolf's spine, going up, down. I thought I'd analyzed every inch of the piece until something caught my eye right in the middle.

His skin bubbled up a bit, and upon further observation, I noticed bubbled skin all throughout the black line that tied the planets on his back together.

What…

I got closer, a breath away. Squinting, I studied that dark line, and eventually, I blinked back.

Scars.

Like a whole line, solid and strategically placed beneath the bold line of the tattoo. It was a full scar, but not like an accident.

Like surgery.

I touched it with my finger.

"What the *fuck* do you think you're doing?"

My hand shot back.

At least, I tried to.

My wrist ensnared, I fell to my back. Wolf was on top of me. He pinned me down with a wild look about his eyes, and mine widened.

"Did I say you could fucking touch me?" He grabbed my throat, and the air flow cut off. I choked, gasping. Hair shrouded his face. "Huh? Did I?"

He shook my throat with every gritted word, both hands around my windpipe now, and I grabbed at them. "You're choking me…"

His grip tightened, and my vision darkened. My legs kicked beneath him, but I only think part of that was voluntary. My natural instincts were trying to get me out, but shock looped its intense hold around me.

Wolf looked deranged.

Crazed, he pressed his face closer to mine. "You don't fucking touch me. You understand?"

I didn't. We were touching a lot earlier tonight.

I mean, we had sex.

I think he just meant I couldn't touch him there, where I had that made him act like this, but I couldn't ask.

My vision was blurring now, his fingers embedded deep in my throat. "Wolf…"

I could barely see him at this point, and he didn't let go. Appearing mad, he only gripped harder, but a knock at the door had him twisting around.

"Wolf? You in there? Someone said they saw you and Fawn come through."

It sounded like one of his friends, Dorian? Honestly, I couldn't even think right now let alone try to match a face with a voice.

The guy chuckled outside the door. "Anyway, we're taking off, so…"

"One sec," Wolf ground out, but he wasn't looking at that door.

Only at me.

It was like I could see through him. He wasn't Wolf, Ares… He was something beyond any of that, and whatever it was had the fear clouding around me in a thick haze.

Another deep chuckle rolled outside the door, and only once it drifted off did Wolf let go.

I coughed, gasping. The bed lifted when Wolf bounded off, and I watched him grab his discard clothes. I blinked through watery eyes. "Wolf…"

It came out raspy, and really, not at all. I rubbed at my throat, the indentation of his nails literally under my fingers.

Wolf covered himself, quick. He got his boxers and jeans on, snapping the latter shut and covering the only other tattoo he had outside of his back piece. He had a small flower on his hip, black and gray, a line drawing.

I hadn't noticed it the night he came on my breasts, but I think his hand had been covering it. I leaned up on my elbows. "Wolf?"

I spoke louder but that didn't matter. I watched as all he did was tug his shirt on and cover that back piece. He toed on his high-tops, then he was out of the door, and he slammed it so hard the sound vibrated in my already spinning head.

I blinked, nothing left to do but that. The party beats bumping the walls, I lay naked in a bed and a room that wasn't even mine. He'd left me here like that.

He just left.

CHAPTER
EIGHTEEN

Ares

The cold stethoscope touched my chest.

"Breathe in."

I did, deep.

"And out."

I did that too, slowly. The stethoscope moved away and landed on my back. Dr. Sturm grinned. "New ink?"

My hands came together. "Recent. Yeah."

Dr. Sturm nodded before requesting I breathe in once more, and I did, my feet firm on the floor. I had to sit on these exam tables during the visits, but I was so tall I didn't bother using the foot rest.

"And out," Dr. Sturm requested, my breath expelling. He told me good job and that I could relax.

I braced my legs. "Can I put my shirt on?"

"Yep. Go for it."

I did right away, wanting to cover that ink. Normally, I was proud of it, a milestone.

Today, all it did was remind me of Fawn and how she'd looked when I'd been on top of her. The fear in her eyes...

I shrugged the tee on quickly, pushing the memory out even quicker. I had no time for it.

Dr. Sturm came around with his clipboard. "Everything's looking good, Ares. Real good, and you're not having any problems? No aches? Pains?"

My fingers threaded. "Nope."

"How about tingling or numbness?"

"No."

He wasn't looking at me during anything I'd said, jotting things down.

I was glad.

I gripped the table, waiting patiently for him to finish. His pen on the clipboard ticked my pulse, but I didn't say a word.

His writing slowed.

"So how are your classes going?" he asked, making small talk. Always did. "Must be intense. Took you a while to get in here."

They weren't that bad in all honesty. School was easy as shit for me. It always had been, and I'd excelled quite well in high school.

It was the art that always challenged me because I cared about it.

I braced the table. "Yeah, and sorry about that."

"No problem. No problem."

More writing, more jotting. Eventually, it stopped, and he faced me.

"I think I'd just like to see some blood work from you, then." He grinned. "Routine and all that, you know? I know you said you're doing well, which is great. Just procedure, as you know. We want to make sure you're still in tiptop shape, of course."

Procedure. Yeah.

I shifted. "Yeah. Sure thing."

"You can do it on your way out of the clinic. You don't need an appointment for the lab downstairs."

"Okay."

He continued to write, but eventually, he stopped, smiled. "I think we're all good for today."

"Great." I got up, and the man's hand came out. I shook it.

"It's always great seeing you, and remember to get that blood work taken care of. I'll have my nurse call you with the results."

"Does it have to be today?" I shrugged, casual about it. "I just got classes and stuff, so…"

He lifted a hand. "Understandable. Take care of it when you can. Just don't forget?"

I tapped my head, making him smile again. He gave me another shake before I headed out, and I didn't breathe until I made it to my truck.

My hands on the steering wheel, I just stared into open air. *Fuck.*

I unstrapped myself, needing a moment. Any doctor's appointments came with a fair bit of anxiety, but this one in particular was fucking my shit up. I hated the doctor. Especially after last year.

Get your shit together.

I eased out a breath, taking my phone out. I checked for messages but ended up just looking at one.

Fawn: I'm staying with Heath. He's offering his couch, so I'm taking it. I think you know why.

It was an old message, and one I felt like I'd looked at a million times since she sent it two days ago.

I wished I could only be mad at her.

I couldn't, though. More relieved she'd left than angry. It meant I didn't have to do this shit with her anymore.

Why did you sleep with her?

Because I was stupid. Because I was fucked up, and if she knew how fucked up, she never would have agreed to the fake arrangement in the first place. That night with her single-handedly blew up everything. A nuclear explosion could have only been worse.

And I couldn't even fix it.

In good faith, I couldn't. Yeah, I could go over to that fucker Heath's place. I could drag her back, make her honor our deal. I could use blackmail, and I had before.

I ran my hand against my steering wheel, my stomach tighter than at my goddamn appointment. I scrubbed my face before I belted myself, but a tap hit my window.

A smile graced the other side.

My mother, Brielle, placed her arms on my ride, her hair up, her grin wide. I put down the window, and her head cocked. "Hey, critter."

My eyes lifted at the nickname, but a noticeable ease hit my stomach after she said it. Perhaps, it was the familiarity of it since she used to call me that as a kid.

Or maybe it was just her.

I was surprised to see my mom, and once I got out, she hugged me right away. She squeezed me, smelling familiar too. Like home.

My stomach loosened more.

"What are you doing here?" I asked her, trying to man the hell up. Puffing up, I was acting like I wasn't completely fucking grateful to see my mom right now in the middle of a fucking breakdown.

Mom shouldered her bag, a petite woman. At least when it came to the Bigfoots in her family. She was actually normal-sized, and even my sister was taller than her. "Was on campus for a bit visiting some former colleagues."

Mom used to work as a professor at Pembroke before she became mayor of our city, Maywood Heights.

"Anyway, I thought I'd visit my son and my daughter. Sloane and I had breakfast this morning. Knew you were busy with your appointment."

Both she and Dad were the first I messaged to let them know about it. I'd been casual about it, brought it up in the group text between my sister, Bru, myself, and our parents. It was my way of letting them all know I was handling my business. It also kept them all off my back.

Mom threaded her arm around mine. "So how about lunch? You wanna take your mama out? I'm buying."

Like I could ever push my mother away. She was worse than me when it came to getting what she wanted.

I mean, that was who I'd learned from.

I took my mother out to lunch and refused her money when I brought her to my favorite spot on campus. For the most part, Pembroke had decent food, but the food trucks on the quad ran supreme.

Mom and I took our chili dogs on some benches under a tree, watching people play Frisbee and just hang out. I didn't see my mom a lot between school and her busy schedule, but it was always nice when we could hang. She pushed more than Dad, not as laid-back as him, but I got it because we were really alike. My sister may be her mini-me as far as looks, but when it came to the insides, I was all Brielle Mallick. I had her fight too, which meant I was always butting heads with my parents on the regular growing up. I hadn't always been the easiest kid to get along with.

Mom scarfed some of her chili dog. "So how did your appointment go?"

I grinned, wiping my mouth. "Just wanted to come out to lunch, huh?"

"Well, I wouldn't be your mom if I didn't ask." She waggled her dark eyebrows. "Anyway, it go well? You're doing well?"

I considered how to answer that. "Yeah. He said I was good."

Doc had said that, the truth, but I didn't miss the tightness that returned to my stomach.

My mom's smile triggered it.

It made me focus on my hot dog, easier than other things. Mom shook my leg. "I'm so glad you got that taken care of. Lots of worry off my and your dad's backs."

My parents did worry a lot. I'd given them so many reasons to over the years, too many. I'd grown up as an only child, and that fact had put my entire family through the wringer. My parents had dealt with Sloane's absence in our lives far better than me.

And I hadn't even met her back then.

I put my hot dog down. "Well, you don't have to worry. I told you I'd get it done."

She wouldn't worry. She couldn't, and I refused to let her or Dad.

I swallowed as her lips lifted.

"You did, but still, I know how busy school can get, and now that you've got a girlfriend, I'm sure your time is very divided."

I'd been taking a bite of my hot dog and nearly choked. I coughed it down. "Girlfriend?"

"Sorry. Cat's out of the bag. Your sister told me all about it."

But I hadn't even told her that, made Fawn and I official-official. I mean, I'd told that bitch at the party that, but... "I never told Sloane I had a girlfriend."

"No, but you moved in with her, so..."

My eyes flashed. I was sure wide as fuck. "She told you that too?"

Goddammit, little.

"I think we all know how serious that makes this," Mom continued. She nudged me. "Sloane said you were just helping this girl out for a term, but come on, Ares. We know you. You don't bring around girls."

I didn't, which meant my parents knew I was just as much of a ho as anyone else.

"This is obviously very serious, and it's okay to admit that." My mother beamed, and she didn't beam. It wasn't like she wasn't a happy person, but emotions certainly came easier to my father. At least, expressing them.

And so, I was my mother's child.

Her head tilted. "Needless to say, your dad and I are elated and can't wait to meet her. She's obviously had an effect on you."

My chest caved, and I wished I had more food. I ate when I was uncomfortable. Like a fucking tick or something. "Actually, Mom..."

"We were hoping you'd bring her down for a weekend soon like we mentioned." Mom finished her food, crumpling her trash. She lifted a hand. "We'll plan it all out. Have dinner and do one of our family hikes."

Fuck.

"It'll be so fun, and my God, Ares, is she lovely! Sloane showed me pictures today. I hope you don't mind, but she looked up her social media."

My head whirled, and my world tilted.

Mom's eyes warmed. "She looks so nice, and a creative like you?" She shook my shoulder. "Sloane told me she takes pictures. Is that true?"

I nodded, on autopilot more than anything else.

"And all those tattoos she has... simply gorgeous. Her flowers actually remind me of the one you got. The ones on her arm?"

My parents knew I had a tat on my hip, but I'd never shown them. I'd shown them the design, though.

I'd designed it.

I put my hands together. "Mom..."

"We are so stinkin' happy for you, critter." Mom's phone buzzed, and her eyes lifted to the heavens. She didn't look like she wanted to check it, but she was a public figure. She took it out. "Dang. Give me one second, honey. It's the office."

She got up to take her call, take that second, and my stomach wasn't just tight this time.

The sickness swirled, heavy. It was like I was on a fucked-up carnival ride that wouldn't stop with an insane carny at the wheel. I couldn't get off this shit with Fawn and me.

At least, not until it was done with me.

CHAPTER
NINETEEN

Fawn

I ignored another call from my mother today, but that was only partially because I didn't want to speak to her.

Ares Mallick was still in my head, and I couldn't shake him no matter how much I desired. The reminders of him were everywhere, the first being I hadn't had a decent night's sleep in days. Being on Heath's couch wasn't ideal, but hell if I was going back to that dorm Wolf and I shared.

The way he'd looked at me...

He'd been insane, wild, and that said something considering how unhinged I'd seen him in the past. He'd acted like I had violated him when I'd only touched him and shared concern.

What happened to him?

The question of the hour, all this history surrounding this guy. I hadn't been bold enough to ask in the past, but maybe I should have. Wolf had some sizable issues, and only part of that seemed to surround his recent insanity.

That bugged me the most, that I wondered about him,

worried about him. This was ironic considering I was the person who was supposed to be alleviating that from his life regarding his family.

I slammed a textbook closed, getting up from my "bed." It was either that or the blow-up mattress, and Heath's roommate (Allen) was definitely giving me the side-eye the last few days I'd been on the couch. Heath told him I was a friend who needed a helping hand like I was homeless.

In a way, I was, I guess.

I needed to brave the hell up and just go get my stuff, speak to housing, but I didn't want to confront Wolf. He'd been crazy the last time I'd seen him.

My phone buzzed.

It was a text this time, not a call, and I was grateful. My mom didn't call often, but she called enough where I always checked before answering. She knew I was busy with school or my photography, so she never got offended, and considering the crickets that sounded during our chats, I was saving her. I never had much to say. We just were like that. Always had been.

Kurt: Hey. It's Kurt from the NY Times.

I shot up, ramrod straight. Even if I hadn't known the number by heart, I knew it was him. Who he was, I mean. Obviously.

Kurt: I'm in town again covering a story, and since you're at the top of my list for the internship, I wanted to see you in action. Are you game? I'll be shooting downtown.

Holy crap. Holy crap. Holy crap. Was my luck seriously changing right now?

I pushed my hair out of my face.

Me: Yes, totally. When and where and what time?

Those details shot over while I rooted around my bag for something other than sweatpants. I'd filled my duffel with as much as I could the one or two times I'd been able to sneak into my dorm. I hadn't wanted to risk Wolf seeing me, and since I didn't have much stuff anyway, I'd gotten most of the things that mattered. Things like my dad's camera and clothes.

Kurt: If you can bring an assistant, that'd be great. You'll be shooting most of the feature, so it'll help you get more angles. I'll be around to advise, of course. ;)

This was wild, and I had the perfect person. Heath would love this and would be completely stoked.

I shot Kurt a text that would be no problem and was barely able to get the words out when I called Heath. He had a class, but he obviously ditched it. We decided to meet downtown since he was already out, and I brought his gear with mine. It'd been awkward carrying it all since I had to take the bus, but I managed.

"Well, this is fucking cool," he said, the moment he saw me get off my bus. He tapped my fist. "And good looking out. This is a great opportunity."

It might even open some doors for him. I had no idea his plans after graduation, but mentioning he worked on a piece with Kurt Ackerman I was sure wouldn't hurt. I grinned. "No problem. I guess I owed you one for letting me crash on your couch. You and Allen."

He'd been very cool about that. They both had.

"Eh. Not a big deal. Though, I'm still wondering about all that." He took his stuff from me. "Any idea when they'll have your place fumigated?"

So I'd had to give him a little white lie, but I hadn't gotten a hold of housing yet. Honestly, I was kind of intimidated by the whole thing considering it'd been Wolf to arrange everything.

He could have easily locked me in to live with him knowing his pull, and any call to housing could be futile.

Honestly, Kurt reaching out to me today in the first place was a surprise. After I'd left Wolf (abruptly), I thought I may see some repercussions from that, and also knowing him, I should have.

He was like a specter hanging over my head, an animal waiting to retaliate, pounce...

I dodged Heath's inquiries and instead had him focus on our shooting location today, which was crazy. Kurt texted later that his story downtown was to cover the city's youth, but I hadn't expected this.

There were kids, many kids spray-painting walls, graffiti. In fact, there were so many I couldn't count, and the dingy back alley couldn't look prettier. Normally, the area held squatters, but today, it was nothing but kids making art. They varied in ages, some teens and others younger.

"Wow," I said, snapping a test shot. Kurt hadn't given me too many details, but he said this was what we'd be covering.

"Wow is right." Heath took a shot himself, quick and probably for lighting like me. "Can't wait to add this to my portfolio."

He wasn't the only one, and both of us took a few more shots. We did this while looking for Kurt, and while we did, I couldn't help but bug my ex-roomie about what I'd seen in the library. I didn't tell him I'd seen him, *of course*, but I did say word had gotten around that he and Wells Ambrose had hooked up.

His face colored after I said it, and mine did too. Though, for other reasons. He passed it off. "Eh. It was nothing. Just a hookup."

"Do you want it to be something more?" I snapped another photo, surprised when he shook his head.

"Nah, I'm good. I didn't go into it thinking it was going to lead to anything."

"Why not?"

"Because he's Legacy." He shouldered his bag. "I mean, it was nice. Fucking awesome, but I'm not trying to deal with the heartbreak if you know what I mean. These guys aren't generally known for commitment, with the exception of Prinze and well, now, you and Mallick."

He nudged me, laughing, and though I laughed too, mine had been dry. He was the smart one, I guess. Not to get involved.

"So, what's going on with you two anyway? You've had campus buzzing since you've been hanging out. I mean, when did it happen? How?"

This wasn't the first time he'd asked these questions, nor the first that our friends had asked. I did keep all that very private. I mean, no one but Wolf, me, and his friends even knew we'd moved in together as far as I knew.

That spectacle had been for them.

I waved what he said off. "Let's just stick to the photos."

His eyes lifted, and I was relieved to see Kurt. He had his own camera, the thing sweet and strapped to his back. He was chatting with some of the kids, but he wasn't the only one.

My steps slowed, the dread in my steps as Heath continued on toward Kurt. He knew who Kurt was. Everyone in our circle did, but I just stood there as he headed that way.

I did for a long time. In fact, so long it took Heath a second to realize he was alone. He looked back. "You okay, Fawn?"

Kurt's head turned in my direction, and needless to say, the guy he was with did the same. He had a box of spray cans in his mighty hands, his hoodie on and his grin wide. His nose rings flicked off the bright sun beneath his dusky hair, and my mouth dried. Ares Mallick was grinning at me.

And so, there was my wolfish specter again.

CHAPTER
TWENTY

Ares

Fawn didn't look particularly happy to see me, but this wasn't surprising. I'd expected it even.

Bracing the box of spray paints, I headed over, casual about it. Kurt approached Fawn right away, shaking her hand, but she was so distracted by me.

This isn't over, Red. Not yet.

This girl and I were in this for the long haul, and as soon as we both accepted it, things would be easier. For both of us, not just her.

My grin stretched, the box of paints on my hip. I gave her a few seconds with Kurt, ignoring the pretentious fuck with her. That dude Heath may not be into girls so much these days, but he still put her up.

He took her from me.

Relax. Fuck.

Things had to be different this time, and I was well aware of it. Kurt told Fawn how good it was to see her, and after

Fawn introduced Heath to him (as her assistant), her attention veered right to me. She came over in ripped jeans that flashed her knees and gave ample views of her tatted thighs.

I dampened my lips. "Red—"

"What are you doing here?" she cut, low. Kurt had his back to us, his hand in Heath's. They were shaking it out, getting acquainted. "Wolf—"

"Nice to see you too, babe," I announced, loud enough for both guys to hear. Fawn's lashes flashed, then she flinched when I eased an arm around her. "Missed you too."

I pressed a kiss to her brow, slow, deliberate. I acted like a guy who hadn't seen his girl in a while, and it felt like that the moment I had those curves of hers up against me again.

It had been a while.

Maybe I'd gotten used to seeing her every day, our walks on campus and hanging out. I'd gotten used to seeing her in our dorm, even though I wasn't there a whole lot with school. I'd gotten *used to her*, used to us. Add to the fact we'd been intimate the last time we'd been together—well, maybe I'd missed her a little bit.

Well, she certainly hadn't missed me, and she fought the width of her eyes the moment I placed my mouth on her freckled skin. Heath and Kurt had ambled toward us, and right away, Fawn pushed an arm at my lower back. Her arm there right away reminded me of other things, us together that last time. Her fingers had invaded places they certainly shouldn't have been going, and best believe the shit going on between us now was one hundred percent her fault. She liked to do things like that, test me.

We got nothing but smiles in our direction from Kurt, aware the two of us were together. I'd mentioned it. He pushed hands in his pockets. "Ares told me you two were seeing each other. A great man this one."

"Oh, go on," I joked, Fawn easing away from me. She'd

obviously felt she'd done enough in front of present company.

Her smile was tight. "Yeah, after we ran into each other at our meeting, Kurt, and things just kind of clicked, I guess," she said, taking it upon herself to give us more backstory. She was lucky I hadn't said anything about how we'd gotten together to Kurt. She eyed me. "But he didn't tell me he'd be here today."

"Really?" Kurt cuffed my arm. "Modest, this one. This whole project was his idea. Called my office about it, which was why I called you." He tilted his head at her. "Figured it'd be a great opportunity to see you in action."

Yeah, Fawn had no idea what the fuck Kurt was talking about, but this wasn't surprising either. The idea definitely hadn't existed before recently. I shrugged. "Just wanted to do something for the community."

"Yeah?" This came from Fawn, suspicious as hell, and she should be. I didn't want to say me putting this community project together in two seconds was because of her. But...

I pocketed my hands. "Uh-huh. These kids are from alternative schools in town." I studied Kurt, who was grinning. "This project gives them course credit and is a great way for them to channel aggression."

I'd actually gotten the idea from my father who had used similar tactics with me in the past. I'd had a lot of anger coming up. He'd called it illegal art therapy, the two of us tagging walls in my hometown.

Of course, I'd gotten all the approvals for this today, nothing illegal here. The city had actually thanked me, an upgrade for this area since it'd gotten so run-down.

Fawn's auburn eyebrows lifted, her red-painted lips parting. She had a lot to say, but obviously felt she couldn't say it in the moment.

Kurt tapped my shoulder. "Just like his father in that right.

A regular philanthropist and always giving back to his community."

Him comparing me to my father was an insult to my dad. Nothing about what I was doing today was genuine, and the person I was targeting definitely saw that.

Fawn was all puffed up like she was two seconds from busting a cap in someone's ass. She had that camera she constantly carried gripped by the strap, and that was when Heath cut in and asked Kurt for more details about today. Yeah, didn't like that fucker and his distraction had Fawn all up on me.

"What is this really?" she asked, that sweet-smelling shit she wore in my face again. It reminded me of when I'd fucked her, warm sugar all around me, all over me… "Why are you doing this? Why are you here?"

She should be thanking me for calling Kurt. "This is an opportunity for you to work with Kurt."

"No, this is an opportunity for you to wave him and my internship in my face again."

She was smart. I'd give her that. "Our deal isn't over."

"Oh, it's fucking over."

"Eh. A call from my editor," Kurt announced, and Fawn and I gazed up. Kurt raised his phone. "I have to take this, then, Fawn and Heath, I'll explain exactly what we'll be doing today."

Heath and Fawn both grinned, but only Fawn's looked crooked. Heath mentioned wanting to talk to some of the students about the project, and Fawn started to go too until I got her arm.

"Red—"

"Don't fucking touch me."

My own words shot back to me, I closed my lips. She'd whisper-shouted them. I passed a hand over my hair. "Look. Shit got crazy the other night. It did, so I get why you're pissed."

"You went fucking crazy," she hissed, glancing around. She lifted a finger. "I can't do this anymore, Wolf. I'm sorry. But no. It can't happen. It won't."

She started to walk away, but I got her arm again. "I don't want to threaten you."

"So don't."

I pushed air through my nose. "So don't make me. Don't do this. I don't want to *do this*. I don't..." My fingers moved over her arm, my hand easing away. "We don't have to be enemies. We could even be fucking friends."

Light laughter hit me, her laughter, and I didn't like getting fucking laughed at. Her expression darkened. "I can't be friends with a psychopath, and someone who clearly has more skeletons in his closet than me."

I clicked my teeth.

"And why would you want that anyway?" she questioned, her laughter audible to everyone around us this time. My pulse spiked, and she sneered. "You wanted a flunky. You wanted a *servant*, and people who serve don't make friends with their employers."

She got bold in the next moment, stepping up to me. I had well over a foot on this girl, but that didn't stop her from putting mere inches between us.

I felt those inches, the heat of them radiating off of her flushed tits and hitting me through my T-shirt. I wasn't sure whether I wanted to wring her neck right now or use it to bring her to her knees.

To make her *bow*.

It was the fact that I didn't know which that freaked me out. This girl was steadily on my fucking mind. She put a finger in my chest. "I'd never be friends with you. Why? Because you're a bully on top of being insane. The fact that you've been blackmailing me is only the cherry on top of your psycho-as-fuck cake."

I wasn't fucking insane.

And she was lucky she walked away.

She headed over to Heath, getting in on the conversations he was having.

I found Kurt instead.

———

I watched Red for the better half of the afternoon, doing that between actually operating this whole event. I did more networking than anything, my other objective for this event outside of getting Fawn down here. My name tied to this drew people from the art community, my background semi-prolific. I wasn't anything like my father in that regard, but people knew me. Knew my stuff.

If anything, I needed practice networking. I wasn't used to that side of the art world, but I needed to get used to it. It was necessary with the changes I found myself making in my life as of late.

Red looked like she was done.

She'd been getting advice from Kurt the whole afternoon, snapping shots, and I let her. I thought I wouldn't. Not with that shit she'd said, but I did want things to be different.

They had to be.

I couldn't mess up this time, and I had to hand it to her. Me being around only threw her off partially. She was professional, focused, and it was only when I was feet away from her that she actually acknowledged my presence. I wasn't doing any spray-painting, but I was advising the kids and their teachers. Teaching had never really been my thing, but I'd worked with some of the best in the world, and there was evidence of my labor out there. I had pieces displayed on several continents. Basically, I'd done my thing in the past, and people liked to pay for it.

My hands worked at my sides. Grunting, I massaged them a bit, and Kurt approached. He had Fawn and Heath in tow.

I handed the supplies I had over to some of the kids. Since this was my idea, I made sure they had everything they needed outside of advisement.

I noticed Fawn and Heath pair off from Kurt, as he came over. The two studied the back of their cameras, and I figured they were going over their shots.

"Got everything you need?" I asked Kurt, glancing away from the two. I still didn't like that fucking dude with her, but I smiled at Kurt. "For the feature, I mean?"

He was doing me a solid by coming down today, and though this had been a scheme to get to Fawn, I was glad I'd done it. I related to these kids, more than related to them. Shit could get real dark sometimes in life, and art, creation was definitely a great way to heal it.

I knew this from personal experience.

My hands worked again, and Kurt grinned in Fawn and Heath's direction.

"We did," he said, answering my previous question. "I had Fawn and Heath do most of the work. Both take great advisement, and I'll definitely put in a good word for Heath when he needs it. He expressed some interest in the film and television sector, and I told him I had some contacts he could definitely reach out to."

Yeah, didn't fucking care about that. "How'd Fawn do?"

I was acting like I cared. Like she hadn't fucking pissed me off before by saying she'd never be friends with me in any type of normal capacity.

Why the fuck do you care?

I braced my arms, and Kurt smiled again.

"Excellent, and thank you again for recommending her. For the internship?" His chin lifted. "I probably would have missed her if not for your insight. These internships are in high demand. I'm sure you can imagine."

I glanced back at Fawn, my eyes on her.

"She's certainly gifted like her father," Kurt said.

Fawn started to come over then, and I let go of the conversation with Kurt. Other things were priority, like trying to make Fawn fucking talk to me.

Having Kurt here as an incentive definitely helped, and I gripped the man's arm. "How about dinner, Kurt? The least I can do for you coming over from New York."

"That would be amazing, Ares. Fawn? Heath?" Kurt questioned, the pair of them blinking. He smiled. "You should come along with us, and I'll buy for everyone. You kids are in school and shouldn't have to worry about it."

He knew I had no reason to worry, but he was obviously trying to be nice for the sake of Fawn and Heath.

Heath's mouth parted. "That would be amazing."

I was sure it would, about to suggest the same before Kurt had invited at least, well, Fawn. We weren't done today, and I hadn't gotten to talk to her.

I stared at her, but her attention wasn't on me. It was on Kurt who had suggested we all follow him.

"I hit up a great restaurant last time I was here," Kurt said, tugging up his camera bag. "And if anyone needs a ride, I'm happy to take you."

"Fawn comes with me. Obviously," I stated, angling over to her. This was obvious. To these two, we were dating. I put my arm around her, but again, she wasn't focusing on me. Her face had turned red, and she was scanning the ground. The fuck? "Fawn?"

She didn't look at me, but she did ease away. She faced Kurt. "Actually, Heath and I have a deadline," she said, glancing his way. "Right, Heath?"

She ground out the words, and Heath's focus was in her direction. His eyes narrowed, but before he could speak, she moved her attention back to Kurt.

"You understand, Kurt," she said, her hand gripping her camera bag. She knuckled that shit, her fist full white. "Heath and I work for our university newspaper. We have a deadline we unfortunately can't miss."

My brow shot up, but Heath's eyebrows just about hit the fucker's hairline. "Yeah, but that can wait, Fawn." He shook his head, slight but I noticed. "Come on…"

I blinked. Why the fuck was the dude pleading with her?

"Sorry, but you know it can't." She swallowed in the moment, her gaze colliding with mine. My head cocking, I moved toward her, but she distanced. Instead, she smiled at Kurt, a false one that didn't quite hit her eyes. "I'm sorry."

"Oh, you don't have to apologize. I totally get it. Editors."

"Yeah, editors."

"And speaking of mine." Kurt studied his phone. His fingers dashed on the screen. "Mine's bugging me about my own."

He chuckled after, both Heath and Fawn laughing, but it was definitely dry on their end. That fucker Heath looked at her again, but Fawn did nothing but shake her head.

The fuck is going on?

Neither said, just looking at each other.

Eventually, Kurt said he had to give his editor a call, but he shook Fawn's hand first, then Heath's.

"I'll be in contact about the photos," he said, putting the phone to his ear. "And great job again today."

"Thanks for having us," Fawn said, watching the man walk away. I started to get closer to her, but once more, she backed off. "I'm going to get my stuff together."

She said this to Heath more than me and what the fuck?

Fawn's sneakers headed in the opposite direction, the rest of her and Heath's gear by the wall. Heath started to head that way too, but I cut him off.

"What's going on?" I asked, and his eyes flashed. "Why aren't you both going to dinner?"

And if he gave me that shit about a deadline, I was calling

BS on that. This was an amazing opportunity for them both with Kurt, networking.

A curse left Heath's lips. "Because she's obviously letting this shit hold her back," he stated, and when my head cocked, he blinked. "I mean, you know what I'm talking about."

I didn't, shrugging, and his mouth parted.

"Wait. She didn't tell you?"

"Tell me what?" I was getting angry now, this dude fucking around too much.

His head shook. "Fawn doesn't do cars," he said, the last thing I thought would fall out of this guy's mouth. His head tilted. "You haven't noticed? How have you both been getting around?"

I was still trying to wrap my head around the first thing he said. Her not doing cars and shit. "What do you mean she doesn't do cars?"

"I mean, she doesn't. Doesn't get in them. Doesn't *drive*," he emphasized, my brow twitching. "At least, not since I've known her. Never has. Not once, and I'm assuming that's why she doesn't want to go to dinner. She'd have to take the bus and doesn't want to be embarrassed and admit that in front of Kurt."

I... I had no words.

The guy started to step away, but I cut him off again. I held up a hand. "Why doesn't she do cars?"

"No idea." He shouldered his bag, sighing. "It's not something she talks about, and I don't ask. There'd be no point anyway. I'm sure you've noticed from dating Fawn, if she doesn't want to talk about something, she doesn't."

I looked at her, frowning. She was on her knees, shoving gear into her bag.

"Anyway, don't mention I said anything, okay? I don't want it to be a thing, or cause drama, but I wish she'd take care of that." He glanced her way. "It's obviously getting in her way."

He stalked off, heading toward her. He bent down and got his own stuff, and I just watched. He'd asked how she and I got around, and I did think back to the few times I'd tried to get her in a car. The last time, she'd said she would just come to that party with Heath. And the first?

Well, she ran from me.

CHAPTER
TWENTY-ONE

Fawn

I shook out my umbrella in the coffeehouse. Rainy days were the worst. I had to take a lot of bus transfers to get around campus, and my umbrella only did so much.

My socks soaked, I squished my way up to the register, the place packed. Another thing about rainy days was that others liked to hide out from the downpours too.

Yeah, I hated rainy days.

For so many reasons, I hated them, my hand on my umbrella as I waited in the long-ass line. I'd been trying to peer around it when someone called my name.

But I didn't recognize the woman. Dark, almost black hair hit her shoulders, her hand up, and when she tugged the guy next to her, I blinked.

So I recognized him, the guy towering over her. A coffee in his hand, Wolf was adding creamer to it from the self-service area. The woman had her hand on his arm, though, and he turned around, his hood up over his hair. His wild curls pushed out the front of a Pembroke University Football hoodie, Wolf's jeans sitting low and tight on his thick legs. I hadn't seen him since the weekend and hadn't wanted to see him.

Well, he was definitely seeing me now, those dark eyes of his flashing. He exchanged a glance between the woman and me, and something akin to panic flashed across his handsome face. He started to touch the woman, but she was already stepping away.

"That's her, right?" she questioned, her hand up again. I didn't know her, but seeing her standing next to Wolf, I definitely saw the similarities. She looked just like him, and the only person who had more on that than him was his sister, Sloane.

The woman was like the smaller version of her. She only came up to about Wolf's shoulder, and Sloane was definitely taller than that.

"Uh, yeah," Wolf stated, his fingers flowing into his feathery locks. He whipped around those thick curls peeking out from his hood before pulling the hood down. "That's Fawn."

"I knew it." And just like, the woman was coming over, and I was frozen with wet socks and no choice but to let it happen. I mean, what could I do?

I was trapped.

The woman smelled like vanilla, the air filled with it when she came over. She put a hand on Wolf. "So, you're going to introduce me, right? To your girlfriend?"

Oh… crap.

It seemed Wolf and I shared the same thought, his expression pinched, tight. He had a hand on the woman too, and he looked about two seconds from tugging her away. "Mom, this is Fawn."

Mother. Mom.

Of course.

Now, I was in a predicament here, but I still had a choice. There were two actually. One was I could blow this whole thing out of the water right now. I told Wolf this game of his was off after how he'd treated me.

The other was me moving closer to Wolf, my arm sliding around him. This was the second option, and I think the only one more surprised I chose that was him.

A stiffness hit his back as I settled my arm there, but only for a second before he hooked an arm around my neck. The familiarity of it touched a quiver in my stomach.

Relax.

Hard to, that weight on my shoulder, his grin on me. He flashed it right in my direction before squeezing my shoulders. "Red, this is my mom."

Red...

I'd hated that nickname when he gave it to me, loathed it, but the jump that returned to my stomach told me right away that had changed. It was like I'd missed being called that.

"Red." His mom's head tilted, a smile on her face. She had a smile like her son and, of course, her daughter. She put out a hand. "Hi, Fawn. My name's Brielle. This one's mom."

She lodged a shoulder into his side, the grin on his face easy now, relaxed. It reminded me of the rare times when he expressed pure joy and how truly handsome it did make him whenever he did it.

Glancing away from it, I took his mom's hand. "Fawn."

"Lovely." I didn't know if she meant me or what, but whatever the case, the sentiment brought the smile out on my face too. I couldn't help it. Something about this woman's energy, and she appeared so happy to see me. "I'm so glad I got to meet you. Ares said you had a class."

"She does." He looked down at me, and I nodded.

"Got out early," I said, but I noticed neither one of us let go of the other. If anything, we moved closer, and the pair of us held on to each other in a death grip. Mine was because of how awkward this was in front of his mom, but I didn't know his reasons.

Perhaps awkwardness too, and I did something weird in that moment. I let go of my death grip and tapped him. I did it softly, assuring him I was okay in this situation and that we were. I didn't know why I did this, but when his hand moved from his own death grip, I was glad I had.

He rubbed my shoulder after that, as if soothing me, and for a second, I forgot we were in front of his mom and this was awkward as fuck. I forgot we'd argued, and he'd been a bastard once again by dangling Kurt in front of me.

I just… forgot.

"Well, how lucky," his mom said, and when the line moved, I moved with it. They both did too, of course, going with me. His mom pocketed her hands in her raincoat. "I don't know if Ares mentioned anything about his stuffy old parents, but I used to work at the university."

Wolf's eyes lifted. "Mom…"

"What? I know parents aren't the hot topic of conversation. Especially in a new relationship."

God, this sucked. Lying to her, but here we were, right? I smiled. "He hadn't mentioned, but that's cool. Were you a professor?"

"Yep, and I come through from time to time. Visiting old work colleagues and…"

"Hovering," Wolf finished for her, and his mom made a face.

"Checking on my kids because I'm a mom and, when you have children, you'll understand."

"Nah, they'll be out of my house and *my hair* as soon as they graduate high school, and that's a promise."

His eyes danced at his mother, the guy actually joking and acting nice. Go figure all it'd take was his mom around. He was such a brute I didn't think he cared about anything outside of himself.

But you know that's not true.

It's not considering the labor he'd gone through to make sure this thing we had worked in front of his family.

"You're lucky your dad and I didn't feel the same way." She poked him, making him laugh, and I did too. These two were kind of adorable together. She faced me. "Anyway, I'm sure my son also didn't mention his *hovering* folks invited you to come down to visit for a weekend."

He hadn't, and that was probably for obvious reasons. Faking dating around here was one thing but bringing that home... to his parents. Wolf squeezed my arm. "Ma, we just started dating."

"But you moved in together," she said, and though I was shocked he'd told her that, I played it off. "Which means you're pretty serious, right?"

I kind of loved how this woman didn't bullshit around things. I admired that since I liked to be straightforward too on my positions, but as I was the central focus of this particular topic, I shifted in my wet sneakers.

Wolf's jaw clicked. "Mom..."

"I won't make you answer that. Though, I do want the answer." She winked at me, and I smiled. "Anyway, I do have to get back on the road, but now that she does know about the invite, maybe I'll see her around?"

She glanced in my direction, but before I could say anything, Wolf lifted a hand.

"You don't have to answer that," he said, hugging me closer. My stomach warmed again despite myself, but he let go to hug his mom. "Have a safe trip."

"Thanks, and good meeting you, Fawn." When she eased away from him, she took my hand. "And please don't let him convince you out of a visit. No matter what he says, his parents are wonderful people and would love to have you over."

She elbowed him after she said it, and his eyes rolled back. He shook his head, and she tugged him to bend so she could give him a kiss on the cheek. He did, which made me smile but him sigh. He mocked fake agitation for sure. Anyone could see how much he cared about his mom, loved her.

By this point, I was nearly to the front of the line, and I ordered while Wolf said his final goodbyes to his mother. I started to pay, but he cut me off before I could.

I watched a silver card pass over the register, something I didn't need but I let him. "Thanks."

"No problem." He kept his distance beside me now, his mom gone and all that. I tried not to think about how it felt to be that close to him again, and instead focused on his lingering presence.

"Your mom seems nice."

"She is, but believe me she takes no shit." He cuffed his thick arms. "And thanks for what you did. Why did you?"

Meaning why did I go along with our fake agreement. I shrugged. "Just because I'm mad at you doesn't mean your mom should suffer for it. She believes, so why complicate things?"

I noticed I was tiptoeing around words in front of others, and people were looking at us. Wolf being Legacy, that was just what people did, and for some reason, I was still playing the game.

"Mad at me, huh?" Wolf cocked his head, his expression curious. He'd stepped out of line with me, and I had to wait for my drink. He angled back against the counter. "Like a real argument in this new relationship."

He was tiptoeing around words too.

Why are we still doing this?

Sighing, I took my coffee, and Wolf proceeded to follow me to the creamer. This was better anyway. We could actually talk without prying ears. I took the lid off my cup. "I think you and I both know there's nothing normal about this relationship."

"Yeah."

He watched me add cream, my awareness of this guy truly unsettling. I decided to redirect, stirring my coffee. "What are you going to tell your parents?"

"Tell them?"

I nodded. "You obviously weren't going to bring me down to see them. You didn't even tell me."

"You would have gone?"

No, but him not telling me was an indicator I was never going. "I guess we'll never know."

I had no idea why I said that, or why I was even still talking to him. I mean, I'd thought this game with him was over, but every time it ended, weird shit just kept pulling me back. Shit like his mom being around and me not wanting to blow this whole thing out of the water in front of her.

Things were awkward now, and I finished stirring my coffee. Normally, I'd take a beat and drink it. Especially since it was raining outside.

But with Wolf here...

I released a breath. "See you."

I didn't wait for his response, edging by him. I brushed up against him, but I ignored that shit too.

"Why didn't you tell me?"

"What?"

"About the car thing."

I paused, my hand gripping my coffee, my umbrella.

Heat hit behind me. His heat. I wasn't sure how close Wolf had gotten, but if I could feel him, his presence...

"That you don't do cars," he continued, his voice low, soft. "That you don't get in them or anything else."

I closed my eyes.

Heath.

Of course, Heath, and I had seen them talking together. I'd been trying to get out of that alley so fast I hadn't cared.

My jaw shifted. "Why?"

"Why?"

"Why would that have mattered?" I angled around, and Wolf was close. The large guy craned above me, and I distanced. "Why would that have mattered that I told you?"

And why are you talking about this with him?

I shifted, my shoes squeaking.

Wolf slid his hands into his hoodie pocket, his big shoulders shrugging. "Because I would have made accommodations for you."

"Accommodations?"

He nodded. "You're my girlfriend, so yeah, I would have made accommodations."

I noticed people looking at us again, *staring* at us. I braced my arms, leaning forward. "So what? You're going to ridicule me now."

"No, I'm just wondering why you didn't say anything."

Because it wasn't his business. That's why. I chewed the inside of my cheek. "So now what?"

"What do you mean?"

"I mean, what happens next? You probing me?"

"Probing you?"

"I'm sure you're curious as to why. Why I don't do cars or whatever."

I had no idea why I was pushing this, but I was agitated and felt cornered. He was real good at that shit, cornering me and making me feel uncomfortable, small.

His eyes narrowed. "Yeah, I'm curious. Of course."

"Of course."'

He frowned. "But I don't need to know why. That's your business." I blinked, and his shoulders hiked. "I just wanted to know why you didn't say anything. Could have made things less complicated like with the bus that day." His tongue eased over his lip. "Could have just not been a thing. A thing between us, I mean."

Why did he care that it was a thing? I'd gotten myself to his parties. Done everything he'd wanted me to do.

His expression shifted, and the next thing I knew, he was getting close. He hunkered down. "Those parties I had you go to were late as fuck, you know. And what? You took the bus to them?"

He almost sounded angry, his jaw piercing his skin.

My head angled. "You care?"

"Red..." My name fell out of his lips low. He fisted his curls. "Like I said, you're my girlfriend. You had no business getting on a late-ass bus in the middle of the night. I can't believe you'd do something like that. Who knows what kind of filth is out. At that hour?"

That wasn't a thing for me. I'd pulled more than an all-nighter or two since coming to college, and I wasn't the only one. The twenty-four-hour buses usually had other students on them coming from the library, not bums.

A shot of red crushed Wolf's chiseled jawline, and he actually looked like he did care.

He'd also called me his girlfriend again.

He'd just said it and hadn't even looked around first. Like he wasn't aware of others around, and we were just talking. The two of us...

My fingers tapped my cup. "What are you going to do about your family?"

He had his hands laced on his head, really stewing, and I'd never seen him this way. His dark eyes flicked down. "My family?"

"The weekend invite? What were you going to tell them about me not showing up?" Yeah, no idea why I was asking. Maybe I just didn't want his focus or concern on me or something.

Yeah, that.

"Uh, eventually, I was going to tell them that…" He was conscious of our surroundings now. He got close. "Eventually, when it was right, I was just going to tell them we weren't together anymore. Why?"

I squeezed my cup. "Well, what if we were together?" His eyes narrowed, and I forced out a breath. "What if we continued this."

"You'd want to?" He stayed close, breathing close. I could feel him, that warm spice all around me, that heat. "You'd want to continue this?"

I mean, I didn't want to. He was terrible, a bully, but I had seen him with his mom.

He'd been so relaxed.

It was a miracle quite honestly, and the first time I hadn't seen him on edge. Something about his mom being happy, happy meeting me and seeing us together had given him peace. It really did seem like he needed her to be okay, his family.

"It's probably all a bad idea." I waved it off. "I mean, your family lives in Maywood Heights, right? Still?" That's where he'd played football. His high school, Windsor Prep, had been there. I knew since they'd played against my high school team obviously.

If that was the case, his hometown was like two hours away, and he knew now I didn't do cars.

"Correct, but if you're worried about getting there, I can take care of it."

His thoughts aligned with mine, I glanced his way. Wolf had his lips tipped up, a true smile, a genuine one on me.

My goddamn stomach.

It flipped seeing the expression. A whirl of excitement brewed inside me in response, and I was well aware it was way more intense than any pleasure I'd gotten by simply getting to him. I kind of got off on annoying him, but seeing him smile? Smile because of me... I tucked hair behind my ear. "You can?"

No way this guy would take a bus two hours.

"Is it just cars you can't do? If so, I can work something out." His head bobbed once. "Just let me take care of it. I can get us there. Get you there."

I noticed he still hadn't asked me why. Why I didn't do cars, or anything like that. I swallowed. "What happens when we get back? With us?"

Meaning our relationship.

His lengthy digits folded over his arms, his head lowering. "Whatever you want, and what I didn't get to say at that art thing was I wanted this to be different. You and me?" He angled closer. "It can be whatever you want this time."

Shocked, I almost took a step back. He'd mentioned he wanted us to be friends, but I hadn't thought he was serious. I mean, how could we in an arrangement like this?

And with all that happened...

We'd crossed a line more than a few times, and Wolf? Well, he was a guy. He had urges but what he could pass off as a casual hookup wasn't so easy for me. I couldn't explain why I'd slept with him beyond the fact that he was, well, gorgeous. Fuck, I wished it'd just been that.

"I just want this to work," he continued, and his proximity flushed warmth across my face. I swallowed, and he noticed, his attention flicking down. "I do, so this time you call the shots. I won't do the blackmail shit. I won't do any of that shit. I just want this to work. You call the terms."

He almost sounded, well, desperate. Hell, he looked desperate.

Why does he need this so bad?

He'd said why he had, his family, but this was so desperate. Like he truly needed me to do this and I had the power when I didn't. He'd always been the one with all the cards, and I'd known that the last time I'd said no to him. I figured

I'd get a call from Kurt saying that internship was gone, or my enrollment at Pembroke would come to an end, but that never happened. Wolf never made those calls or cashed in those favors even though he did have all the power.

I wondered when that had changed.

CHAPTER
TWENTY-TWO

Ares

I had to pull some strings to get the Coach bus but not many.

My grandfather even hooked me up with a driver.

Lucas Gray worked for my grandpa, and though I didn't have much of a relationship with my gramps, he'd been very adamant about calling when I needed something. Things with him and my whole family were complicated. He hadn't always been around, but when my parents had become open to him being there, I'd decided I didn't have much of a problem either. I wasn't best friends with my grandfather or anything, but we'd had coffee a time or two and some good conversation. He'd had reasons for not being around, and when he'd come back, he'd done all he could to make that up.

He'd done more than enough.

Of course, that was a story for another day, and I was happy to see Lucas. He worked as my grandfather's security, and just like my grandpa, he extended himself to myself, Sloane, and our younger brother, Bru. I hadn't seen Bru in a while, but this was expected considering how far he'd gone away for school. He probably wouldn't be coming through until around holiday break, and I wasn't disappointed the visit wasn't now.

I already had enough to juggle.

Lucas took my hand outside the bus, grinning. "Everything's all set for you, Mr. Mallick."

"Come on, Luke. You know you can call me Wolf or Ares." I was trying to get better about being open to my real name. Being vulnerable or whatever. I'd had a tough year, but that didn't define me. I grinned. "How's Grandpa?"

"Doing well, and he's looking forward to hearing from you. Says he hopes your return to school has been a good one and hopes that referral he gave you worked out. For the doctor?"

I could hear my buddies and Sloane in the bus. We were all hitching a ride to town together for the weekend. Sloane, Dorian, and myself because we usually did, spending time with our folks and all that. Wells and Thatch did because, once again, they were lazy fucks and brought their laundry home for their staffs to do.

Their laughter loud, I angled close to Lucas. "Thank him for me."

"Will do. I'm sure it makes things a lot easier for you. No more scheduled appointments and all that."

Grandpa Mallick had hooked me up with my own personal doctor, someone whose job was to make me a priority and abide by my schedule. I had a busy one, so that's what I told my grandpa when I asked him for the referral from Johns Hopkins.

"Definitely works better for your schedule," Lucas said, the two of us on the same wavelength there. He smiled. "And remember Dr. Easton can make house calls whenever you need him. Your grandpa told me to mention that to you."

We'd been doing mostly virtual up until this point.

I shook Lucas's hand, thanking him again. By then, we

both heard the rolling luggage, and when I glanced back, I frowned.

Red…

She was supposed to tell me when she was ready, not dragging her bags herself.

But that was exactly what she was doing, her mouth dropped open. I hadn't told her how I'd be getting her to Maywood Heights, but I guess she could see now.

The Coach bus took up a good portion of the dorm's parking lot, but surprisingly, not many stares had been in its direction. People probably figured one of the university's teams or clubs was using it.

Not my friends and me.

"Wolf." Fawn paused on the sidewalk, her hand on her bag. She had those jeans on again, the ones that made her ass look thick as fuck and had my eyes wandering. This probably wasn't a good idea, us traveling two hours together, but I wasn't going to turn away from an opportunity to keep her close. We needed to be together, as much time as we could.

If I had it my way, that time wouldn't be spent with my parents, *lying to my parents*, but I was looking at a bigger picture here.

Staying focused on that, I sprinted over to Red.

She pushed her sunglasses into her vibrant hair. "This is our ride?"

I told her I'd hook her up, grinning. "Good enough?" Honest to fuck, I was still curious about why we needed the accommodation, but I didn't and wouldn't bug her about it. I was trying to earn a semblance of trust with her.

Like stated, we needed to be together.

I wasn't sure for how long it'd be, but she had moved back into our dorm. Our shared space smelled like warm sugar again, and I was completely aware that I didn't mind that. I had missed her in a weird way.

A fucked way…

I eased her bag out of her hand. "This good, then?" I'd figure out something else if it wasn't.

Her lashes flashed, as if surprised I asked. She folded her arms. "Uh, yeah."

"Really?"

She nodded, grinning. She had subtle makeup on today, and her freckles were full out. On her face, her lips... "I mean, yeah. It's perfect. You got a bus?"

"Called in a few favors."

One in particular with Lucas who, again, had extended himself to me. It wasn't a thing, and he took Fawn's bag when we arrived at the bus.

"Nice to meet you, Ms. Greenfield. I'm Lucas, a friend of the Mallick family, and I'll be driving you this weekend."

Good ole Luke was sacrificing his whole weekend to cart around my friends and me. He'd be staying overnight and everything before taking us back to campus on Sunday.

Fawn extended a hand. "Nice to meet you, and thank you."

Lucas took her bag, but before getting on, Fawn faced me. "All this is really for us?"

My friends chose to laugh in the next seconds. Wells and Thatcher were always loud as fuck. Fawn blinked, and since we were about to board, this was a good time to let her in on the fact they'd be coming along with us.

"Us, my sister, and the guys," I said. "Sloane, D, and I always go back home for the weekend, and Thatcher and Wells are hitching a ride to do their laundry."

Again, they were fucking lazy, and a second ago, Fawn had looked a little excited about leaving. Now, she had those freckled lips of hers turned down.

"What did you tell them? I mean." She paused, her face all red and looking cute. Red could look cute when she wasn't letting my ass have one. "What did you tell them about me?"

Well, there was nothing really to tell. She hadn't told me

anything about her or the situation. I propped an arm against the bus. "Sloane and D know I got the bus for you. We always go home together, so yeah, I had to tell them." She looked worried about that, but I got her shoulder. I brought her close by both. "It wasn't a thing, though. I swear. They're not like that. As far as Thatch and Wells, they just think this is me being spontaneous."

They actually said this was me being fun again, but I was fucking fun. Last year had just been shit.

Quite frankly, I'd had a few years like that, but things had been looking up. When Sloane had come back and Bru had arrived into our family, yeah, things had been good. Great.

They'll be that way again.

They would be if I had anything to do with it, and I realized I was rubbing Red's shoulders. I was squeezing them actually, but not only was she letting me, she had her eyes closed.

I brought her even closer then. "Red?" Something had me brushing her cheek, her hair in her face. I touched this girl in the most intimate of ways, but for some reason, just touching her fucking cheek shot excitement into my fingers. A tingle hit, and I couldn't stop it. "Fawn…"

Her lashes fanned open, and she looked a lot better when she gazed up at me. Less worried, more relaxed. "I'm okay."

"You're sure?" I hunkered down. "We can do anything you want."

I wasn't lying. She had the cards here, hers. I'd probably do anything this girl fucking wanted to keep our arrangement up.

I mean, I had up until this point.

I'd gone down a rabbit hole I couldn't back out of. I was in this shit for the long haul, and when Fawn nodded, I pushed it even more.

I put my hand out for hers, and a part of me hoped she

wouldn't take it. A part of me wanted her to tell me to fuck off. I wanted her to leave me. Leave this.

But she didn't, though. She took my hand, and when she smiled, I made mine bigger. This girl and I had a counter on us. We had the moment I'd crashed her internship interview, but I was going to make those fucking seconds count.

Everything depended on it.

CHAPTER
TWENTY-THREE

Fawn

"Fawn?"

Rough fingers ghosted my cheek, and my eyes fluttered open. Wolf stared at me, his lips tipped up in a smile.

I'd fallen asleep.

I was as aware of that as I was his fingers gliding across my skin. He'd done it to obviously wake me up, leaning in. His grin hiked. "Can't even make it two hours, huh?"

Shit.

I scrubbed my face, groggy. Upon sitting up, I noticed Wolf take back his arm, and I realized now I'd been laying on him. I pointed at him. "You let me sleep on you."

"Let you is a strong statement. More like was forced to when you fell the fuck asleep after about ten minutes." He said this, but his thick eyebrows danced. He tucked hands under his arms. "Must have been comfortable."

Yeah, must have.

I pressed a hand to my face, still feeling him there, *smelling him.* He was like all around me, and I tried to angle out of the way of it.

We were alone.

Like no one was here, and there'd been plenty of people before. Wells, Thatcher, Dorian, and Sloane had definitely been on this bus, and I was surprised I had fallen asleep. They'd all been playing cards and had really gotten into it.

Wolf had asked me if I wanted to join, but I was awkward since I didn't really know them. I'd opted to stay in my seat, and he'd surprisingly stayed with me.

I guessed that'd been when I fell asleep.

It'd been a nice gesture, and I guess something a boyfriend would do. Also something a boyfriend would do was book an entire Coach bus for his girlfriend to ride two hours in because she didn't do cars, the reason for which he still hadn't asked. I pushed my sweatshirt back over my shoulder. It'd fallen a bit with the wide neck. "Where is everyone?"

"Lucas dropped Thatcher and Wells off at their places," he said, stretching that long wingspan. He dropped an arm behind me. "Dorian and Sloane are inside."

"Inside?"

Chuckling, he pointed out the window, and I blinked.

Holy fuck, this guy's house...

I assumed this was his home, a large colonial-style mansion through the window. It had white columns and an expansive array of flowers surrounding the property, the lawn large and the house completely gated in. Spiked, iron gates gave the whole place a European feel, and my mouth parted. "Your house?"

"My house." He grinned. "Anyway, you ready to go inside? Everyone is waiting for you."

Everyone meaning his entire family.

And I'd been sleeping.

"Why did you let me sleep?" I asked, instantly feeling

embarrassed. Visions of people on the couch wondering what was up with Wolf's high-maintenance girlfriend swirled me. I pressed hands to my face, and Wolf chuckled.

"We haven't been in here that long."

Long enough where he felt the need to wake me.

The ghost of that digit still on my cheek, I dropped my hands and found him looking at me. "What?"

"Nothing," he said, though he didn't stop. That sizzle hit my cheeks again, but for a different reason.

What's his deal?

He didn't say, his head tilted. He backed out of my airspace eventually, but I found myself edging into his. He frowned. "What?"

I didn't know what, but I did see myself getting closer. Wolf let me and didn't move an inch when I grabbed his shirt.

Nor when I pressed my mouth to his.

He froze, of course, stilled. He had his hands up like he didn't know what to do, but he didn't have to do anything.

I was directing this, his lips full and hot beneath my mouth. Eventually, he let me coax my way inside, and a zing hit my body when our tongues brushed.

Christ.

I'd kissed Wolf before, but it hadn't been like this. He'd forced it and basically treated me like a feast he had to devour. It'd been hot too, but it hadn't been intimate. Well, not like this.

A noise rolled from his chest as I deepened it, but I noticed he didn't grab me back. He just let me kiss him, and his eyes were closed when I pulled away.

"What was that?" His voice had lowered an octave, his pupils dilated. He wet his bruised lips. "Red?"

I touched my own mouth, warm. I shrugged. "I guess I just figured we should practice."

"Practice?"

I nodded. "We're dating, right?" And a part of me wanted him to know it was okay, what we'd just done. He said I was directing this. "We can kiss. It's okay, and I just... I guess I wanted to let you know that. We can kiss, and it's cool."

Though, I didn't know why. Maybe it was all the sentimental shit he was doing for me. Shit like this bus and letting me sleep on him.

Lengthy digits touched his mouth too, his grin wiry. "Doubt we'll be making out in front of my folks." He edged forward, a breath away. "But thanks for the consent."

I thought he may kiss me again, and my heart hammered at the prospect.

He didn't, though. But he did take my hand. We were doing that by the time we entered his big-ass house, and he said the driver had already taken our things to our rooms. Apparently, I got my own room, and I honestly didn't know what to expect. I could have easily gotten a couch to lie on, so yeah, having my own room would be cool.

We heard laughing once inside and didn't make it past the foyer that led to a large staircase. It was one of those statement staircases like on the Titanic and opened up the entire room more than it already did. A glistening chandelier shined above it, and two people in athletic clothes were beneath it. The couple literally looked like an ad for The North Face, and I recognized them both.

Wolf's parents were gorgeous, much like their kids. His mom had her hair up in a low ponytail, her windbreaker matching Wolf's dad's. Mr. Mallick was dressed in black down to his sneakers, his hand in his pocket. The other arm was around his wife, and the two stood there laughing by themselves. It was quite sweet actually. His mom was in hysterics at whatever Wolf's dad had said.

Of course, they noticed both Wolf and me when we came in, and we were immediately showered with greetings.

"Dad, this is Red," Wolf introduced me as, and his family

always did get a kick out of the nickname. I really did used to hate that.

How much had changed. I shook Mr. Mallick's hand, but when I referred to him as that, he told me to call him Ramses.

"Mr. Mallick is my father," he said, his arm returning around his wife. Apparently, Mrs. Mallick was the *mayor*, which was something Wolf had warned me about on the way in.

The power this guy had.

It was everywhere and in bounds, and I tried not to be intimidated by it. I wasn't poor, but my background certainly wasn't his.

The house was filled with an array of smells, many in fact, and I was informed staff was preparing dinner. I was told the first thing the family did when Sloane and Wolf came back home was go for a hike, which was why his parents were dressed in such a way.

I wasn't too keen on a hike, but if that was their family tradition, I was game for it. Especially since they were letting me stay for a whole weekend.

Wolf had warned me to pack something to move in, and that his family was athletic. He said they liked to run and do hikes together, so I had prepared for that.

I didn't feel as bad about sleeping in the bus when I found out Wolf's parents were waiting for Sloane and Dorian to get dressed for it. Dorian was coming too and had a room in their house, which didn't surprise me. Wolf had said they were brothers.

It was all a lot to take in. Especially when we did hit the trails behind their house. I'd overhead from his folks they normally drive to some of the better ones in town, but that didn't seem like the case today.

And so, Wolf struck again.

He didn't say this, of course, but I figured he arranged this alternative hike. He kept making these accommodations, and it was blowing my mind right now.

And then him on the trail...

He kept checking in with me, and I was sure everyone knew hiking in the fucking woods wasn't my strong suit. These people were built like beautiful machines, but Wolf was there with me the whole way. Even when his family got a little ahead, he held back, and Sloane was often back with us too.

"Yeah, I'm not a runner," she was quick to admit, laughing. Everyone was resting by a creek, and she had her hands on her hips. "I've been training, though. I even beat Ares in a foot race once."

"Fuck. Really?" I asked, the guy chuckling over by his dad and Dorian. His mom had to take an urgent call, which was one of the big reasons for the break. She hadn't taken any calls since we'd left the house, and I think the only reason she did now was because she said it was an emergency.

"Yeah, and once I won that shit, believe you me I rubbed it all up in his face." Sloane laughed, pocketing her hands. "I also wasn't stupid enough to challenge him again, so I got that win for life."

Smart girl, and something I totally would have done if I, well, fucking ran. I didn't, though. Definitely not my wheelhouse. I was active enough with my travel photography, but nothing like that.

I'd spent most of my summers on a bus. My camera and I just went wherever the stories were. We went wherever the people were, and I continued the work my father and I had done before he'd passed. He used to be the yin to my yang.

My everything.

I wished I'd taken my camera now, my gaze gliding over to Wolf. He stood on a rock, just chatting with his dad and Dorian, but what I wouldn't give to capture him on film. He had his hair down, his curls wild and his face flushed. He was too beautiful for his own good, and maybe even too beautiful for my camera.

I grinned away, but it fell upon noticing Sloane. She had a knowing smile in my direction, but let me off the hook when she noticed her brother.

"I'm glad you're here," she said, her smile a subtle one. "Here for him? He's smiled more during this hike than I've seen him in months."

He had?

"You're good for him, and I was wrong," she said, her voice serious. "And I never apologized for that. How I treated you…"

"I definitely didn't give off the best first impression." I rubbed my hands on my knees. "I could have been better that night. I hate that I made you think less of me, and I really do care about your brother." I did, which was crazy.

I mean, I wasn't even lying to her.

I rubbed my legs again, glancing up at Wolf. Sloane sat beside me on my rock, which effectively cut me off from my viewpoint.

I was glad.

Using my sneaker, I kicked some pebbles into the creek, and Sloane studied me.

She chewed her lip. "I guess I was just worried before. About you coming around? Being in his life…" She stared at her brother. "This whole family has been through a lot, but especially him."

I wondered if she was referring to his last year, which was definitely something he didn't talk about.

I wanted to ask her about it, but how could I? He'd been so cool about my bullshit, my trauma.

My lip moved over the other. "I'm sure that was hard."

I didn't know why I lied and played it off like he'd told me.

My gaze flicked to Wolf, but this time, we clashed. His

sight on me, we were like two mountains colliding into the other, two volcanoes ready to explode, and I wondered how long we'd both maintain being dormant. We had our shit stacked in a house of fucked-up cards, but at least some of his was out in the open. He had people in his life to vent to, people he *wanted* to vent to.

I guessed therein lay the difference.

CHAPTER
TWENTY-FOUR

Ares

Red did good today, and when I knocked on her door that evening, I had full intentions of telling her that. She called me in, and I edged a grin inside. "You decent?"

What started as a joke ended with me watching her pull her sleeve over her tatted shoulder. She wore an oversize shirt and tiny shorts to bed, something I'd seen her in before since I lived with her but tried not to notice more often than not.

Yeah, good luck with that.

This girl couldn't help but flash skin, ass. She had an abundance of it, and my dick definitely knew it. Her lashes fanned. "You decent?"

She was flirty about her statement, teasing, but her grin slipped when I came inside. I typically slept naked but did bother to put on a pair of gray sweatpants and a tank before coming down to her room.

Red's gaze instantly homed in on my cock. The dude was half-mast at the sight of her flesh but half-mast for me was like full out for most guys. I'd been told my dick was the thing of legends, but Fawn had taken that shit and beautifully.

I twitched now under her gaze, my digits fingering through my hair when I came inside. By the time I closed the door, she wasn't looking anymore, but that didn't mean I hadn't caught her. I cuffed my arms. "Sure you don't want another peek?"

I thrust my shit for emphasis, and Fawn's eyes rolled.

"I'm good." In response, she picked up her phone, something she'd been scrolling on when I came inside. "What are you doing in here anyway? Why are you up?"

It was late, the middle of the night actually. I shrugged. "I'm usually up at this hour."

Not a lie. I typically was to work on my art, and my circadian rhythm was shot because of it. I was hard-pressed to get to sleep before 3 AM most days, even though these days I didn't have a paintbrush or charcoal in my hands.

My jaw clicked, as I eased forward. I tipped my chin. "Why are you up?"

I'd seen her light on, but I'd been about to come inside anyway. No one in this house would believe my girlfriend was sleeping down the hall and I didn't at least try to visit her.

"Unfamiliar house. Unfamiliar bed," she stated, watching as I lounged against the wall. "I mean, it's a nice bed, but my body doesn't know it."

My attention moseyed over that body, that flesh.

Cool it.

I'd been trying to cool my shit since she'd kissed me on the fucking bus. It'd come out of nowhere and, honestly, would have been something I would have done to prep her. Red was getting bold and making moves. These were things I definitely didn't approve of, but for some reason, I wasn't putting her in her place.

Nor was I fighting her.

I pushed off the wall, coming closer. She had people up on her phone, and she let me look.

"My mom and stepdad," she said, my stance staying put. She tossed the phone on the bed. "Just watching them globe-trot. Don't mind me."

My sight stayed on her and away from the smiling faces in front of some kind of museum. "I sense a little bit of sarcasm there."

I kept my voice light, made sure of it. Fawn's screen went dark, and when it did, I took a seat on her bedside table.

"Caught that?" She hugged her legs, those flowers tatted down to her toes. She wiggled them. "I'm not mad that my mom travels. And my stepdad's cool. He's fine." She paused before pushing all that red hair back. "I'm sorry. You don't want to hear this."

She got restless then, fingering all her hair. She pressed her face to her legs, and the girl looked like the Little Mermaid with her naked toes and vibrant hair. I tucked my hands under my arms. "Shoot."

No idea why I said this. I was the last to get into someone's business. This was mostly because I didn't want people in mine, which was why I never asked her about anything regarding her life. Not the things I'd read and dug into her past to get. This girl had a locked box of fucked-up secrets, and not a whole lot of it made sense. The things I'd found didn't make sense. Especially as I'd gotten to know her over the past few weeks.

Again, it wasn't my business to know, yet here we were now.

She faced me. "You don't want to know."

"I wouldn't ask if I didn't." I tapped the bed with my foot, making her smile. "Why are you in your feelings about them?"

"It's not about them per se. Like I said, my stepdad is cool. I've never had a problem with him or my mom and him together." Her shoulders lifted. "I guess I just wished it were that easy."

"Easy?"

"To forget? To *be* easy." Her eyes fluttered closed. "My mom has moved on, and I'm so happy she has. It's just harder for me."

She was speaking vaguely, but I was sure she knew that *I knew* exactly what she was talking about.

"I'm sure you heard about my dad's accident," she said, sighing. "You know he's gone? That he's passed."

I had read something, yeah. It'd been in the stuff Thatcher had gathered about her, but I didn't know too many specifics besides how it happened. I kicked a foot over the other. "A car accident?"

She twitched once I said it, and I wondered in that moment if that had something to do with her aversion to vehicles. Her dad had died that way, but it did seem extreme to avoid cars altogether.

But who was I to judge trauma?

Who *was I* to judge pain when I'd gotten up to all kinds of fucked-up shit in my past due to mine. At one point, I wasn't even sure I'd get on the other side of it. I had so much guilt back then surrounding the void my sister being gone had left in my family's lives. I knew it wasn't my fault Sloane was gone, but it was my fault for the shit I put my family through. I was depressed and had so many issues.

"Do you know the details?" she asked, and when I shook my head, she nodded. She hugged her legs closer. "Anyway, yeah, I wish it were that easy for me to move on, and I hate myself that I do."

"Why?"

"Because some people don't deserve to be right on the other side," she said, the frown hitting my face. "Some people deserve everything they get."

I didn't understand, watching as she stretched out.

"Anywho, I'm sorry for all that. And I am in my feelings." She pressed the heel of her palms to her eyes, laughter in her voice. The dryness shifted a clench in my gut, the same when that smile made it nowhere near her eyes. "So forgive me."

She had nothing to apologize for, and once upon a time, I would have agreed with her. I punished myself for a long time for things I wasn't responsible for. I'd actually wanted to die for all the shit I'd put my parents and my friends through back in the day. I'd been terrible in my grief, crazy and rageful.

I didn't know why Fawn herself felt that way about her particular situation, but once again, I wouldn't let myself ask.

You should.

Like a few other occurrences, things were starting to feel a little too serious here, and it was one thing for us to hook up. That was just physical shit. Pleasure, flesh...

But this?

This was some next-level, real shit, and my hands pushed me off the end table. Fawn watched me, her head lifting, and my stomach spasmed again.

Distracting myself from it, I looked away. "You don't have to apologize, and I'm sorry I just barged in here." I played that off, waving. "I saw your light on and wanted to say you did a good job today."

She did do a good job, a great job. Everyone was thoroughly convinced we were together, and Fawn had been great at dinner.

She'd even laughed at my dad's jokes.

My father was terrible about it, corny as hell, and though I'd cringed through most of it, Fawn had seemed to get a kick out of it. Really, it'd been fun seeing them all together with her, and I liked having her there.

You more than liked it...

Distracting myself from that too, I scrubbed my hand into my hair.

"It was fun today. Reminded me of family and the things my mom, dad, and I used to do." Her smile stretched, real this time. "And thank you for that. For today. It was fun."

Yeah, too much fun.

I started to leave her, but when she watched me again, I ended up sitting down on the floor.

"What are you doing?" she asked, and I reached over, snagging one of her extra pillows.

I propped it under my head. "Going to chill in here for a bit. It's more believable if people think I snuck in to see you."

I'd be hearing this shit if my parents caught me. They had a time or two in the past when they'd caught me sneaking a girl out, and I didn't envy Sloane or D for shit. Dorian had a room here from when we were kids, but once my parents had found out they were together, his overnights were few and far between. It certainly didn't stop D from sneaking back over *tonight* and crashing in Sloane's room, but still, they had to be secret about it now.

I supposed when it came to Fawn and me, it would be good if people knew I came in here. It would if I cared about that shit. If it mattered in the grand scheme of things, but it didn't as much as something else this fake relationship was establishing. It was doing a lot, and that extra shit should probably have me leaving right now. I needed to leave.

But that wasn't what I was doing, stretching out. Fawn's feet touched the floor. "You're going to stay there all night?"

I closed my eyes. "Just a few hours. Like I said, it'll be good."

Go to sleep, Red.

I heard no movement, though, and when I opened my eyes, she was smiling. She waved a hand. "Come on."

"What?"

"Come *on*." She eased back on the bed and under her bedding. "There's plenty of room up here. Especially if you're only going to be in here for a few hours."

I got up on my elbows. "You want me in your bed?" That didn't feel like a good idea...

Turned around, Fawn's shoulders bumped in laughter. "I don't necessarily *want* you in here, but since you are, you don't need to lie on the floor." She shifted, facing me. "Besides, I'm not going to be responsible for your back hurting."

A twitch hit my eyes, but she didn't stay facing me long enough to see it. She just got back on her side, and using a hand, she flattened the other side of the bedding out.

"You can lie on top," she said, creating that distance between us. Not disagreeing with the need for that, I did get up. I returned the pillow to the bed, and the mattress dipped when I got on.

My feet hung off the side, her queen smaller than my California king. "Night, Red."

"Night."

I watched her. Though, I didn't know why or what I was waiting for.

Go to sleep yourself.

I turned off the light but had no intention of sleeping. I wasn't sleeping a lot these days *because* of my back. It ached sometimes.

Something told me she knew that.

CHAPTER
TWENTY-FIVE

Ares

The storm hit sometime after I closed my eyes. I'd fallen asleep.

Well, would you look at that…

I guess I could sleep, stretching. I shifted under the torrents of rain hitting the roof, and it took me a second to realize it hadn't been the actual storm or even my back to wake me up.

Red's shoulders shook.

She hugged them beside me, her arms tight around herself. A clap of thunder hit, and those shakes hit her body harder.

"Red…"

She stilled, a gasp in her voice. "What, Wolf?"

Agitation touched her raw voice. Her tone was as thick as it was emotion-filled, and I'd definitely heard her crying a second ago.

It'd woken me up.

I edged close. "You okay?"

This was a stupid question, of course. She'd been crying, and upon another thunderclap, her hand tightened on her body.

"Fine," she lied, pressing her face into the pillow. "I'm fine."

She wasn't, and that was obvious. I leaned up on my elbow. "You scared of storms?"

My gaze hit the ceiling when another roll of noise slammed through the room. It accompanied lightning through the curtains, and Fawn didn't even move this time. Like she was frozen and too still.

"No." Another gritted word fell from her lips. "I'm not a child, Ares."

She didn't have to be a child to be scared of storms. I mean storms fucking sucked and could be scary, loud. "Well, what's the problem, then…"

"Just go back to sleep," she growled, her head shaking. "I'm not scared of storms. I just don't like them, and they suck."

I smiled a little, thinking the same thing. I waited a beat, still on my elbow.

"Are you still awake?"

"Yes."

She growled again, turning around, facing me. She'd rubbed her face before she did, but even in the dark, I made out a face charged with color. Not to mention, her eyes were bloodshot.

"Red," I started to reach for her, but resisted. My jaw clicked. "Tell me what's going on."

She could very well tell me to fuck off again and had before. Her eyes escaped. "Why?"

"Because I asked." I did touch her then, stupider than shit, but I couldn't help it.

She looked so sad.

She was sad, and her eyes closed when my fingers flicked

her hair. A tear squeezed out of them, and she didn't stop me when I touched that too.

"Red," I repeated, so close to her now. We were even sharing the same pillow. "Talk to me."

She didn't, sighing. Her skin flushed, so red under my fingers.

"It's my dad," she admitted. Upon opening her eyes, she rolled them back. I figured she did this to avoid looking at me. "It's my dad. It's my... It's my..."

Her voice cracked, her face all screwed up. She pressed her sleeve to her face, but I got a hand there. I got her tears for her and whatever they surrounded.

"What about him," I said, going there. I didn't want to push her, and at this point, she was crying so much she couldn't even talk.

She mashed her palms into her eyes.

"I killed him," she croaked, gasping. Her shoulders shook. "I killed my dad, Ares. It's my fault he's gone."

Confused, I just lay there, waiting. Another clap of thunder ricocheted off the walls, and when Fawn curled up, I wanted to enter the heavens and strong-arm that shit down myself. I spread a hand on her face, making her focus on me. "What do you mean?"

"I mean, I was the one driving," she admitted, causing me to blink. She nodded. "It was me behind the wheel. You didn't know?"

I hadn't. The only thing I'd found out was that her dad had passed in a collision. I'd read the byline about it, but it hadn't gone into details about the who and what.

I swallowed. "You were behind the wheel? But you were only like..."

"Fifteen. I had my permit." She sniffed. "A lot of good it did me."

I cringed. "Your dad obviously thought it was okay."

"Yeah, but he shouldn't have. It was a storm just like this."

She glanced up, wincing. "It was raining so bad, and I couldn't see… I couldn't see…"

She was talking to herself, and I let her. Her focus was on everything but me again, and though I tried to capture it, she wouldn't allow it. My throat flicked. "It was an accident, Red."

"Yeah, and I survived, and my dad didn't." Her head shook, angry now. "The thing is, that trip had been my idea. They were *all* my idea. I had to go take pictures. I had to get the story, and my dad always took me. It was the thing we did together. He taught me everything."

"Because it was your thing, the two of you," I said, and obviously something they shared. "But it was an accident, Fawn."

"I didn't have a scrape." She wasn't listening to me, clearly. She closed her eyes. "Truck hit my dad's side, and I didn't have a *fucking scrape*, Ares. How does that even happen?"

Because she was lucky. She'd been lucky. "It wasn't your time."

"And it was his?" She cringed now, but it wasn't because of the storm. "Why wasn't it *me*? It should have been me. I was driving. Why wasn't it me!"

She screamed above the roar in the heavens, none of this fazing her now. Her anger seemed to have risen above it, and I leaned in. "Don't say that about yourself."

"Why not?"

"Because it wasn't your time." A grit hit my voice, and I wished I didn't understand it. I wished I had zero emotion when it came to this girl. I wished even more I didn't understand this. I wished I didn't get *her pain*, but I did. "You're supposed to be here, Fawn. You are, and you shouldn't feel guilty for that. You shouldn't any more than I do."

Her lashes flashed up, red fanning above nut-brown irises.

I glanced away, her gaze probing. "It wasn't long ago I felt the same way about myself. Why I got to be here and my sister taken..." My attention shifted to her. "I used to feel like for a long time it should have been me who got swiped. I wished it was."

Desperately, I had. I'd actually been resentful of my own existence and harbored even more guilt when I couldn't find her myself. I'd searched for years before she came back.

Fawn looked at me, scanning my face. "How did you get through it? That feeling? That guilt?" Her expression twisted. "It hurts so much."

I could hear it in her voice, that hurt, and I appreciated she didn't console me. That she didn't feel the need to tell me it wasn't my fault. This was a given and something I was so glad I was on the other side of now.

I touched her then, again probably dumb but couldn't help it. Her red hair looped my finger. "I guess I realized one day I was here for a reason," I stated, focused on her. "I was and had an obligation to myself and the people I cared about to live my life. That *I mattered*, and I needed to live *for* my sister. I owed that to her and myself."

It'd been a long journey and one I really hadn't seen the other side of until Sloane came back. There'd been a start, though. A turning point, and that was the day I was referring to.

I kept that time to myself, that day. I didn't want to talk about it and one hundred percent couldn't with Fawn.

She wouldn't understand.

My fingers weaved through red tendrils. "I don't know your dad. I don't, but you being here... living life and honoring him in every photo you take and every day you fight is a win for him. You gotta fight, Red. You have to, and you can't harbor that guilt."

It wouldn't help her, and it didn't me. It just made me angry, mean. Nah, it didn't help, and she couldn't take on that weight.

I think the storm had stopped, and maybe she was right that she wasn't scared of it. It might just bring back some memories, and my thumb touched a wet trail on her freckled skin. Her tears had stopped but still coated her cheeks.

I eased the trail away, my fingers brushing it. I was so focused there, and it took a beat to notice her proximity. The heat of our breaths intermingled, and when I gazed up, Fawn had her eyes shut.

She did before she closed the space.

Red had kissed me before, and it surprised me now just as it had on the bus. I didn't know what to do with myself, not able to actually kiss her with a clear head and no excuse.

Stop this.

Growling, I shifted her to her back, separating us.

It was needed.

My fingers bit into her arms, my breaths husky, labored. Fawn lay with wide eyes and parted lips below me.

At least, at first.

Eventually, she reached up, her fingers hesitant.

"Don't," I gritted, actually speaking this. My tongue eased out. "No."

She wasn't listening to me, not giving a fuck, and I really didn't know what I was telling her not to do. I just knew this was a bad idea. It'd been one before.

But the way her fingers felt in my *fucking hair*.

Her soft digits danced in it, playing with it. My hair had fallen forward, and Fawn played her fingers all up in that shit.

Stop.

I wasn't telling her now, her touch electric in my hair. She pressed her fingers into my scalp, and next thing I knew, I was sinking teeth into her arm.

I was kissing her.

I got deep in the crook of her arm, tongue flicking, mouth

moving. She moaned and stopped playing with my hair to touch her breast.

Fuuck.

I watched her as I tasted her flesh, her top in the way. Letting go, I shoved it above her breasts, and my dick kicked at my sweatpants.

Braless, flushed tits. Her creamy pinked flesh lay on full display. I tugged her shirt off, then gathered her breasts in my hands.

"Ares..." She moaned out my name, her hands on my shoulders. "Do what you want."

She didn't want to tell me that, literally groaning on this girl's fucking tits. I buried my face in them, an easy death well worth the suffocation.

I couldn't get enough of them, licking, pulling. I took in large bites and small ones edged out noises from her freckled lips.

I bit there too, being stupid. My tongue tunneled inside her mouth the same time I posted elbows into the bed. I locked her underneath me, crowding her.

"Stop me," I ground out, begging, pleading with her. "We shouldn't be doing this."

I shouldn't be doing this, not the point of all this. I needed us to be friends.

But I didn't need this.

I needed her to know me, but I couldn't get what I wanted this way. No, this shit would drive her away, and it should.

She placed hands to my face, not stopping me, drinking me in. She lifted her hips off the bed, and I grabbed them to turn her around. I shoved her shorts and underwear down, ripping them off and making her yip, but I needed to see that ass.

I needed to bite it even more.

I indulged, my hand down my fucking pants. I fisted myself, angry about it when I licked and kissed her ass cheeks. Fawn had a gorgeous ass, full, thick. Like the rest of her, she had that shit in abundance, and I jerked my cock so hard I thought I'd shoot my load at just a taste.

"Wolf..." Her hand maneuvered between her legs, her back arching. Shit, was she touching herself? "Fucking hell. Wolf."

Her fingers played between her thighs, and I gripped her ass, arching her, spreading her. I kept her exposed this way, fascinated by that shit.

She strummed her clit, my tongue dipping down to lick the essence off her fingers from time to time. I watched more than anything, pervy about it. I sat back on my haunches jerking myself.

"That's it, Red," I gritted, her fingers in her cunt, her ass coated in bites from *my mouth*. "That's it. Fuck yourself. Get yourself ready for me."

I hadn't taken her lightly before, and my cock was easily big enough to split a girl in half. It hadn't with Red before, hadn't even fazed her.

"Fuck, I'm close." Her digits picked up, actually fucking herself. It was the hottest shit I'd ever seen, and I pressed my mouth to her cunt, sucking around her fingers, tasting.

"Fuck, you taste so good, baby." My fingers pinched her ass, my nose up and down her sex. I teased her with my tongue, and she cried out.

"I can't. I'm gonna..." Her ass lifted, her cheeks pushing against my face. "I'm gonna..."

She came apart over my mouth, gushing all over my face, down my throat. I lapped that shit up, not wasting a drop.

"Yes," I ground out, the howl restrained in my throat. I didn't want my parents to know what we were doing in here. The storm had basically stopped, our coverage gone.

I craned my body over Red's, working her hair around my fist. Licking my lips, I jerked her back to look at me. "Taste yourself."

She did, pressing her lips to mine. She appeared sex drunk and completely hot, her body red all over, and freckled, well, everywhere. There was barely a place this girl existed where she didn't have any.

Why hadn't I noticed?

I had noticed. I noticed too much of her beauty, her strength. She didn't put up with my shit, and I had to fight against that bullshit every day. She commanded me with every part of her.

I hadn't stood a chance.

I turned her around, her thighs in my hands when I spread her. Her tattoos lined her rosy skin, and really, the only place she didn't have them was her stomach.

"Wolf..."

I kissed her, right there. Soft flesh trembled under my mouth, and I groaned.

"Fawn..." I brought her to me, close. Pulling her up, I slid her on my lap, and we fit so well together.

We were perfect.

My tongue hit hers, dancing, dueling. I was getting so drunk off her, physically aching when I lifted my cock into her through my sweatpants.

"You're wearing too many clothes," she said, but she didn't go for my pants. Her fingers looped around my tank, and my mouth stopped on hers.

She noticed.

Her lips stopped too, swollen, bruised. She backed off, studying me, and didn't move an inch.

"Can I?" she asked, fingering under my tank. "Please, can I see you?"

The fact she felt the need to ask should bother me. I should be over this shit. It happened, my past, and I should be over it.

My hands moved up her waist, her body warm. She was still naked on top of me, and I did something I never believed I would. Not with her and after our last time together.

I nodded, giving her consent and even helped her. She pulled my shirt off, and we just sat there together.

Fawn's fingers explored, her small hands on my biceps, squeezing. She pressed a hand down my abs, but before she could loop around my waist, I laid her to her back.

I kissed her, not ready for any more of her exploring. I put a hand down my pants but Fawn's replaced mine.

"Let me see it," she said against my lips, pulling me out. She worked my cock, and I growled into her mouth.

"Taste it," I gritted, guiding her up. I wouldn't fuck her mouth. I might kill her, but when her tongue flicked across the head, I thought she might kill me.

I watched her, again fascinated. She parted those bruised lips of hers against my shaft, her bottom lip dragging on it. Her tongue eased out, tasting, and when she gathered my balls, I thought I'd break down and actually fuck that mouth raw.

"Fuck, fuck, Fawn."

She laughed against my cock, kissing it and being arrogant. She knew she was getting to me. "He's a human again. Where is that god, Wolf?"

I didn't know. I was losing that part of myself every day with her, my strength depleting, waning. I drew her back before she could put her mouth on me, kissing her, our tongues flicking.

"Watch your mouth, Red," I stated, biting her. I covered her with my body, then reached into one of the bedside table's drawers. I kept condoms in all these spare rooms for the parties I used to throw in high school. I grinned against her mouth. "Only use it if you're going to scream."

I'd make her scream, my sweatpants shrugging down. I kicked them off, then sheathed myself.

Fawn looked ready for the challenge, and I bet she would

try to fight me and keep herself from screaming. I lifted her leg, angling into her with a hard thrust and hadn't been gentle about it.

We both choked down our sounds.

Fawn had actually bitten her arm, and I lodged teeth into her fucking neck. We really were perfect, fit perfect. I picked her up, putting her on my lap. I fucked her hard and fast below, and Fawn gathered her hair up above her head.

Her tits bounced, slapping her chest and making it red. I caught a nipple in my mouth, and she did scream then.

I held a hand over her mouth, catching it. Her teeth lodged into my palm, and I removed my hand, biting the shit out of her mouth.

Fuck, we were so toxic.

We were both a hot fucking mess but I loved every minute of it. I loved it too much really.

Way too much.

Enough to try to look past her. I did before the last time we were together and tried again.

Red wouldn't let me.

Fawn put hands on my face, her fingers in my hair again.

"You don't get to leave," she said, calling me on my shit. She always did. She shook her head. "Not this time."

She kissed me, as intensely and mercilessly as I fucked her. I thought I had the upper hand here. She was on my cock, but here she was lassoing me with a single kiss.

And who was the god now?

She was the one owning me, a goddess in my arms, and I squeezed her. I let myself give in to her. I let myself bleed with her.

What are you doing?

I wasn't listening to myself, ignoring the signs. I was letting myself give in, and when Fawn's hips worked against me, I pushed her to do the same. I wanted her to give in too.

I was stupid enough to want that too.

I was stupid enough to want that for us, as if we weren't ill-fated. As if this whole arrangement wasn't bullshit, and we could have something more. Like this could be us forever.

As if I hadn't already damned us from the start.

That didn't stop me from taking her and bringing her to the brink. I rocked her against me, and her face lacing in complete pleasure had my balls tightening.

That's right, Red. Come for me...

She did and beautifully. Her back arched, her cunt squeezing and choking me. I brought her to her back and held her on that final wave.

I wasn't far behind.

I flooded the condom shamelessly, my muscles locked up, my body rigid. I opened my eyes to find her beneath me.

I opened them to see her kissing me.

She felt brave enough to, and if I hadn't known before this shit had gotten too deep, I did now. I did when I noticed her hands roaming. They moved to my shoulders, my arms, and when they eventually eased around to my back, that was the something interesting I noticed. I noticed I actually let her.

And that I didn't flinch this time.

CHAPTER
TWENTY-SIX

Fawn

The storm stopped, finally.

And Wolf was gone.

His scent wasn't, my body bathed in it. His musky aroma surrounded me, and it wasn't quite daylight yet.

I wasn't sure what was happening between us or what had happened, and when I heard water running, I pressed the comforter to my chest.

Is he in the shower?

I'd seen I had one, no reason to leave this room really. The bedroom I'd been given had a private bathroom.

I edged out of the bed, taking a sheet with me. I wrapped myself like a burrito, then followed the sound to the bathroom. I thought to knock but decided against it.

I mean, it was my shower.

I told myself that, and that I wasn't a Peeping Tom. In any case, the shower walls were opaque, but an outline could easily be seen.

And how was he gorgeous even through that?

Wolf's solid form radiated through, unmoved, his head hanging. He had an arm on the wall, and though I couldn't see him completely, that didn't stop his figure from displaying through the glass. If anything, it made him look like a work of art, abstract.

Perfect.

He literally did look like a painting, my heart racing.

"Wolf?"

He said nothing and didn't even move.

I stepped on warm tiles. "Ares?"

His head lifted a little then, but only slightly. He passed a hand over his hair, the room filled with mist, heat. After that, he pressed both palms on the wall, and I came closer.

"Ares?" I repeated, so close to the glass now. "Can I come in?"

I wanted to for some reason, curiosity pulling me. He could have used his own shower, not mine.

His response to this was just to look back, his blurry form in my direction. He turned back after that, and I took the initiative.

I dropped the sheet, the thing pooling at my feet. One would think I'd be shier about joining probably the most gorgeous guy on earth in the shower… with the lights on.

I wasn't, though, and I think earlier tonight gave me confidence. He actually seemed more reserved than me this evening, vulnerable.

I eased the door open, the heat cracking out. Like I'd witnessed on the other side, Wolf had his head hung. His muscled frame rose up and down with heavy breath, and I wondered how long he'd been in here.

My gaze glided over him, his ass… Everything about this guy was perfect. His chiseled legs were as solid as his arms and back, and I definitely focused there. His back piece was on full display again, but I passed over it quickly, pushing myself to approach.

"Ares, are you okay?" I lifted a hand over him, stopping just shy. I wanted to touch him so bad.

I wanted to wrap my arms around him more.

I didn't want to piss him off, though, and he was so good at terrifying me. He liked to be that Big Bad Wolf, so I just stayed in place.

"Can I..." I started, and his response to this was to glance back. His hair had clumped, his thick tendrils wet, soaking. He appeared like a fatigued animal after a fight.

Like a warrior who'd found defeat.

His tongue eased over his lips, his head down. He nodded, but I didn't go for his back.

I pushed my arms around him, hugging him. I just wanted to squeeze him until he didn't feel whatever he was feeling anymore. He'd helped me so much tonight. I actually felt... *better* after our talk, and I'd had no idea he'd experienced similar things.

Though, I shouldn't have been surprised.

This guy packed away a lot of hurt, and even though things seemed perfect now with his family, I couldn't deny that'd been there. He had a lot of trauma too. Both of us.

I kissed his back, unable to help it, that scar so close. He'd had some kind of surgery, and I didn't know what it was, but I didn't care.

I just wanted him to feel better.

My hands roamed, pressing my naked flesh against his. It was crazy, but this guy and I fit together so well. Even with as big and solid as he was.

His chest lifted, heavy breaths again. He got one of my hands, and soon, he laced them. He eased them onto his hip, making me grip him there, bone, muscle.

My palm heated, and my other moved to his dick. I fisted him, and a low noise vibrated into my cheek, my nose. I kissed his back again, and he turned around.

His pupils had dilated, and I could barely see them through all his hair. His thick curls shrouded his face.

He approached, our hands still laced. The tattoo on his hip shifted with his strides, a single line drawing. Without knowing, I'd just had my hand there. He had a line drawing of a wild flower.

Wolf pinched my chin, playing with it. Something of a debate was in his eyes, but he craned his body to meet me halfway.

And the kiss he gave me...

So soft, full. I didn't even *know* he could kiss this way, and when I eased my arms around his neck, he picked me up.

The groan from his hungry lips fell into my mouth, my feet literally off the floor when he pressed me into the shower. Whatever he'd done to his back obviously was a thing of the past because he never, not once, had issues picking me up. He was always so strong.

"Let me inside," he said, his hand between my legs. His fingers played at my opening, and my mouth fell open. "I'm clean. I haven't been with anyone after you."

That was one thing I hadn't asked, if he'd been with anyone else while faking things with me. In the past, I would have told myself I didn't care what he did outside of our fake relationship, but that'd be a lie.

I did care. I cared *so* much about him.

"Please," I ached, widening my legs. "Please. I'm on birth control, and I'm clean too."

My recent history with all that had been pretty dry anyway, and I couldn't even *think* about anything before this.

I couldn't think of anyone before him.

This felt so real, was feeling *real*. I wanted to fight it. I wanted to hate it, but as Wolf hiked me against the wall and spread me wide, all I could do was let him angle inside. I wanted him.

I fucking needed him.

When I cried out, he caught my lips, wrapping my legs around him, his dick tunneling, *ripping*. He was so goddamn big, but the hurt burned just as good as the pleasure.

"Red, fuck." He kissed me, fucking me. He let me hold on while he pressed his hands to the wall. "How are you everything?"

The words felt so real, raw. They danced something warm in my chest, but I wasn't strong enough to think over what that was. Heath had said dealing with Legacy was heartache, and he wasn't fucking wrong.

I hated that he wasn't wrong.

I held on to Wolf for dear life. Like I could flip the script. Like I could make this real. A desperate attempt backing me, I let him fuck me like I was his.

And he was mine.

My fingers buried into his hair, I kissed everything I could find. I tongued his shoulders, tasted his neck. My brain was seeking something only he could fill, and I didn't care that it was only fleeting.

"You feel so good." He hugged me, gasping like he needed me too. "How is it possible? How are you..."

For some reason, what he said pricked something at my eyes. He had a desperation in his voice, and it felt like it matched mine. Like he was trying to make this last.

When I knew it never could.

Wolf and I were a game and always had been. This was reality.

That was just how it was.

My head touched the wall, Wolf's mouth on my neck. He bit, sucking too, and I bet I'd have so many scars when I looked at myself in the mirror. I had the Big Bad Wolf's bite on me.

How had I let him eat me alive?

"Fuck, Fawn. Fuck..." He shuddered, actually shaking. He

fused me into him, gripping my hair, my shoulders. "Fuck, I'm..."

Little warning before his dick vibrated inside me. He shuddered again, and my walls closed so hard around him. I called his name, crashing right there along with him.

We were wet, both of us. My body slid and sloshed against his as he fought to keep us pinned. He had his head down, the two of us literally one body.

A curse fell from his lips after. I didn't know if he was cursing himself or what, but when he grabbed my face, I let him ease inside my mouth again. He didn't pull himself out.

And I didn't fight when he ultimately moved to take me again.

CHAPTER
TWENTY-SEVEN

Ares

"So, um, Sloane and I heard you guys this morning."

I froze, my hands on Fawn's bag.

I'd been loading it on the damn bus.

Lucas was inside the house talking to Mom and Dad. They were catching up since he was a family friend. Dorian and I had offered to get things started in regard to the packing.

My friend had a knowing look after what he said, his hands buried in the front of his Pembroke Football hoodie. I stood back. "You think my mom and dad heard…"

"Nah. Your parents are heavy sleepers."

I fought myself from gagging in that moment. He would know that personally since he was boning my sister.

"I will say, though." He paused, posting an arm on the bus. "That you're real fucking lucky it was late, and Ramses wasn't working in his office." He pointed at me, laughter in his voice. "That's how he caught me that one time."

Yeah, really wouldn't get over my sister and my best friend were fucking. Like ever.

I did dry heave, and he shoved me.

"Sounds like you two had fun, though." Dorian cocked his head at me. "And where did you two sneak off to after breakfast anyway?"

That was also something he'd know since he showed up at the door this morning to get breakfast, even though he'd clearly stayed the night.

I supposed he wasn't the only one sneaking around these days. I'd left Fawn's room early too, and we did have a good morning after breakfast. A great morning actually.

Fighting the grin, I slid her bag under the bus. "Wasn't anything."

"Yeah?" Dorian's smile widened. "Well then, tell me."

I shrugged. "May have taken her to Windsor Prep. Just showed her my stomping grounds."

That'd actually been kind of weird showing her my high school. I mean, the stadium fight hadn't been there but we had met at her school on a similar field. I brought that all up, our history, and what was funny was we did have a laugh about it.

We'd walked around the campus after that, just shooting the shit, and I even got her out on the football field. I tossed her a ball, and we just kind of chilled.

It'd been easy.

We'd done some general walking after that, around the city. I even worked out renting some bikes so we didn't have to drive or anything.

Like stated, it'd been easy, nice and certainly wasn't worth all the ragging my buddy was doing on me now. He was fake-hitting me upside the head while I was telling him everything, getting a good jostling in, and I rolled my eyes. Fawn and I had a good day and the rest of it we just spent with my family. We only all broke it up so us kids could get back to school at a decent hour. Typically, we stayed until Sunday but Sloane realized one of her art projects was due early Monday morning, so we all agreed to come back early to give her some extra time to finish it.

"Weird to see you like this."

I looked up. "Like what?"

"Happy?" He stated this like it was obvious. We had a few bags left, and he handed them off to me. "I haven't seen you smile like this in, well, forever. You don't smile like this. *Ever.*"

All my buddies were making it sound like I really was unhappy with my life, but I just didn't express emotion like they did.

"Always so serious." He posted fingers in his face, doing a fucked-up Joker smile, and I kicked at his ass. He barked a laugh. "Anyway, it's nice to see."

We'd been talking lightly up to this moment, and my smile fell away. The tone had ironically grown serious.

Dorian might have said something more, but Thatcher showed up, and I found myself relieved by that.

"The fun has officially arrived," Thatch announced, waving a hand as if he were royalty. He had a neck pillow on like some fucking goober, and if this guy wasn't a prima donna to the highest fucking power. He was always extra as fuck and shameless about it. He pushed a hand over spiky hair, intentionally messy. His sharpened earrings flickered off the sun. "Y'all miss me?"

I was sure his staff didn't, and I took his fresh laundry shit from him. He had a big-ass mesh bag that smelled like country cotton. I lifted my eyes at it. "Hardly, and definitely not your staff with all this shit. You need to start doing your own laundry."

He made a *pssh* sound. "Can't see why when they'll do it." He flicked a finger at me. "Also, I heard it from my sister this morning about you bringing a girl to town and not setting up a meet and greet." He grinned. "She said the next time you bring Fawn around, she wants to meet her."

I was sure Bow Reed did, nosy like the rest of my brothers. She'd be coming along to Pembroke U next year I could imagine. She was a senior in high school right now.

In any sense, Bow shouldn't get her hopes up. Fawn and me definitely wouldn't be a thing next year, and the more people I kept out of all this, the better.

My jaw shifted. "Where's Wells?"

"Said he'd catch up," Thatch said, smirking. "Had a thing or something."

Meaning he was fucking someone, and Dorian and I both lifted our eyes to the heavens. Between the two of them, I was honestly surprised Thatcher had shown up on time to depart.

Dorian barked at Thatch to get Wells's ass on the phone. Meanwhile, I was trying to ignore the fact that Fawn was approaching with my parents and Sloane. Lucas was behind them all, but I wasn't focused on him.

Fawn was basically arm in arm with people I cared about so much in my life, and my mother actually did have her arm around her, rubbing it. Of course, the bus thing had come up, but I'd warned her and Dad about it.

They'd thought I'd been just doing something fun too.

People really were worried, at least about how I'd been, and I hated how it felt to see Fawn with Sloane and my parents. They were all grinning around her, and Mom and Dad's especially couldn't be denied. If I'd been smiling since we all got to town, my parents had been fucking beaming, and my selfish heart loved that. I'd do anything to make them happy.

Anything to keep their world right.

———

Fawn

I kept falling asleep on this guy.

He certainly made it easy.

His arm around me, Wolf brushed his fingers casually against my elbow. He stared out the window, seemingly in his thoughts.

At least, until I adjusted.

His attention flicked away from the dark world, the bus humming around us. I didn't know how long we'd been driving, but we'd left Maywood Heights pretty easily. No traffic or anything. A grin touched Wolf's lips. "Didn't even make it an hour this time, Red. I'd hate to see you on a real road trip."

My finger lifted, flipping him off, and he laughed albeit lightly. Something told me I hadn't been the only one asleep.

I gazed up to find Sloane's dark head against Dorian. He had his arm around her too, holding her. The couple was about four seats up, and Wells and Thatcher were toward the front. I couldn't really see them much, but they looked like they were playing another card game. Hard to do on a moving bus but they obviously managed.

I lay back down. "What can I say? I fall asleep when I'm bored."

And warm.

I kept that last bit to myself, definitely aware Wolf hadn't moved his arm when I lay back down. I also noticed neither one of us had talked about what had happened this morning, and we'd certainly had a lot of time to do it.

I mean, he'd shown me his life.

At least, a snapshot of it. We'd gone to his old high school, and he even showed me some sites where he'd tagged graffiti in town. I'd gotten to see his work for the first time, and that'd been amazing. He tended to use both dark and vibrant colors, geometric scenes and not far off from the piece he had on his back. He gave the world a glimpse into the universe through his art. The work I'd seen displayed constellations like his tattoo.

A lot had happened today. A lot *had been happening*, and not once did either of us address it. I wasn't sure of Wolf's reason, but mine surrounded fear. Fear that I'd let this guy in a bit.

I'd more than let him in.

I let my eyes close, the crook of Wolf's arm hugging my neck. As solid as this guy was, one would think lying on him would hurt.

I wished it did.

I was too selfish to move away from him, and if we only had one more hour on this trip, I didn't see the point in wasting it. I wouldn't waste it.

"It was cancer."

My gaze flicked up, eyes narrowed. "What?"

"Cancer, Red. It was *cancer*." His fingers folded on my arm, his eyes avoiding. He stared out the window. "My back. It was cancer. A tumor. That's what the scar's from. I know you saw it."

I had seen it.

A tumor...

I didn't move. I didn't breathe. I simply watched him, his digits restless against my skin.

"What's crazy is, I didn't even notice through football or anything. Not the intense training. None of that shit." He lifted his hand, the one holding me. "It was my art. My hands..." He formed a fist. "The work was getting all fucked up and wasn't coming out right."

Oh my God.

"Anyway, that's what it was." His hand returned to my arm, dark eyes finally looking at me. "A tumor. Spinal cancer."

I swallowed, not really knowing what to say.

I mean, why did he tell me?

He certainly didn't have to, and I shifted against him. "Are you okay now?"

Mine were the restless fingers now. They clenched his hoodie a little, and he noticed.

Our fingers danced, his smile a subtle one.

"I'm sitting here, aren't I? With you?"

"That's not what I asked."

Our gazes clashed again. "Doc says I'm fine. Just had an appointment actually. Went well."

But there were multiple ways to be fine. There were, and they didn't always surround the physical. My throat thickened. "Christ, Ares."

"Christ." He said the word as if considering it.

And I noticed his digits didn't escape mine.

They continued to play, and he wore that Court ring today. The thing was thick around his lengthy finger.

"That's all you can say?" His head cocked. "Not *I'm so sorry that happened*, or *I can't imagine what you went through*. That's what everyone says when they find out. Feeling sorry for me."

I was sure they did, and I guess I got now why no one I knew gossiped about all this. His life. He'd obviously kept a lock on the information.

His fingers folded with mine, and I liked it so much I didn't make him stop. He studied us both together, and I wondered if he even realized what he was doing.

How crazy something like that could be so intimate. I didn't feel like I knew his body, but I was certainly getting there. Hard not to lately.

"Ares, are you okay?" I asked again, and his chest lifted.

"Surgery took care of it, Red." He lowered our hands. "The recovery period was a bitch, but I'm good. Didn't take me out."

My tongue ran across my lip. "Why did you tell me?"

"Why not?" His shrug was casual. "After all, we're sharing, right? We're friends."

He was sounding very cynical right now. Like he wasn't

all right, and I hadn't shared what I had about my dad to make him share. I hadn't expected anything at all and really hadn't wanted to share.

I sat up, and his arm moved from around me. I felt the heat of his stare on me, but I didn't address it.

"You okay?" How funny he was asking me that. "Fawn…"

"Remember that girl from the pictures." I studied his prickled jawline, his expression curious. I opened my hands. "The one you said didn't even look the same after what I did to her."

I didn't know where this was coming from, and maybe there was a part of me who didn't want him to feel vulnerable by himself. I certainly wasn't okay either.

But maybe we could be not okay together.

Wolf sat back, his arm hooking on the top of the seat. "Yeah."

I forced out a breath, breathing into my hands. "Well, she bullied me. Was a bully." I cuffed my arms. "She never liked me, but she never went out of her way to do anything to me. Not until I got in her way."

"What do you mean?" He leaned forward, invested now.

"There was this boy. This new kid." My stomach clenched. I really didn't want to talk about this shit. "He was cool, and the two of us started talking."

"Talking? As in you were seeing him?" His dark eyebrows drew inward. "Okay."

His voice had deepened, rough. He sounded like he cared about that, and maybe before a few things had occurred between us recently, I'd think the opposite. Things were certainly changing with us and so quickly.

Too quickly.

My lips moved. "It hadn't really gone that far. He was nice to me and was about the only person who didn't look at me like the train wreck that I was. My dad had just died, and I didn't handle that shit well."

I was sure he could fill in the blanks there. He knew about the alcohol abuse…

He knew about the drugs.

Wolf had access to my entire life, all my secrets at his disposal. He'd used those secrets to blackmail me, and oddly enough, once he put that out there, he'd never brought it up again. It was like he just needed me to know he knew.

I certainly did, my hands rubbing. "Anyway, this girl, my bully, was into this new kid." I lifted and dropped my shoulders. "But he wasn't into her. He was talking to me."

"And she didn't like that." His head touched the seat, and mine nodded.

"Apparently, the new guy picking the 'chubby girl' over the cheerleader isn't a thing." I'd air quoted the chubby bit. I was aware of what I looked like, but the only people who seemed to take issue with it tended to be girls like the one who'd bullied me. They hated that I didn't care what they thought.

They hated even more if I got something they didn't.

The girl's insecurities had bled through her and were so obvious.

Wolf leaned forward then, his big body hovering over me. I didn't know what he was doing, but I didn't fight that masculine aroma that surrounded me. I liked it too much, just like his touch.

"What did she do to you?" he surmised, my lips parting. He frowned. "That bitch did something to you, because otherwise, you never would have done what you did to her."

And how would he know that? I could be just as wild as him. Crazy…

But I wasn't, though, and as his eyes scanned mine, I wondered if he could see that. My fingers bit into my arms. "She locked me in a car."

His nostrils flared a little, his gold hoops still there. His hands came together. "For how long?"

Long enough where I remembered the scratches on my arms and my legs. At one point, I think I'd thrown up, but I couldn't remember that part.

I'd blacked out.

A girl had locked me in a car. She had *knowing* I didn't do cars. Everyone did.

They felt sorry for me.

Wolf and I shared more similarities than I ever wanted to admit. I didn't do cars, not since the accident, and I too had lots of people in my life throwing their remorse at me. I had it twice over. They felt sorry about my dad, but they also felt sorry for me. I had been a train wreck back then, the addict whose daddy died.

The one who wore her trauma all over her.

"Long enough where I blacked out," I said, and Wolf nodded. I swallowed. "I honestly don't remember much. I was told what happened, but she knew what she was doing. I hadn't even gotten *in* a car since the accident."

"Of course, she did." He glanced up. Some laughter occurred up front, his friends. Thatcher and Wells were getting into their game again, but Wolf wasn't paying attention to them.

He had a way of using those dark eyes of his to probe me. They gained secrets, and between us, the pair of us had enough to write a book.

He put his hands together. "Why did you tell me?"

"Well, we're sharing, right?" I touched his chest, teasing. "We're friends."

I teased that too, joking. We weren't friends, and he hadn't sounded like he'd been for real either when he said it.

"Right," he said, his voice low again. His expression went serious. "Right. We are friends, and you didn't deserve what happened to you. That girl was jealous of you and everything you are."

My heart leaped, not expecting that.

"You were right to kick her ass," he continued. His tongue eased over his lip. "I'm glad you kicked her ass."

No one else had been glad. "I had to leave town after. Couldn't stay there."

My stepdad had actually made it all go away. Though, at the time, he hadn't been my stepdad. He'd just been a family friend then, helping me, my mom.

Like a lot of things, I hadn't gotten to express my feelings back then. Not to my stepdad for helping in the way he had, or my mom for ultimately getting me into rehab. She'd saved my fucking life.

And you can't even talk to her.

Again, a lot of things were unsaid, and gratefully, Wolf didn't make me say any of them. He just put his arm around me again, and this time, I didn't let myself fall asleep. I just hugged my arms around my friend.

And wondered how that had happened.

CHAPTER
TWENTY-EIGHT

Fawn

"Who got you smiling like that?"

I walked out of my bedroom to find Wolf on our shared couch. He had books stacked around him, a frown posted on his lips.

Was I smiling?

Maybe I was, my cell phone in hand. I closed out of the text, and Wolf arched a thick eyebrow.

"Better not be that fucker Heath," he bit, eyes on my phone. He grunted before returning his attention to his books, and I laughed.

"You don't like Heath?" I sauntered over to our couch, then made a seat out of the armrest. Wolf certainly had the rest of the couch covered. He was literally surrounded by books while he jotted something in a notebook.

His look was passive. "Dude's nothing but an opportunist."

I couldn't help my smile, wondering what this was about. I propped a leg beneath the other.

Wolf's frown deepened. "He was quick to let you crash with him full well knowing you and I were together."

"Okay. Okay. Wait." I lifted a hand, seriously laughing now.

Especially with how cute he looked.

This large guy who covered well over half the couch—with just his body—was completely simmering. A flush of red crept up to Wolf's hairline, his fingers working through his chunky curls when he adjusted on the couch.

My God is he... jealous?

I dashed a finger in his direction. "Holy crap. Are you jealous?" And of *Heath* of all people? I wasn't his type, at all, and there'd been zero sexual tension there on both sides.

Wolf snorted. "I'm simply making a statement. You and I got something going." His eyes flicked up. "We did but he was quick to come on his white horse for you."

But all this was fake, though. At least, it was supposed to be. Wolf and I certainly hadn't addressed what had happened last weekend at his family's house, but a lot of real things had been felt. Especially on my end.

I fidgeted on the couch myself. "It's called being a friend."

"Yeah, well, I'm your friend."

I blinked at another thing not addressed, a friendship, him and me. We'd said as much, but still that was... different.

Wolf's eyes averted, most likely similar thoughts about our sudden friendship going on in his own head. His fingers lodged into his hair. "I just mean..."

I knew what he meant, a lot of lines blurred recently. We'd had a long bus ride home over two days ago, and neither one of us had brought up anything that had happened between us. He'd just held me, my arms around him. We'd enjoyed the moment with no talks about further secrets and definitely not the hot sex that had occurred between us.

Real hot sex.

Wolf was quite frankly a god in the sheets, and my face

heated at just the thought of him. Him thrusting that powerful body inside me had hit my brain more than once, and since we'd gotten back to the dorm, we'd basically been playing house. We were passing ships for the most part due to classes, which seemed to be a necessity. If we both took a second to stop and smell the roses, we'd have to have a needed conversation. One that involved what the hell was going on with this "fake" relationship.

And why suddenly neither one of us was brave enough to talk about it.

Maybe because it had gotten real. It *felt* real, and because it did, I wasn't brave. If I said something about it, things might get weird again. He'd be his wolfy self, and I didn't know what that would mean to this new juncture we'd stumbled on. I feared the result.

I feared his shutdown.

Wolf gripped his pen. "Anyway, the guy knew about you and me." He waved a hand. "But that certainly didn't stop him from stepping in."

That was because he was being a friend like I said. I glanced up. "You're really sounding jealous, Wolfy."

His dark eyebrows flicked up, and I really wasn't sure if that was because of what I'd said or the flirting. I was flirting.

I couldn't seem to stop.

When I wasn't flirting with this guy, I was calling him a friend and actually feeling legitimate about the thoughts and feelings. I chewed my lip. "Well, you are."

"Yeah, okay." He said this, but a ghost of a smile tugged at his lips. He definitely knew I'd been flirting a moment ago. "Anyway, who were you on the phone with?"

He sounded more curious than anything.

He moved some of his books, and I sat on the couch. I asked him about them in the process, and he said he was studying.

He really does take school seriously.

It was funny that was how all this had started. He'd wanted a fake relationship for his family, yes, but clearly, his initial excuse of school was a part of that.

I sat back on the couch. "I was talking with my mom actually. Well, I responded to one of her texts."

That was kind of a big deal since I never did, and I'd been surprised I had.

Wolf's attention drifted from his books. "Everything okay?"

"Mmhmm. I just never do. Respond to her texts." I put my phone on the coffee table. "Anyway, I did today."

I had no idea what had compelled me, and it hadn't been a big deal. She'd actually just sent me more pictures about what she and my stepdad were up to. She sent those a lot, and instead of ignoring them, I said something today.

"She sent photos from a trip she'd been on, and I said *nice*," I stated, then laughed. "I think I made her day."

Hell, I'd made my mother's year. She asked me how I'd been after that, and I said okay. The conversation hadn't really gone anywhere after that, but it had started.

So I guess that was a big deal.

Wolf had his legs crossed at the knee, and he posted both feet to the floor. "I didn't know you didn't talk to your mom."

I waved a hand. "We've just been distant. After Dad passed and all that." Wolf's head cocked, and I scrubbed into my hair. "The conversation we had wasn't much, but it was nice, and she sounded happy I said something."

More than happy.

"What made you want to talk to her?" Wolf angled in my direction. "If you usually don't, I mean."

Well, *that* I didn't know, but I felt a sneaking suspicion it had to do with him. I nudged him. "Maybe spending some time with the happy, perfect Mallicks last weekend did that."

His family did seem happy, was happy, and they certainly had plenty of reasons not to be.

Maybe, in a way, that had me looking at my whole family dynamic. If a family like that could heal, why couldn't mine?

Why couldn't I?

My fingers grazed my arm, again fidgeting, and I noticed Wolf's doing the same.

"We're not perfect," he said, his attention falling back to his books. "And certainly not me."

But he was trying, and they did all seem happy. I nodded. "Anyway, yeah. Mom definitely loved hearing from me, and I said I'd talk to her again. Told her I planned to call sometime." I think I actually would.

Crazy.

I really did feel myself changing, which was insane. I was feeling open to addressing some things in myself for the first time.

I had no idea if that had to do with Wolf or not but I hadn't felt that way *at all* before our fake relationship.

"That's real good, Red. Good," he said, his smile returning. "Family is important. Family's everything."

His voice sounded a little far away, and I scooted closer. "I'm trying to get back there. To what my mom and I had?" I smiled. "And it was nice to see what she and my stepdad were up to. They were just in Bali, but they're back in New York now. That's where they live. My mom's a party planner. Did I tell you that?"

Yeah, didn't know why I was telling him that, sharing more of my business.

Wolf's head shook. I grinned. "She plans these huge parties for celebrities, and my stepdad is a surgeon."

He was one of those TV doctors, and that was how they'd met. Mom planned all kinds of parties, and their paths had just crossed.

Wolf's pen slowed. "That's cool," he said, his voice sounding far away again. "You said they're back in New York?"

"Mmhmm. New York City. My stepdad's German, though. Did I mention that?"

His head shook once more before his attention returned to his work. I was probably bothering him with this, and he had been working when I came into the room.

I got up. "So, um, I guess thank you."

His sight fell on me, and I played with my hands.

"I feel like I only responded to my mom because of last weekend. It really was nice to be around family."

So nice, amazing.

Wolf's mouth moved but he didn't say anything. Maybe he didn't know what to say, and I was still bothering him. I backed up. "I don't want to bother you, so I'll let you get back to work."

He wasn't now, his pen tapping his notebook, and I felt bad. I started to go, but he told me to wait.

He had his books off his lap when I turned, and when he asked me to come here, I did. He put his hands together. "So, we never talked about last weekend. All that happened."

I froze. "We haven't."

I had to admit the words came out brave, and I also had to admit I wasn't ready for any of this.

That didn't mean *this* wasn't coming, and as I watched Wolf's hands rub, my heart raced. He could literally say anything. Say last weekend was fun and all that but it was time to get back to reality. That he was good on that front with his family, and he didn't need me anymore. I didn't think what occurred between us was a part of the act, but it would definitely be an incentive to end all this.

He might end it.

I think that was what thudded my heart the most, but of course, I'd never admit that.

"We should talk about that. It's important and..." He wasn't looking at me, his eyes on the floor. "And, uh, yeah. We got a lot of things to talk about."

Though, as per usual, neither one of us were saying them. A pregnant silence occurred, and the next thing I knew, Wolf was stacking his books.

"I'm on my way out, though," he said, getting his things together. "Meeting the guys to play billiards."

I didn't know why, but I felt relief by him saying this.

Yeah, you know why.

I shifted on my feet. "That sounds fun."

"Yeah, we do it every once in a while." He stopped, facing me. "You should come. It'd be a good time. I can have Dorian bring Sloane."

My smile was shaky. "Like an assignment?" I had to admit in that moment I wasn't up for it. I wasn't sure I was strong enough. I wasn't strong enough. "Actually…"

"No, like because you want to," he said, and I blinked. He nodded. "Because you just want to hang out. No pressure, and I'd like for you to come."

"You would?"

His smile was easy. "Yeah. Like I said, it'd be fun, and we could chat later."

Chat about us, he meant.

I really wasn't sure I wanted to go now, but I found I couldn't even turn down an opportunity to hang out with him. This guy had me completely gone.

And let's not even talk about the job he was doing on my heart.

CHAPTER
TWENTY-NINE

Fawn

"The drinks have arrived." Thatcher Reed had his beefy arms lined with beers. He handed mugs off to Wolf's friends one by one, and apparently, the student rec center didn't mind selling to the underaged.

But I guess when one was Legacy...

Wolf and his friends really did do what they wanted around here. Dorian, Sloane, and Wells crowded Thatcher. They got their beers, but when Thatcher tried to hand one off to me, I passed.

"No, thanks," I said, and when I did, Wolf raised a hand too.

"I'm good," he stated, looking delicious in a pair of black jeans and a gray shirt that hugged his muscular frame. He'd changed before going out, a visual feast, and I tried not to notice just like the fact that we hadn't had any kind of talk. We walked over to the student union from the dorm but strode in silence for the most part.

I'd liked it that way.

Thatcher shrugged after Wolf gave him permission to basically take two beers. He offered Wells the other, and with their newly acquired bounty, they certainly didn't linger on the fact that both Wolf and I refused to drink.

I faced Wolf. "You didn't have to do that."

He obviously picked up on what I'd done, and he did know my history with drug and alcohol abuse. I'd gotten really into the party scene after my dad had died, and though this wasn't something I'd been forthcoming about, it seemed I didn't have to.

Wolf's refusal on my behalf said as much, and my stupid heart pattered at his solidarity with me, his support. We both lounged against a high-top table, and his big shoulders bumped. "It's not a problem. I got used to not drinking anyway last year."

Oh, right. With his cancer. My hands touched the table. "Did you have to like get chemo or anything?"

I said it low. Dorian, Sloane, Wells, and Thatcher were chatting, and even though we were only here with his friends, I was sure it was a tough subject to talk about.

Wolf noticed my resistance, as well as my wandering gaze to the others around us. He barked a laugh. "You don't have to talk about it like it's taboo, Red."

I mean, well, didn't I? I chewed my lip. "Sorry. Just didn't know if you wanted all that out there."

He angled forward, his shoulder brushing mine. A harsh heat touched my body, and my stupid heart shot up in beats again.

Cool it.

I really needed to. I was acting so weird with him now, and I didn't like it. I was always aware of Wolf. But these days...

"I appreciate that, but I did tell you about it." He smiled a little. "Because I did, I'm open about it, and no, I didn't have to have chemo."

I figured as much. I didn't know a damn thing about cancer but I'd seen his chest and hadn't noticed any kind of port.

"Gratefully, the surgery took care of it," he continued, his gaze suddenly taking the table. He stood. "Anyway, let me get you a soda or something since you're not having a beer."

He started to walk off, but I pinched his shirt between two fingers. "I'm okay. You don't have to."

I liked him here anyway.

Wolf's tongue ran across his lip, an action that never ceased to bring a dance to my stomach. "Okay, cool."

His attention lingered on my fingers. I did like him close and hadn't let go.

"So that talk," he said, my stomach dancing for a different reason now. It was more like a twitch, a twist. His dark eyes found mine. "I was thinking we could go for a walk. Just when we get a moment. Or…"

He might have said something else, but his sister came over. And God, I'd never get over how tall she was. Really, any of his friends. Sloane's shoulders alone were like well above mine, but the guys had shoulders above her. It was crazy. She tossed long arms across both Wolf and myself. "Talked with the guys, and we're thinking guys against girls," she stated, grinning at me. "We obviously have an odd number, though, so Fawn and I get Thatcher."

She pointed at him, and Thatcher's grin was so cocky behind his beer mug. Wells Ambrose was standing next to him, and the stark-white blond tucked hands under his thick arms.

"Yeah, and that shit's no fair," Wells said. "Thatcher's like way better than all of us."

"I can't help it if ladies love me, my guy." Really fucking

cocky, Thatcher angled over. Sloane had dropped her arms from between Wolf and me, and Thatcher took the opportunity to place his weighted biceps on the only girls in present company. One of those girls was me, and I nearly succumbed to the weight. He squeezed us both. "Let's win this thing."

His smile coy, he started to squeeze us again, but Dorian and Wolf tag-teamed the guy. They literally ripped him off both Sloane and me, which made Sloane howl in laughter. The two immediately started punching at Thatcher, and though I probably should have been horrified, I was laughing too.

It was funny.

It was nice to just be a part of something light and nothing stressful. Of course, I had my own friends, but I'd always been uptight. It was hard to let people in, but these particular people made it easy.

He made it easy.

Wolf had Thatcher in a bear hug. Probably because he was so tall but that got him restrained enough for Dorian to hit Thatcher over the head repeatedly.

"What did I say about that handsy shit?" Dorian barked, but he was laughing, smiling. Honestly, Wolf was laughing too, and though Thatcher was basically being assaulted, it didn't stop his own laughter. Thatcher's face had charged like a million degrees in color while he pleaded for his life, but that seemed to no avail. Dorian and Wolf didn't stop until they were good and ready. Meanwhile, Wells gave zero aid.

He was too busy laughing himself.

This was obviously the dynamic between these boys, these brothers. Eventually, Wolf and Dorian pushed Thatcher away, but even after they did, Thatcher was still laughing.

Thatcher's long earrings danced, his dark hair all over the place. He worked his hands through it. "Uh-oh. Wolfy's joined Dorian in the ranks with that territorial shit."

His eyes blazing, Wolf darted in that direction, but Wells did step in this time.

"Relax," Wells said, chuckling. "Save some of it for the game."

"Yeah, there'll be fucking plenty." And suddenly, Wolf was with me. He brought an arm around me, a *territorial* arm, and those goddamn butterflies struck again. He angled a look down at me. "Watch that fucker. He does get handsy."

Thatcher made kissing noises, and Wolf growled again. I patted his chest. "It's okay."

"It's not, but it fucking will be if this guy puts hands on you again."

Thatcher mocked faux fear, and even Dorian (who'd definitely returned to Sloane and put an arm *around her*) was laughing again. He certainly found all this funny too. He found Wolf funny, and I could see why.

Wolf held me to the point of fusing himself to me, and suddenly, I was dreading our talk so much. Maybe it wasn't what I thought it'd be. Maybe it wasn't this whole thing crashing around us, our relationship. Maybe it was this, laughter and lightness.

Maybe it was him being as foolish as me.

———

So, um, Thatcher was awesome. The dude basically killed it half the night, and it took Dorian, Wolf, and Wells just to keep up with him. I mean, Thatcher was pretty much carrying Sloane and me, but that didn't seem to matter to him. If anything, he got off on embarrassing his friends, and Wolf, Dorian, and Wells were getting increasingly frustrated as the night went on. There were a lot of grunts and growls on their end. Especially from Dorian and Wolf, who did it any time Thatcher got anywhere remotely close to Sloane and me. Sloane was obviously used to this because she took every opportunity she could to "poke the bear." At one point, she even hooked her arm on Thatcher's shoulder, which got her Dorian's arm permanently around her waist. The two were freaking hilarious, and I'd pay attention more if I didn't have my own distraction with Wolf. His disagreement with Thatcher's proximity was minimal since I didn't poke, but that certainly didn't keep his attention off me.

I seemed to have it every shot either he or I took, and I was starting to want this game over to talk to him.

Did he want to make this real?

He might. He could, and if he asked, I wondered what I'd say. I mean, did I want this to be real?

You know that answer.

I studied him across the pool table, all smiles after the shot he made. He even did a little victory dance, and I saw so many changes in him. He wasn't nearly so abrasive. Especially when it came to me.

I mean, he had his arm around me all night.

He had, a permanent fixture like Dorian and Sloane. The only reason he wasn't doing it now was because it'd been his turn.

Our gazes clashed just then, a hard hold. He passed a wink at me over the table before Dorian said something to him, and I think the only reason I looked away was because Sloane poked me.

"I got an idea," she said, exchanging a glance between me and the other side of the table. I was sure she caught me looking. She smiled. "It'll get us a leg up. Just watch and learn from me."

We were actually pretty even in the game. Dorian, Wolf, and Wells were holding their own against Thatcher, and this really could be anybody's game.

Curious, I studied Sloane. She lounged against the pool table the same time Dorian leaned down to make his shot. Thatcher and Wells had brought Wolf into conversation, and the only one really paying attention to what Sloane was doing was me.

Well, Dorian and me. The dirty-blond's eyes flicked up upon his girlfriend placing herself in his line of sight. He definitely picked up on that, grinning at her before pulling his pool stick back. Sloane had her stick too, and when she pushed off the table, she brought it to her mouth.

Her tongue dragged up it, licking it and right in front of Dorian. The guy had been mid-shot, and his stick hit billiard cloth the moment Sloane licked her stick.

"The fuck?" he gritted, and the other three guys whipped around. Blinking, they transferred immediate attention to the scene at hand, and Dorian's stick which had gotten a piece of the cue ball on its way toward the cloth. He'd essentially scratched and stood. "Sloane—"

"What happened?" Wolf asked, and Dorian tossed a hand at him.

"She licked her pool stick in front of me!"

Wolf's eyes shot in Sloane's direction, and cheeky, Sloane angled in beside me. "He's completely overreacting."

Well, Dorian sure didn't think he was. He charged over to her, but Thatcher got there first.

He actually cut between them.

"Chill, bro. I still need my teammate," he stated, basically laughing, and Dorian's eyes blazed.

"You better back the fuck up or I swear to fucking God you'll lose both your arms." He cut a look around him. "What the hell was that, Noa?"

Brilliant was what it was, and the girl wasn't fighting her laughter. Those two seemed to have just as much push and pull as Wolf and me.

Dorian bumped Thatcher's chest to get to Sloane, but Thatcher made a man wall. In a fit of chuckles, he refused to let Dorian through, and that was when Wolf and Wells stepped in. They were basically trying to pull Thatcher out of the way for Dorian. Fighting laughter myself, I whispered to Sloane, "I can't believe you just did that."

I mean, it was brilliant, but who knew where those sticks had been. I wouldn't have licked one just because of that, and when I joked about that, she spoke behind her hand.

"Yeah, I definitely scrubbed the shit out of it in the bathroom," she said, obviously two steps ahead. The girl really was brilliant.

She got the words out just as Dorian barreled his way through Thatcher. This was no easy feat considering how big the guy was, but Wolf and Wells gave Dorian the edge. They got Thatcher out of the way, then gave him swift hits in the arm.

"We're talking. *Now*," Dorian ground out in front of Sloane. The guy was intimidating as fuck, but all Sloane did was tip her chin at him.

A sly grin tipped her lips. "What if I don't want to talk?"

"Noa…"

She put a hand on his chest, and a noise rolled in his chest. Like an actual noise, and his dark pupils even dilated.

Next thing I knew, he was directing her away, and when she asked where they were going, all he did was make another noise. He had her by the shoulders while he quick-stepped her away but not before Sloane made eye contact with me.

"It's up to you now," she mouthed, making me laugh. At this point, Dorian was rushing her away, and when he barked the two were going for a talk, chuckles sounded from the other side of the pool table.

One of them was Wells, who propped his pool stick against the table. "Yeah, those two are definitely about to go fuck." He nudged Thatcher after he said it, and Wolf made a face.

"One hundred percent don't want to hear that shit," he stated, coming over to me. His hand found its way right away to my waist, which shot a laser of heat directly into my skin.

As well as my pussy.

I ended up rubbing my thighs together through my jeans, and it only got worse when he tucked me into him. He smelled fucking good, and though I wanted to be a team player and give him and his boys a fighting chance against Thatcher, I realized I wanted something more in that moment.

Quite frankly, it excited the shit out of me to get a rise out of Wolf. It always had, and an opportunity came up the moment it was Wolf's turn again.

"It's up to you now."

Sloane's voice in my head, I lounged against the pool table like she had. I knew exactly what to do to get a rise out of the Big Bad Wolf, and I waited until he leaned forward to make his shot.

Wolf pulled that long reach back, and the moment he did, I leaned forward myself.

I pressed my breasts together, hugging them in his direct line of sight. I basically had my boobs on the table, the swell spilling slightly over my tank top, and Wolf's stick hit the cue ball so hard it went flying over the table.

"Jesus, Wolf!" Wells shot a leg up, the ball missing him by inches. Meanwhile, Thatcher was dying. He had his hands on his knees, seeing the whole thing, and Wolf was just standing there craned over the table.

He was still staring at my boobs.

His mouth agape, he blinked out of whatever daze he'd been in at the sound of his friends. Wells was laughing now too despite being on the wrong side of all this. He was on Wolf's team, but I guess the fact a pair of tits drove his friend to fuck up his shot superseded any disappointment he might have from the missed shot.

"Shit. These girls have you guys acting straight stupid," Wells announced, and Thatcher looked literally on the brink of throwing up. He was roaring at this point, and Wolf did seem like he was still in his stupor. It took him a second to realize he'd shot the cue ball to the floor.

And when he did…

"The hell? That didn't count." He fisted his chunky curls, eyes wide. "No fucking way I…"

"Oh, you did, my good sir," Thatcher stated, tears in his eyes. I had a hand over my mouth, trying not to laugh myself, and I think the only reason Wolf's focus wasn't on that was because he was too busy watching Thatcher. The bulky frat boy leaned down, taking his own shot. He sunk it in, of course, and when he stood, he had a large grin on his face. "And that's game. Sorry, my guy."

"No, that's…" Wolf studied the table, the evidence before him. His eyes flashed. "That's…"

"What? Cheating?" Thatcher's large shoulders bumped, still fucking laughing. "Take that up with your girl, man. Has nothing to do with me."

Shoved under the bus, I backed up but couldn't help grinning myself. "Sorry, Wolf."

"Sorry, huh?" His eyes were wild looking at me, feral. He stalked toward me, slow and so much awareness shot into my pussy I thought I'd keel over. "Yeah, real fucking sorry."

A wolfish grin hit his bright white teeth, and I backed up a little more. I wasn't going fast and kind of wanted to get caught.

He noticed.

His stick hit the floor about the same time he grabbed the back of my neck.

"You'll be fucking sorry," he said, my heart leaping, my clit buzzing. His digits lodged into my flesh. "Come on."

Directed away in a similar fashion as Sloane, I forced myself to move with jellied legs. Wells and Thatcher were still laughing, but I really wasn't paying much attention to that.

Neither was Wolf apparently, his eyes hungry. His grip on

my neck danced the line of painful, but I think that only added to the electricity moving through my legs. I was wet, *slick*. My thighs rubbed together with an attempt at relief, but he had us moving too fast.

We hit the bathrooms. Like legit, Wolf tried to barrel into one, but the door wouldn't give.

"Someone's in here!" grit from the other side, Dorian's voice. Husky, the sound followed feminine laughter, and Wolf snarled at the door.

So... that was his sister.

Wolf gave no more of his energy to that, too busy throwing the door open of the other bathroom. He jerked me inside with him, and when he kicked the door closed, he pressed me against it.

"You think that shit out there was funny? Playing with me?" He rested heavy arms on the door, smelling like heaven laced with hell. His full lips were so close, and I popped on the tips of my toes to bite them. He held me back by my neck. "You obviously do. Aren't taking this seriously. Me seriously..."

I wasn't. I wanted him too bad. I lifted my chin. "It is funny."

I tried to touch him, but he grabbed my wrist hard. His next move was to yank my tank's straps down, my bra straps with them. He bared my flushed breasts, then after, just stood there with them between us.

"I don't think it's funny." He tweaked one nipple, then the other. He pulled, and my thighs clenched. "You know how much I like these?"

I had a feeling. He buried his whole face in them whenever he could. I arched my back, giving him a better view.

The feral noise that lifted his chest built pressure between my legs. I squeezed my thighs tighter, but Wolf pressed a hand between my legs.

"You're evil, you know that?" He gripped my pussy, his

digits still pinching my nipple. He had one tight between his thumb and index finger, and I called out. He leaned forward. "And cheaters never prosper."

"Are you going to fuck me or what?" It was like I was a fly on the wall hearing myself. I sounded needy as fuck, but I didn't care.

I wanted him to fuck me.

I literally needed this guy inside me right fucking now and could totally hear Sloane and Dorian on the other side of the wall. They were laughing before a door slammed shut, their laughter fading away.

Like they'd finished.

Wolf and I were just getting started, and bold, I put a free hand on his chest. He watched my fingers on his pec, solid through his shirt. "Are you, Wolf?"

"You'd like that, wouldn't you? A reward?" He brought his eyes up, his hand still on my pussy. He gripped it. "Right here like a dirty little whore in the bathroom."

I should slap him for what he'd said.

Not be *dripping*.

I think it was the arrogant grin that teased his lips while he said it. Those beautiful fucking lips. I angled forward to taste, but he kept us separated.

He had me by the pussy.

His other hand was still preoccupied with my breast, his thumb flicking my nipple.

I sucked in a breath the same time his grin widened.

"What if I don't want to give you a reward? What if I want to teach this pussy a lesson?"

A shudder hit me. "What are you going to do?"

Because fucking me wouldn't teach me a lesson. I wanted to be fucked.

I wanted to be owned.

When that happened, I didn't know, and I watched as he

took his thumb and pushed it across my mouth. I wore my red lipstick today, and he was easily smearing it.

"Suck," he said, using that thumb to part my lips. He shoved two long digits into my mouth and immediately hit me deep, not being shy. "Let me fuck that evil little mouth."

I did let him fuck me, so deep my gag reflex went off. Wolf didn't stop, though. If anything, he kept hitting my throat on purpose. He snapped his jeans open while he did, and when he pulled his cock out, I gazed down.

I sucked him harder then, envisioning the length in my mouth. I hadn't done that with him before and honestly wasn't even sure I could manage the feat.

He was so big.

"That's it, Red," he coached, and I gagged so hard tears pricked my eyes. "Get yourself ready for me."

My lids flashed open, a flutter in my chest, and I got my breath back when he removed his fingers. He guided me to the floor, my kneecaps hitting tiles.

He was right in front of me now, long, thick. His balls hung heavy, his aroma heady. My mouth watered at just the thought of tasting him, and he angled forward with the mass in his hand.

"I want this lipstick on me," he said, using his dick to outline my lips. Pre-cum dewed the tip and ran slick above my trembling mouth. Wolf grinned. "And you won't stop until that red is all over my cock."

Holy hell.

He arched forward, forcing himself past my lips with a growl. I grabbed his hips out of sheer surprise and attempted to use them to distance. Again, this was due to surprise. My mouth and throat were suddenly filled, too filled.

Wolf wouldn't let me back off, his hand in my hair. He worked red strands around his fist in a tight grip as his hand landed on the back of my head.

"Just relax your throat," he coached, his tone rough but even. His digits gripped my scalp. "Relax it, and let me in."

He felt the resistance obviously, my resistance. Even without his size, I could count on one hand how many blow jobs I'd done.

I closed my eyes, determined to make this work. My knees digging into the floor tiles, I used his hips to keep him to me now and opened my throat.

"Christ." Wolf's hand hit the wall, his hips thrusting. "Yes, that's it. Fuck."

Adrenaline slammed into me in a rush, sucking him harder, faster. I pulled him in as deep as I could, and I swear to God, this guy was down my esophagus.

"I knew you'd be fucking good at this." He smoothed my hair away, and I moaned. I pulled off him just for breath, but then, Wolf had me right back. "No you don't. I told you not until that red is all over me. You don't get to walk away from what you just did out there."

What he said hit home more than I wanted. I'd been hard-pressed to walk away from Wolf since this whole fake dating thing began.

And damn had I tried.

I'd resisted him. I'd *fought* him, but no matter what I did, I couldn't escape him. It was like he'd imprinted himself on me. He'd ruined me, but what was worse was I wanted to be ruined. I wanted him.

I needed him.

I pulled him back into my throat, in and out until my throat was raw and tears escaped my eyes. They weren't just watering, and I pushed myself past the point where I believed my breaking point was. I was determined, needing to make this guy come with my mouth. I wanted to make him fall apart...

Just like he was doing to me.

I had his balls in my hands at this point, massaging them,

and Wolf groaned so loud I thought he'd bring the place down.

"Fuck, don't do that. I'm going to fucking come," he ground out, but I didn't stop. I continued to work them, but he fought my hands away. "I said don't fucking do that. This isn't your fucking reward. It's mine. You're mine."

I'm his.

He pulled himself out then, brought me up. His hands caged my face, and he slammed his mouth on mine so hard our teeth clacked.

God.

I loved this, was drunk off this. I hooked an arm around him, and he picked me up. My ass hit the sink as Wolf devoured my mouth, and it seemed he forgot about punishing me.

His mouth was on my nipple so fast, sucking, teasing. My eyes rolled back, and my head did too. At one point, I was watching him suck my chest through the mirror, and I noticed my lips.

My lipstick was like gone. Not completely but smeared so bad. I barely had any of it left.

It seemed he'd gotten what he wanted.

"Fuck, Fawn. Fuck…" He breathed so much heat over my nipples, tonguing them. He really loved my breasts, and when he fisted them, my flesh spilled through his fingers. "God, I fucking love these." He laved an areola, and a noise left my throat. His mouth covered one whole. "So fucking beautiful. So perfect. You're perfect."

He proceeded to make me feel that way, kissing his way down my chest. He pushed my shirt off, my bra with it, then tugged me forward.

His mouth landed on my stomach, sweet kisses across my soft flesh. I didn't even know he could be soft, sweet. I moaned, my hand in his hair.

"Yes," escaped my lips, his hand between my legs. Upon unzipping my jeans, he told me to hold on.

I did, steadfast. My heels hit the floor when he picked me up, so strong. I had my arms hooked around his neck while he worked my jeans off me.

I kissed his neck. "You're perfect."

I couldn't believe I actually said that, but it was true. He was perfect. He was perfect for me, and that scared me.

Wolf's chuckle was deep in my ear. He pulled me away to look at me, his hands on my hips. I thought he'd have some kind of smartass retort, but he didn't.

He kissed me, as gentle and soft as he'd done on my stomach. He had to have tasted himself, but he clearly didn't care.

"Red," he said, strong-arming me to him. He used just one arm to hold me up while he peeled my panties off. My bare ass hit the sink before he parted my legs. "Let me have this."

He could have anything he wanted, and my mouth fell open when he dipped between my legs. He pressed hard kisses to my sex, making love to it.

"Ares..." I trembled, his big hand fisting my mound while he tongued his way between my lower lips. I couldn't take much more of this.

"So fucking sweet," he growled, his tongue flicking my clit. He used two fingers to probe me, and I shuddered so bad I thought I'd fall off the sink. "Don't you fucking come. Not yet."

He was teasing me, getting me to the brink before pulling back and breathing heat over me. Eventually, he had his mouth completely sealed over my sex, his hands gripping my thighs. I groaned. "Stop fucking playing with me."

"So greedy." He chuckled, rising above. He rose like a literal mountain, his cock in his hand. He pumped himself. "You want this?"

He knew I did, but I refused to say. I simply lounged back, gripping the sink. I widened my legs. "Do you want this?"

Two could play this game, and his pupils dilated accordingly. He jerked my head back by my hair and didn't ask permission before arching and thrusting himself inside me.

I kept my face stoic, as much as I could. Wolf's hips slapped my inner thighs, his expression the same. He was playing the exact same game with me.

But he wouldn't win.

He stretched me, pulling, tearing. He fucked me raw, but all I did was hold on to the sink. He wouldn't crack me.

"Give in," he announced, his hand in my hair. Dipping my head, he made me watch him fuck me, but in response, I just worked my hips. I fucked him right back, the growl in his throat. He brought me close by the skull. "Give in, Red."

He bit me, my lower lip, as if an incentive. Unable to help it, I trembled, and when I did, he smiled.

"That's it. Show me what I do to you." Caging my face, he made me look at him. "I want to see it on you. All over you."

I was sure he could, and I was always so bad at fighting him. Our hips slapped between us, my mouth open. I licked my lips, and when he did too, I bit him.

His roar hit me in the back of my throat, just as unleashed as me. He'd been fighting too, I'd give him that.

But he wasn't now.

He was right here with me, the two of us fucking each other like animals. I couldn't tell where we were divided, literally the same person. We didn't even have a fucking condom on between us.

"Don't stop," I coached him, my fingers twisted up in his belt loops. He still had all his clothes on, and I used that shit to my advantage.

"Not on your life," he said, his tongue basically down my throat. His hips picked up, and when they did, he buried his face in my neck. "Not on either of ours."

He sounded desperate, like he truly did need this, needed me. The rawness of it sent me over the edge, and I squeezed his dick so hard between my legs. My fingers dug into his shirt as my walls gripped steel.

"That's it, baby. Come for me." He pushed my hair out of my face again, guiding me to look at him. "You come so beautifully for me."

He said that the same time his hot cum filled me, his mouth on mine. He drank me in, our tongues dueling. He kissed me through his entire high, and I thought I'd die.

I wanted to. Right there because if this was death, I'd take it. It felt so good, amazing.

Wolf laughed after. We both did. We just held each other on a fucking bathroom sink, and I burrowed into his chest.

"I think you may have actually ruined me that time," I said, slipping my arms around him. I fisted his shirt. "I may actually love you."

The words slipped out in the same laughter as before, my head hazy. I was basically sex drunk on that sink, but I certainly realized when I was the only one laughing.

He'd stopped.

He stopped everything in fact, and though he was holding me, he wasn't moving.

Only his heart was.

Hard thumps hit my cheek, still rapid from before. I eased away to look at him, but he was already separating us.

"We should probably go back out to the others," he said, cold air hitting me immediately from his absence. He'd been so warm, and I watched when he reached for toilet paper.

It was for me.

I was well aware of the cum dripping between my legs, my naked ass still on the sink. I was the only one naked between us and suddenly felt exposed.

Wolf handed the toilet paper to me, his eyes averting. He helped me down off the sink, then immediately proceeded to get my clothes. He got them off the floor, then turned around while I wiped myself.

Like he hadn't just seen every part of me.

Feeling really naked now, vulnerable, I cleaned myself up quickly. He was very ready to get out of here, and not knowing what to say, I simply got myself together, then got myself dressed. I'd obviously said the wrong thing earlier but was too scared to do anything about that.

Mostly because I knew I couldn't take it back.

CHAPTER
THIRTY

Fawn

Wolf and I never went for our walk. In fact, after we got back to the others, we didn't talk at all.

And he didn't touch me again.

A sharp distance occurred between us, and I was too chickenshit to say anything about it. I just let the night roll on and figured, afterward, we'd talk about what had just happened.

That never happened.

Wolf walked me back to our dorm, and though we had ample time to talk, neither of us did. For me, personally, I believed we had plenty of time, but Wolf cut that off right across the threshold of our place.

"I'm going for a walk," he said, nodding. "Just need a second."

I let him go, not thinking much of it.

I should have.

I waited up basically all night for him to come back. I waited so long actually I ended up falling asleep. My phone woke me up for class, but I didn't have any missed text messages.

At least, not from the person I wanted to hear from.

I had to admit I was hurt. I was *pissed*, but I wasn't brave enough to be the one to say something. It was me saying something that made him start acting weird.

Why the fuck had I said that?

The words had just slipped out. We'd been in the moment, I guess, and I couldn't help it. That was apparently how I felt, and I'd just gone with it.

And why doesn't that scare you more?

It did scare me. It scared the absolute shit out of me, the things I was feeling, saying. I hadn't meant to say I may love Wolf because I didn't want to feel like I loved Wolf. I didn't want to feel any of this. I didn't want to want him.

But I did.

I knew that now every hour I let pass without seeing him. I sent him a few text messages since last night, and though he responded to every one of them, they weren't things I wanted to hear.

Me: Where were you last night? Where are you now?

Wolf: Stayed with D. Just needed a second. Right now, I'm in class.

Me: Well, can we talk later?

Wolf: We will. I promise.

We will.

Famous last words, and he swiftly left me on read after that. I mean, he hadn't technically but he certainly hadn't expanded. I didn't want to be *that girl*, so I waited for that talk and some kind of anything back from him.

It ended up coming on Friday.

This guy let two freaking days pass before he got back to me, and once again, it'd been texts.

Wolf: Hey. Can you come by the dorm? I'm here, and we'll talk.

I should have been pissed at him. I was pissed at him, but I wanted to see him more.

I missed him.

Of course, I had a game plan when going into this. This guy had run like a freaking gazelle the last time we'd spoken, and honestly, I wasn't sure I wouldn't by the end. I was scared of these feelings, and I didn't want to have them.

We were both so fragile.

Wolf and I both needed healing and ways to channel our feelings in a healthy way. We both avoided tough issues like the plague, and I personally wasn't ready to bleed my heart out, but I'd be willing to try. I wanted to, for him and us, yes, but mostly for myself. I was screwed up.

But he made me feel not so alone in that.

"Excuse me."

The words came across the threshold of our place. A big guy in a Pembroke University Football hoodie said them, and he had many boxes in his hands when he waltzed past me.

He was excused... I guessed. I did let him pass me, and the dude was flanked by a couple others. They too had boxes.

And Wolf was directing them.

He had his hands in his own university hoodie, standing in a room filled with boxes and not much else. There was our dorm furniture, of course, and a few of my things. I'd left some books out and personal items, and though those were still there, his stuff wasn't.

What the hell?

I strode inside, stepping over more mess. He had things scattered about, open boxes mostly. "What's going on?"

I got the attention I aimed for, deserved. Right away, Wolf looked at me, and when he did, he stood tall. He lifted a hand. "Hi."

Hi. Like he wasn't in the middle of a move and failed to tell me about it. "You're leaving?"

I said this in front of all his friends, apparently football players? I recognized some familiar faces, but not from the football field. A few of these guys had helped Wolf move in here in the first place, and they'd had football hoodies on that day.

Wolf navigated between them, easy since they parted like the Red Sea for him. Our small dorm was chaos with them there, but eventually, he made it over to me. "Yeah, I am."

He said this with his hands in his pockets. Like this wasn't a thing when it fucking was. I opened my mouth to say something, but someone tapped him on the shoulder.

"We don't have any boxes big enough for this. What do you want me to do?" The guy had some bedding, and Wolf waved him to the kitchen. He told him trash bags would do. Meanwhile, I was just standing there. Fucking waiting.

Wolf noticed. He eased me out of the chaos, but I angled away when he tried to touch me.

He noticed that too, his gaze flicking down. "I'm glad you came. We need to talk."

I actually had to laugh at that, a real belly laugh. "You want to talk?"

"Yeah, I do."

Was that before or after he was going to tell me he was moving? I angled forward. "What the hell is all this?"

And even with my voice low, we had more than one eye on our conversation. This was Wolf, and everyone wanted to know his business.

"This is what we ultimately planned," he said, still not fucking looking directly in my eyes. He nodded. "And I wanted to let you know I made a call today."

My eyebrow arched, confused. "A call?"

"Yes. To Kurt?" He glanced round. "Everything is squared away there. You don't have to worry about anything."

Out of all the things I believed would come out of his mouth, it wasn't this. It wasn't that. "Okay."

People still moved around, still in this conversation, and I didn't *get* this. Why would he want to do this here? This made no sense. He tucked hands under his arms. "So that's done. You're good, and I didn't want you to worry."

I still didn't get this, my heart racing. Someone else came to ask him a question, but when they did, Wolf waved the guy off.

"We just need a second. Please," he said, like this would take a second. Like the talk we ultimately needed to have would only be seconds.

Like it was nothing.

Angry now, I faced the room. "Everyone get out."

They all stopped. Everything stopped, and Wolf eyed me. "What are you doing?"

I was doing what he obviously couldn't. I pointed toward the door. "I want everyone out of my dorm room. *Now.*"

Everyone but Wolf, I meant, and he definitely knew that, his attention still on me. He started to say something but ended up facing the room too.

"You heard her," he said, his jaw tight. He clearly didn't want to do this, but I didn't care.

We were going to do this.

All his foot soldiers cleared the room in an assembly line, and I stared at the ceiling.

Calm down.

But I was screaming inside, livid. I gazed at Wolf. "Now, say what you have to say."

"What?"

"Say what you have to say. What you clearly felt you couldn't say, which was why you filled this room up with so many fucking people."

It was a cop-out, and he had to think me stupid to believe otherwise.

He laced fingers above his head. "Fawn…"

"No. Don't fucking do that." I approached him, pointing at him. "You eased in here *with all these fucking people* so you could run out of here and not have to answer to shit. Not have to answer to us."

I hated I raised my voice. I hated I was hurt, but I couldn't help it.

I just couldn't.

He couldn't deal and went running like a fucking jerk away from me.

"I just didn't want you put on the spot," he admitted, and I blanched. He lowered his arms. "With people here, *you* wouldn't have to say anything. Address anything."

I wouldn't have to…

Right.

I laughed now, really laughing. I shifted in my sneakers. "I can't believe you're doing this. Really doing this."

"What?"

He was really going to make me say it. I swallowed. "I said I may love you, Wolf," I said, and he twitched. I nodded. "I said that, and you couldn't fucking deal, so you went running for the hills."

I think that hurt the most. That he left me high and dry with all these *feelings*. I mean, did he think I was dealing with this on my own?

Did he not feel it too?

I didn't believe that, refused even. This guy was a goddamn brick wall, but he'd shared so much with me. He'd been vulnerable, and something told me he didn't do that for everyone. He was private just like me.

He said nothing after my statement, and I laughed again.

He frowned. "Fawn…"

"Well, I'm sorry, Wolf." I raised and dropped my hands. "I'm sorry that I have feelings for you. I'm sorry I *may* love you. I'm fucking sorry!"

I was sorry. He was the last one I wanted to love.

My throat jumped again. "I'm sorry I love you."

He didn't twitch this time, but his expression twisted so

hard. His hands came together. "You don't know what you're saying."

Oh, I think I did, nodding. I breathed into my hands. "I don't want to fucking feel anything for you. If you haven't noticed, you're a fucking jerk, and what you did today is only solidifying that."

He made eye contact with me again, his lids narrow. "Which is why it'd be stupid for you to feel anything for me."

"And what? You don't?" I stepped up to him, right in his face. There was a time I'd been scared of him. Now, I was just scared to be with him. "You can honestly tell me you feel *nothing*." My nostrils flared. "Nothing for me?"

I truly didn't believe otherwise. I just couldn't.

Our time together wouldn't let me.

We'd experienced something in this fake relationship I didn't think either one of us was ready for. We weren't, but it had happened.

Wolf's jaw shifted slowly, clicking. "You and I aren't anything."

My heart clenched, tight, but that wasn't what I'd asked him. "What do you feel, Wolf? Nothing? Because if so, you're going to have to fucking tell me."

His eyes cut to me, dark, cold. He was reverting back into that Big Bad Wolf again, but I didn't back off. I wouldn't. He put his hands together. "You and I were a *business transaction,* Fawn. We were, and there was never any chance of anything happening between us. Our relationship served a purpose. One you fulfilled and one I concluded the moment I made a call to Kurt."

He was trying to hurt me here, but he made a mistake. I wasn't a weak bitch.

That was why he chose me.

My smile wasn't weak either, strong. I distanced. "Can't really say it, can you?" I gazed up. "You can't because you do feel something, and no matter how much you say this was business, it obviously turned into something more."

"It didn't, and you're an idiot for thinking anything else." He was trying to hurt me again, stepping up on *me* now. "I don't do girlfriends, and even if I did, no way in the goddamn stratosphere would she be you. She wouldn't because you're a fucking workout, and I try to live my life with as few complications as I can."

I had to say, he was good, but he'd already made a mistake. Two in fact. The first was bringing people in here as a buffer to protect my feelings. Like he cared.

The second was still not telling me what I needed to hear.

For some reason, the Big Bad Wolf couldn't do what he needed to do to end this, and no matter how many mean things he said, he wasn't fooling anyone.

Let alone himself.

"You're going to have to do better, Wolf."

"Better?"

I grinned. "Better to hurt me. You're going to have to do better because I call bullshit on each and every *piece of shit* that's coming out of your mouth."

He wet his lips, and my grin hiked.

I lifted my hands. "Now, you may not want this, but you got it, and I certainly didn't want this shit." I laughed, dry. "But guess what? I got it too, and maybe when you're ready to man up and deal with that, you can come talk to me."

His growl was low. "We are nothing, Fawn. Zero. Nada, and this relationship? Was *fake*. It was bullshit, and just as much work as you, and I'm beyond happy to be rid of it."

And yet, I still didn't believe him. I didn't because he still couldn't say the words. He couldn't say he didn't care.

He couldn't say he didn't love.

Ares may not love me, but he certainly didn't feel nothing. I knew that just as well as the red that crept up the side of his neck. He was trying to justify something.

But I had a feeling that something wasn't to me.

Nodding, I folded my arms. "And maybe one day you'll actually believe all that," I said, and he twitched again. I smiled. "And hopefully, by then, I'll be over this bullshit too."

I didn't want to love him. I didn't want to care, but since I did, I left to spare my own feelings. This fucker wasn't going to see me cry on top of everything else.

I think it was safe to say I'd already given him enough of me.

CHAPTER
THIRTY-ONE

Ares

The seasons changed really quick at Pembroke. Sharp winds hit, and before I knew it, I was back home in my own bed for holiday break. The house filled with twinkling lights, my parents' staff quickly got into transforming our home into the winter wonderland it always was every year. My folks really got into that shit, and it was the first time we'd all be under the same roof since my siblings and I went off to college. My adopted brother was flying back, today actually.

Sitting on my bed with a novel, I let more than one thought play out. My thoughts hadn't stopped since I'd gotten home, and unfortunately, I didn't have the distraction of school to keep them away. I continued to think. I continued to stew, and also unfortunately, a few too many of those thoughts revolved around a certain someone. I, of course, had to tell my folks about what happened with Fawn. They wanted updates, and I couldn't hide from the reality of that with the two-hour distance of school. I had to address things once again like I had with my buddies and Sloane.

I had to deal with it again.

I thought it'd be easier to lie to everyone. I mean, I'd been lying all semester. One more lie should have been easy, but it was hard to see my parents' disappointment. In fact, they looked the same way Sloane and the guys had once I'd told them I'd cut things off with my fake girlfriend. I had told them all we were different people and things just didn't work out and had expected a few reactions. I was the guy who prepared for all scenarios, but one thing I hadn't anticipated was their confusion.

Let alone their remorse.

It was like someone had died, and that morose tone lingered in the house. It was so bad I'd decided to spend the majority of my time in my room since I'd gotten back.

Hence the fucking thoughts.

I shouldn't have thoughts about Fawn fucking Greenfield. I'd gotten over that shit when I had cut things off, and this had been a necessity. I thought about her and I might change my mind about a few things. They were selfish things and stuff I couldn't entertain.

For her sake.

Fawn and I weren't anything. We weren't because we couldn't be anything. I'd put a nail in that coffin the minute she'd become a project over a person. She fulfilled a need, and I'd decimated that the moment I allowed us to cross a line. It wasn't just that I'd fucked her, or we had a good time together. Good fucks came a dime a dozen, a good time the same. That hadn't been what blurred the line.

"Can't really say it, can you…"

Growling, I ignored the voice in my head and turned a page in my book. I'd been on the same page for what felt like a goddamn hour, and it took me a second to realize someone knocked on my door. I barked for whoever to come in, but had no idea who was here.

The house should have been empty.

Because it was supposed to be, I put my book down, surprised when my buddy Dorian eased his blond head into my room. He supposedly should have been shopping for Christmas presents with Sloane and my folks.

"Hey," he said, his football hoodie on and keys in his hand. "Thought I'd pop in on you before I take off."

"What are you still doing here?" I took his hand, shaking it when he gave it to me. We both shook with a snap before I lay back. "Thought you were out Christmas shopping."

There wasn't a place my sister went where he didn't. The fucker even texted me goodbye when they'd all supposedly taken off earlier.

D's grin was wiry, and I watched him scrub in his hair before he lounged against one of my bedposts. He shrugged. "Stayed behind. I was in my room watching TV."

He did still have one at my house, a room. It went unused these days since my parents weren't trying to provide a hookup spot for him and my sister, but it was still there.

My brow twitched up he'd been here and hadn't said anything, and when I asked him why, he laughed.

"I guess I wanted to be around in case you wanted to be social." He lifted his big shoulders. "You've been spending a lot of time by yourself."

I had, and that was necessary too but for a different reason. I couldn't be around my family or friends for longer than a few minutes within the imploding feeling of guilt.

I only wished that was because I'd lied to them about Fawn.

The lies, unfortunately, only started there, and I knew with Bru coming home I was hitting a deadline. With him here, my family and friends literally all here now, I had no choice but to face a reality I'd definitely been trying to run from. Fawn Greenfield had provided a distraction, but it had ended up being for me more than my family.

It had been for you.

I think I knew that and long before going into it. I knew exactly what would happen when I found out certain things about her. She had fulfilled a need, but it wasn't to be my fake girlfriend or serve a purpose.

It'd been for me.

"Can't really say it, can you…"

Her voice in my head again, I watched my buddy take a seat on my mattress. He flicked at my book with his car keys. "Where's your sketchpad? I feel like I haven't seen you sketch in months. You're always reading now or doing homework."

Of course, he noticed. He was one of my best friends, and he wasn't the first to say something.

Thatcher and Wells weren't here, but they too had commented that they never saw me with my sketchpad or charcoal anymore. I never went out of my way to work in front of the guys. Actually, I went out of my way *not* to work in front of them. When it came to my art, I'd always been private about it, my process.

Even still, they did see me with my sketchpad from time to time, and my sister did all the time. She did because she was an artist too and was about the only one I'd sketch around.

We didn't do that anymore.

We didn't because of me, and I picked up my book. I closed it. "You didn't need to stick around. I'm okay by myself."

I realized I avoided answering his question, and he obviously did too, eyeing me. He shook his head. "That's why I was here without actually being here. Just in case. It was either that or let Thatch and Wells bum-rush you. When you mentioned you weren't going shopping with your family in the group chat, they almost came over here and forced you into their cars. They wanted to get you out of your mood."

"I'm always in a mood." I smirked, and Dorian lifted his eyes.

"Yeah, but you were in less of one when you were dating Fawn."

The smile instantly left my face. I started to open my mouth, but right away, Dorian raised a hand.

"Don't. I'm not trying to get my head bitten off today. I'm just saying…"

"Well, don't," I gritted. He knew that was a forbidden topic. We didn't talk about Fawn because there was nothing to talk about. As far as he or anyone else knew, I'd dated someone. It ended, and that was it. "There's nothing to say, and Fawn and I ended amicably."

Again, as far as he knew.

I fought the jump in my throat. "We were two different people."

"Yeah, well, whoever that person was happened to be a lot happier than you as of late." He sighed. "Anyway, I'm not going to argue with you about this. Like I said, I just came to check on your ass."

"Well, don't do that either." I opened my book. "And tell Thatcher and Wells to stop texting me."

After I'd mentioned I wasn't going shopping, they'd called me the Grinch and shit. I just wasn't in the fucking holiday spirit.

Kind of hard to be.

A tingle hit my digits, a tingle I once again ignored. I squeezed a fist until it disappeared, then quickly got back into pretending to read a book. The words blended into one another on the page, but that had nothing to do with my eyes. Focus lately was impossible. I was too frustrated. Too…

Angry.

It was like I was in a haze all the time. Rageful. Because I was, I constantly did push people away, but they hadn't done anything wrong. My anger mostly surrounded myself and how I'd decided to deal with the issues in my life. I hadn't done things well and still wasn't.

My thoughts did hit Fawn then. Again, too many thoughts happening in this bed. Fact of the matter was, the best thing I could have done for her was let her go. I'd made a lot of poor decisions when it came to my life lately, but one wasn't cutting things off with her. It'd been the right thing.

It'd been the only one I'd actually done right.

Fawn did fulfill more than one thing for me this semester. She allowed me to be in denial and even entertain a reality in which she and I actually had a chance. For an iota of a second, I'd actually considered it, but then I remembered what I was to her. I wasn't the good guy.

And bad people didn't get good things.

I spared her from a reality of bullshit, my shit, and after she found out about all of it, us being something would have never happened anyway.

My chest locked in front of my friend, and barking at him did exactly what I wanted. Pushing off my bed, Dorian mentioned he was heading out, heading home. It seemed his own family wanted to go shopping, and he was using the time as an opportunity to get something for Sloane. They always were together, and he hadn't had time to get her something yet.

I said nothing in response, watching him shake his head again. He started to close the door, but then I lowered my book.

"Can you come over for dinner tonight?" I asked but couldn't face him. I stared at the book's cover. "I already texted Thatcher and Wells."

I did between them calling me the fucking Grinch, then quickly tossed my phone someplace where I couldn't see the alerts.

"You sure? Aren't you and the fam having a big dinner with the kid tonight?"

The kid was Bru, and though he was the same age as Thatcher and Wells, that was what we called him. I gave him the name in high school. I looked up. "Yeah, but I want you guys there. You wanted me to be social, right? Well, I'm being fucking social and asking you to hang."

I needed them all here, my buddies. I had something to say at the dinner table tonight, and I needed their support.

Just say yes. Fuck.

If he said anything else, I didn't know what I'd do. I did need him, but I wasn't brave enough to say or push harder.

Dorian's nod was subtle. "Sure. Just text me when."

He had no reason to do anything I'd asked of him. I'd been treating him and my other buddies equally like shit lately. I did when I was going through it.

Swallowing, I mumbled a thanks to my friend. He studied me for a moment, and I was afraid he'd ask why I wanted him and the guys to come over. I was afraid he'd *poke*, but in the end, he didn't. He just left me to my own devices, and I sat on that bed, again with more thoughts. I felt like they'd rip me apart, and I think the only thing that kept me from collapsing beneath them was the text I got. It came from my brother, and I had to get my shit together.

Bru: Hey. You home?

I was and attempted to get out of the bullshit in my head. I scrubbed my face.

Me: Yeah. What's up? Aren't you supposed to be in the air?

If he was, he obviously shouldn't be texting.

Bru: No, I'm in town. Caught an early flight.

Which meant he needed a ride from the airport.

Really making myself get my shit together now, I got off the bed. I couldn't let him see me this way. I was supposed to be the older brother and taking care of him.

Calm down.

I was prone to panic attacks, and I'd had more than my fair share when my sister had been gone and I'd basically hated my existence. I'd had a series of so much head shit before she came back, and because I had, I knew when I was going down a dark hole.

Calm. Down.

I had to, important. I couldn't break. Not when things were about to change and I needed to be the strong one in my family. I had to take care of everyone. I had to be their reason for stability. I'd done the opposite for so long when it came to my friends and parents. I was the topic of worry.

I was the reason for breaking my folks.

My parents were strong as fuck, *stable* as fuck. They were a united front of strength with equal parts love. They created a harmony in this house, and overcompensated for me, the darkness in this house. I had been the darkness for a time, and I'd never forget how the stress and strain of it had affected my parents. It was something the world probably never saw. They kept that shit locked up and behind the beautiful walls they provided for me. They *created walls* for me and shielded me from the world. Meanwhile, they themselves were going through it, but they never, not once, let people see.

I only had because I lived here.

I saw my mom crying. I saw my dad locked up in his office and burying himself in his work. I saw them both distract themselves and the harmony of this house decimate. Again, it was something they didn't want me to see, but of course, I saw it. I was the source of it. I was that angry kid whose parents had to worry about him. *I* was the fucking basket case they had to watch. My parents *literally* had to keep tabs on me.

Because if they didn't…

I wouldn't be that source of worry for my parents again, refused. I had to nut the hell up and be a man, and I would for my family. I wouldn't be the weak link this time.

Me: One sec. I'll come to get you.

Bru: No, you don't need to. I'm almost home. Sloane says she's out with Mom and Dad. She said you stayed home.

Me: Yeah, I did, but why didn't you call any of us? To come get you?

Bru: Wasn't a big deal. Took the bus.

He took… the bus?

I shook my head. Bruno Sloane-Mallick and his independent shit. Like me, he didn't like to be a bother and my little brother had obviously spent a little too much time overseas. He went to school in a small country off the coast of Europe, and some of the pictures he sent had double-decker buses like in London.

It seemed the kid was acclimating to his environment well, but I couldn't help but be dragged back to unhelpful thoughts at the mention of a bus. I'd obviously had some experience with that in recent months considering everything with Fawn.

Don't do that. Don't go there…

Because if I did, I knew exactly what would happen. I was already fighting stability, and if I allowed my rogue thoughts to go to Fawn Greenfield and everything I forced on the regular to leave behind regarding her, I would hit that dark place. I'd break and I…

Bru: Is it just you there?

Get out of your head. Get out…

I realized now I was gripping into my hair. I had my hoodie half on, acting all weak and shit.

Bru: Dorian or the other guys?

I took a breath.

Me: Just me. Why?

Bru: I'm almost home. Be in soon.

Our texts came in about the same time, and instead of berating my kid brother for not waiting at the airport again, I took the seconds to get my shit together. Since I had been through all this before, I breathed it out. I actually managed not to look like a head case by the time I hit the stairs.

Voices drifted inside when I arrived at the bottom. It was more than one, which confused me, but I noticed Bru's phone in his hand when he eased inside. He didn't look like he was talking on it, but he might have had someone on speakerphone.

I picked up my pace. "Kid, why didn't you wait for me at the airport—"

His head lifted the same time I caught another coming in behind him. A ghost of sweet scent hit the air right after.

A flash of red hair...

Both hit me like a brick fucking wall, a girl following my brother. She eased inside my house too, and the moment we locked eyes, my entire body went ramrod straight. My lungs ceased to function. Like I'd been bucked in the chest by a fucking bronco and the impact collapsed a lung.

I had to say, she looked the same. Her face instantly took that sweet flush that blended into all those fucking freckles. She wore no makeup today, and every single one of those freckles exposed. On her flushed cheeks...

Her lips.

Blinking, it took a second for my thoughts to catch up. Because if they had, my firsts wouldn't have been taking inventory over the entire length of her and how it felt to see her somewhere besides her classrooms or from across campus. I'd seen her more than once since things had ended. Though, she'd never know that.

I'd made sure.

These things had been stupid, and I was aware of that now just as I was she *shouldn't* be standing in my fucking house. Tingles hit my fingers again, but I knew that didn't have anything to do with her. I gripped my fists. "What are you doing here?"

She shouldn't be here, but when I approached, I noticed

something else. My brother promptly cut in front of the new arrival, his hand up. Bruno Sloane-Mallick wasn't a small guy, and even though we called him *kid*, he wasn't one. He was just as big as me and my boys and actually played football with us in high school.

"Bro," he said, looking at me. He passed a glance to the girl who lingered there. He passed a glance to *Fawn*. She stood by the door, and though she'd frozen at the sight of me, she quickly got her bearings.

Her tongue eased over her freckled lips, and even though I stared directly at her, she gazed at my brother. She braced her arms, not looking at me.

What the fuck is this?

I stepped forward again, but *again*, my brother got in the fucking way. "Bru, what the hell?" It was like the two were in their own little world, a silent exchange between them. They passed long glances, and not one of them was in my direction. My nostrils flared. "What the hell is this?"

They looked at each other like they knew each other.

And when he touched her...

My brother put his hand on Fawn's shoulder, easing her the rest of the way inside. The contact sent my back up, and when he closed the door, he stayed behind her. He was bigger than her, though, and appeared like some kind of protective force.

Like a bodyguard.

My back rose higher. I started to speak but noticed Bru. I had to say, when he'd come in, I hadn't been paying too much attention to him.

I was now, and I noticed the chilling look on my brother. His dark eyebrows knitted tight, his lips pinched too. He looked pissed, but that didn't make any sense.

I faced Fawn, but once again, she wasn't looking at me. She had her little arms crossed, her chin tipped like she was about to tell a motherfucker off. She had that fiery look about her that never ceased to shoot my cock up. I liked her fight. I liked her lip.

I liked...

"Well, it's nice to see it for myself."

My attention drifted to my brother again. He'd spoken and, currently, had his arms crossed too.

His frown deepened. "I guess I don't have to introduce you. You clearly know Fawn."

I did know Fawn, and considering the way she was locked up, that history could be seen. She did not want to be here and especially not with me. My jaw shifted. "Why are you here?"

She finally brought her eyes my way, ice in her gaze. If looks could shatter, I'd be in a million fucking pieces. She looked at me like she had that last day.

Like she hated me.

Of course, that'd been the point. I'd said a lot of things to hurt her. She said I hadn't, but I'd called her on her bluff. I'd left her pretty fucked up.

But she had nothing on me.

This girl unnerved me, and I was secure in myself enough to only admit that to myself. She'd said I hadn't wanted to deal with my feelings, but the truth was, I had. I did have feelings for her.

Which was why I'd protected her from them.

Fawn started to say something, her lips moving. Instead, she just opted to look at my brother once more, and this time, he came around her.

"She's here because I asked her," he said, eyes narrowed at me. "Fawn's spending the holiday with us. My guest for Christmas."

His... guest.

A few things took my attention in that moment. The first was that my brother referred to Fawn as his guest, but that wasn't what had me gripping my fists again.

It was his hand.

He placed it on Fawn again, around her and on her shoulder. He held her like he not only knew her but did so intimately.

A dark haze hit me then, confusion, anger. My little brother somehow knew my ex-*fake*-girlfriend, but I didn't currently have the mental bandwidth to question the how.

I was too busy looking at his hand on her.

Wondering how Fawn knows Bru? How about the moments that lead up to the two of them appearing together on the Mallicks' doorstep? You're in luck because there's a bonus chapter to *Eat You Alive*! This is a FREE download and it's available exclusively to my newsletter subscribers!

Join my newsletter today to get your free bonus chapter told from Fawn's POV!

Get here:
https://bit.ly/3PtpDr7

Thank you so much for reading *Eat You Alive*! Get the next book in the Court Legacy saga, *Eat Your Heart Out*, on Amazon today!